I heard a low growl behind me. ChaCha immediately stiffened, the hair along the back of her neck bristling. She bared her teeth, but stayed silent.

I heard the crackle of leaves behind me and then that deep, low growl again. My heart started to beat a tiny bit faster and I tightened my grip on my dog as I slowly turned around.

I had never seen eyes like that before. Black, as though the iris covered everything. Flat, but focused, as though there were one thing—and one thing only—on his mind. The dog's black lips curled up, exposing incisors that looked as sharp as any vampire's and he growled again. Only this time, it seemed to come in stereo.

In a split second, I heard another bark, another snarl.

A pack of dogs?

I started running, my thighs burning, the hand that held ChaCha soaking from my sweaty palm. I glanced back.

One dog. One thick, well-muscled body. Red-black fur stretched across a back that seemed as wide as a horse. Snarling, snapping jaws just at my waist—at my hip, at my flailing right hand.

One dog. Three heads.

Books by Hannah Jayne

UNDER WRAPS

UNDER ATTACK

UNDER SUSPICION

UNDER THE GUN

UNDER A SPELL

UNDER THE FINAL MOON

PREDATORY
(with Alexandra Ivy,
Nina Bangs and Dianne Duvall)

Published by Kensington Publishing Corporation

UNDER THE FINAL MOON

The Underworld Detection Agency Chronicles

HANNAH JAYNE

KENSINGTON PUBLISHING CORP.

http://www.kensingtonbooks.com

KENSINGTON BOOKS are published by

Kensington Publishing Corp.
119 West 40th Street
New York, NY 10018

All Kensington Titles, Imprints, and Distributed Lines are available at special quantity discounts for bulk purchases for sales promotions, premiums, fund-raising, and educational or institutional use. Special book excerpts or customized printings can also be created to fit specific needs. For details, write or phone the office of the Kensington special sales manager: Kensington Publishing Corp., 119 West 40th Street, New York, NY 10018, attn: Special Sales Department, Phone: 1-800-221-2647.

Kensington and the K logo Reg. U.S. Pat & TM Off.

ISBN-13: 978-0-7582-8114-2
ISBN-10: 0-7582-8114-5
First Kensington Mass Market Edition: August 2014

eISBN-13: 978-0-7582-8115-9
eISBN-10: 0-7582-8115-3
First Kensington Electronic Edition: August 2014

10 9 8 7 6 5 4 3 2 1

Printed in the United States of America

ONE

I could feel the cold stripe of fear going up my spine—like icy fingers walking slowly up vertebra after vertebra.

"Is she dead?" The voice was a faint whisper, but it throbbed through my head, singeing the ache that was already there.

"Maybe we should go."

I hoped that they would. I prayed that they would. I remained as still as possible, breath barely trembling through my body, willing my heart to thrum silently because I knew that vampires could hear everything. Every little whisper, every little thought. *Please go, please go*, I pleaded silently.

And then the icy breath was at my ear. "Sophie!"

Now the voice was incredibly loud and I jumped straight up until the tops of my thighs mashed against the underside of my desk. I missed the chair coming back down and flopped unceremoniously onto my ass.

"What do you want?" I glowered, rubbing my

tailbone and seeing Nina and Kale through narrowed dagger eyes.

"Were you asleep?" asked Kale, the Underworld Detection Agency receptionist with a newly pink pageboy haircut, cocking her head so that her hair brushed against her cheek.

I pressed the pads of my fingertips against my temples, making small circles. My head kept aching.

"I was trying to. I have a headache."

Nina rolled her eyes and hopped up onto the corner of my desk, her tiny butt and weightless body not making a sound. "Are you still trying to claim PTSD for the whole back-to-school thing? Get over it. You closed up the Hell mouth or whatever, and never even had to wear the school uniform."

"What do you guys want?"

Nina whipped out a nail file from I-don't-know-where and began working on her right hand. She blew a bubble from the wad of gum she was chewing. After twelve years with Nina LaShay as my coworker, roommate, and best friend, I'll never get comfortable seeing a vampire blow purple Hubba Bubba bubbles through blade-sharp incisors. It just looks *weird*.

"I'm hiding out from Vlad. He's got an all-fangs-on-deck VERM meeting and I have much better things to do than sit in a stuffy conference room with a bunch of dead guys talking about ascots and their graveyard dirt and glory days."

I grinned despite the nap interruption. The Vampire Empowerment and Restoration Movement (or VERM, for short), was Vlad's baby. Vlad, Nina's six-teen-slash-hundred-and-thirteen-year-old nephew, my boss, Kale's paramour, and the roommate who would never leave, pushed the movement, which sought to restore vampires back to their broody, Count Dracula countenance and insisted its adherents wear fashions that Nina couldn't abide. She was a member by virtue of being a vampire and being Vlad's aunt, but she studiously avoided their meetings.

"And I came in to tell you that Sampson wants to see you," Kale said, swishing her hair from side to side.

Kale might be a teenager with hot-pink hair and a stomach-churning crush on a brooding vampire with a penchant for draconian clothing, but she is also strong. Supernaturally so. While some nineteen-year-olds dabble in Wicca and black eyeliner, Kale likes to keep things fresh with frilly skirts, cotton-candy-colored hair, and an inner power so tremendous she can blow the doors off metal lockers with a swish of her hand. She is under the tutelage of our other resident witch, Lorraine, who can conjure up anything from Tom Cruise to Tupperware. The latter because in her cauldron-free time she's the number-one Tupperware salesperson in the whole of Santa Clara County.

But, I digress.

While Kale looked at me earnestly, her pierced dimples twinkling, my heart lodged itself in my throat. A meeting with Pete Sampson, hometown werewolf and head of the Underworld Detection Agency, could only mean one of two things: I was fired, or yet another mysterious, gory, and seemingly supernatural murder had happened within San Francisco's seven square miles.

I would much prefer the former.

I'd like to say Sampson called on me because I could sniff out bad guys like a mouse sniffs out cheese, but that wouldn't be quite right. I find the bad guys all right, but usually just seconds before they try to bleed me dry, blow me up, or stake me through the heart. That last one is particularly bad since I am not a vampire. Or a werewolf. I'm just me, Sophie Lawson, sole breather in the Underworld Detection Agency, runner of the Fallen Angels Division, Sub-Par Napper.

"Do you know what he wants?" I asked, looking from Nina to Kale.

Kale just shrugged, but Nina looked over her shoulder at me, her ink-black hair falling over her slim shoulders. "Someone's probably dead again."

Nina LaShay: not one for pep talks.

Though the Underworld Detection Agency had a fairly decent record of "Days Without a Workplace Accident," our clients never fared as well—which isn't actually as bad as it sounds. Since most of our clients were dead already, second time round was par for the course. But, while we were the number-one agency for afterlife insurance, general demon protection, and keeping all the things with extra eyes, teeth, or horns on the down low, we were also number one with the repetitive paperwork.

I got carpal tunnel syndrome just thinking about it.

I headed down the hall toward Sampson's office, holding my breath as I passed the break room, where the VERM meeting was in full swing. Though our bylaws clearly state that vampire employees are not to eat, taste, or kill me, you know there's always one nutter holding a grudge and that the rule had to come from someone not abiding by it. No one looked up as I passed, and I sported a seconds-long inner grin until I almost ran headlong into a sweet, sparkly little pixie who made a cut-throat motion when I glanced up at her.

Pixies can be total bitches.

I went to make my usual shimmy around the hole in the floor where a senile wizard had blown himself up—like everyone else, the UDA was low on funds so the hole was last on the fix-it list—but stopped dead, my mouth dropping open.

"What's this?"

There was actually a piece of caution tape up, slung on a couple of folding chairs to make a work zone. A guy in a hard hat was up to his knees in the hole, diligently sawing away at one jagged edge.

He looked up and I could see from his gaunt, slightly green face and the hard cleft in his pointed chin that he was a goblin. From what I'd heard, they were brilliant at precision work.

"We're fixing the hole," he told me, his gray-green eyes widening as he took me in. I flushed, sudden embarrassment burning the tops of my ears and, I was certain, turning my pale skin an unattractive lobster red.

"So it's true." The goblin pushed back his hard hat and scratched at the little tuft of hair on his head. "The San Francisco branch really does have a breather on staff."

The Underworld Detection Agency is like the

clearinghouse for everything that goes bump in the night or bursts into flames during the day. We service everyone from Abatwas (teeny, tiny little adorable things that could unhinge their jaws and swallow you whole) to zombies (who most often leave a hunk of their jaw while trying to eat a Twix in the lunchroom).

We don't, however, serve humans. As a matter of fact, the Underworld Detection Agency—and all of its clients—are relatively unknown to the human world. I know what you're thinking—how do people miss a three-foot-tall troll walking down Market Street? The answer is a thin, mystical veil that prevents humans from registering what they see. You see little person; I see troll. You see homeless guy pushing a shopping cart full of cans; I see zombie pushing a shopping cart full of collectable zombie body parts (seriously, they drop stuff *every*where).

So what makes me so different? I can see through the veil. And in case you're thinking I'm some medium or Carol Ann or ghost whisperer, let me tell you that I am not. I'm a one-hundred-percent normal breather who is immune to magic: I can't do it; it can't be done to me.

Okay, so maybe I'm only ninety-nine percent normal.

I steeled myself as I approached Pete Sampson's office and knocked on the door's frame before popping it open.

"Ah, Sophie!" Sampson looked up when I walked in. He grinned widely, tugging at the collar of his button-down shirt. He was a werewolf, but only after business hours. And he was incredibly responsible about it, too, which was why there was a set of industrial-strength shackles double bolted to the wall behind the credenza. But right now he was regular old Sampson, close-cropped, blond hair, sparkling eyes that crinkled at the sides when he smiled, pristine dark suit.

I sat down with a nervous smile pasted on my face. "You okay?"

I nodded, fairly certain that if I opened my mouth the words *who's dead now?* would come springing out.

Sampson went immediately business-y. "So I was going over your third-quarter performance review and I have to say—"

I felt my spine go immediately rigid. Vlad was my boss at the office, but I screamed at him to pick up his socks at home. He may have been one hundred and thirteen chronologically, but he would always be a sloppy, leaves-crap-all-over-the-house, sixteen-year-old boy in looks and at heart (if he had one). Weren't teens revenge seekers?

"Uh, sir, about that," I said, toeing a line in the carpet. "I can explain."

I couldn't, but I was just trying to buy some time.

Sampson's dark brows went up. "Explain? I was just going to say that I am really impressed with your progress. Not just in the community, but in the office, and personally as well."

I let out a breath I hadn't known I was holding, and every bone in my body seemed to turn to liquid. "Really?" I grinned.

Now, most bosses wouldn't wrap "personal growth"

up into the employee ball of wax, but Sampson and I went way back. Not in years so much as in near-death experiences, but one was very much like the other and I had come to think of Pete Sampson as a father, since mine was an absentee dick.

"Of course. You've worked on cases diligently and successfully. You've got glowing reviews from two of your clients, which is especially good because—"

"I know." I wrinkled my nose. "Because most of our clients give me a wide berth, thinking that I bring death and destruction to creatures of the Underworld."

I'd had a very hard time convincing my previous clients that I didn't bring death so much as it followed me around, like I had some sort of hell-fury GPS tracker shoved in my gut. It took a bit of a toll on my client list—especially when my clients kept dying.

"So, taking all that into account, I'd like to congratulate you on another successful year here at the Underworld Detection Agency."

I gaped. "That's it?" The words tumbled out of my mouth before my brain had a chance to examine them or reel them back in.

Sampson's eyebrows went up. "Uh . . ."

"No, no!" I jumped up. "I didn't mean that like, 'That's it? How about a raise?' I meant, *that's it?* You know, every other time you've called me in here someone was dead or I ended up back in high school. Which was kind of like dying a little myself." I felt the trembling terror of mean girls in pleated plaid skirts wash over me, and I snapped the bad-memory rubber band I kept around my left wrist.

Sampson shot me a relaxed smile. "That's true. Why don't you take the rest of the day off since I terrified you, and I'll see what I can do about that raise?"

I was stunned. "Really? Really, Sampson?"

"Yeah, take a long weekend. You deserve it."

No sea of death, murder weapons, or crazed schoolgirls *and* a long weekend? My eyes went to the ceiling.

"What are you doing?" Sampson wanted to know.

"This can't be right," I told him. "I'm looking for the piano that's going to fall on my head."

When none did, I grabbed my shoulder bag, said something that may have sounded like, "See you Monday, suckas!" and hopped into the elevator. As the Underworld Detection Agency is a cool thirty-five stories *below* the San Francisco Police Department, I used the long ride up to mop my red hair from "business chic" into "reality-TV marathon ponytail," and shrugged out of my suit jacket. I was halfway to couch bound when the elevator doors slid open at the police station vestibule, to perfectly frame Alex Grace.

Alex Grace—fallen angel, delicious earthbound detective—the man I had an on-again, off-again, more-off-than-on-or-something-in-between relationship with over the last few (mortal) years. We had moved past that awkward, bumbling, he-caught-me-in-my-panties stage of our relationship and into a more mature, open, adult one.

But I tended to have a habit of crashing us back down to bumbling and awkward every spare chance I got.

"Alex!" I said, trying to keep my cool as every synapse in my head shot urgent and improbable messages: *Kiss him! Tear his clothes off! Maniacally mash the* CLOSE DOOR *button and hide under your desk!*

Alex had his hands on his hips, his police badge winking on his belt, his leather holster nestled up agat the firm plane of his are-you-kidding-me chest. His shoulders looked even broader, even more well muscled if that were possible, making his square jaw look that much more chiseled. His lips—full, blush-pink lips that I had pressed mine against more than once—were set in a hard, thin line. His ice-blue eyes were sharp.

"We need to talk."

While normally those words would make me swoon and rethink today's lingerie choices (white cotton panties dotted with pastel pink hearts; no-nonsense—and no cleavage—beige bra), the set of his jaw let me know that this wouldn't be a tea-and-cookies kind of chat.

My stomach flopped in on itself.

"And a kind hello to you, too."

Alex led me to his office, one hand clamped around my elbow as if I might dart away or steal something at any moment. It was awkward and annoying, but I guess he had just cause: I may have pilfered a cup of coffee, a jelly donut, or a piece of pivotal evidence in an open investigation once or twice.

I sat down in the hard plastic visitor's chair, and

he sat behind his desk in his I'm-the-boss chair, arms crossed, eyes holding mine.

"What do you know about Lance D. Armentrout?"

Heat pricked all over my body. Though I had just finished that case at a local high school, going undercover as a substitute teacher, I'd "taught" English, not social studies.

And either way, I had never done well on pop quizzes.

"Uh, he's the prime minister of—"

Alex cocked a brow. "I'm not testing you, I'm asking you. Never mind. Armentrout was a homeless vet who took up residence at the bottom of the Tenderloin."

San Francisco's Tenderloin district is just north of Market Street, sitting somewhere between seedy and squalid. Most tourists avoid it and some youthful hipsters or city planners were always trying to gentrify it, but nothing ever took. It was generally a spot where the homeless gathered, some drugs changed hands, or a hooker shivered on a street corner, but not necessarily a hot spot for major crime.

I felt that unfortunate spark of bad walking up my spine. "Was?"

Alex opened his ever-present manila file folder and handed me a photograph. "It was two weeks ago Sunday. The ME's report just came in."

I glanced down at the photo and immediately wished I hadn't. It was a half-charred body sitting on the sidewalk, what remained of his torso propped up against a pink stucco wall advertising *Panaderia Chavez*. Bile burned at the back of my throat. I slid the photo back to Alex.

"What happened? I mean, he obviously was burned to death but . . ."

Alex shook his head. "Witnesses said it was spontaneous combustion."

"Spontaneous combustion? That's not a real thing—is it? And wouldn't that mean—" I made the kindest gesture I could think of for a person exploding.

"Yes, it exists—sort of, and no, it doesn't always involve exploding. But it wasn't the fire that killed him."

"It wasn't?"

"No. Witnesses said he was sweating, then he started to shake. They said his skin was hot to the touch and, according to this person," Alex read from his file, "'his skin was smoking. Smoke was coming from his arms and his clothes started to burn. We tried to get his shirt off, but it stuck to him.'"

I pressed my hands against my mouth, willing the sick to stay down.

Alex continued reading. "'It was like he was boiling, first, and then he was on fire. I never seen anything like it.'"

"That's awful. So, wait, if the combustion didn't cause his death, what did?"

Alex pulled out the medical examiner's report and slid it toward me. I glanced over it, clamping my jaws shut. "Oh my God—his blood actually boiled?"

"The ME had never seen anything like it either, but apparently, it does happen."

I immediately felt heat shoot through my body. "What causes it?"

Alex shrugged. "Don't know. Neither did the ME. He is going to do some research and get back to me."

I could feel the sweat beading up at my hairline and moistening my upper lip. I could feel the flush in my cheeks and I used my hand to fan myself before going to the water cooler and drinking a full glass.

"You okay?"

I batted Alex away, waiting for the flames to start shooting from my eyes or wherever spontaneous combustion starts, but nothing did. Finally, I said, "That's awful, but if spontaneous combustion can happen, then what does this have to do with me or with the UDA?" I shifted my weight, thinking. "I am almost totally positive that there are no demons who spontaneously combust as a means of death. The guy is dead, right? Still?"

Alex nodded casually as though we were having a perfectly normal conversation. Which, unfortunately, we were.

"Yeah. Guy's still dead."

I shrugged. "So, why the sharesy?"

I know it sounded callous, but Alex and I worked together on a strictly supernatural basis. I was called in if there was evidence of magic, witchcraft, Satan, or some idiot's need to rule the world with a couple of black IKEA candles and some virgin's blood.

But if a case was standard, that was all Alex and the San Francisco Police Department's jurisdiction.

"Well, Armentrout was ultimately identified by his dental records." Alex then passed me that sheet, stamped with a military ID and government info. There was the standard image of disembodied teeth—top set and bottom—teeth randomly marked by ballpoint-ink X's for a missing molar and a handful of cavities. But the ballpoint pen had been used for something else, too—Ford's dentist had drawn two narrow images, one on each incisor. Rounded at the gum line, then each tapering to a fine point.

"He had fangs."

Alex nodded.

"Vampire."

"That's what it looks like."

I stood. "I'll bring this down to Sampson. I can't recall a Lance Armentrout in any of our records, but Sampson's got that bear-trap memory. Maybe he'll know."

Alex stood, but his face remained unchanged. "That's not all, Lawson."

Fireworks shot through my body as thoughts pinged through my brain. *Let's get back together! Let's make wild monkey love on this desk!* Yes, my pre-pubescent twelve-year-old-boy mind could go there sixty seconds after seeing a photo of a charred dead guy.

I wasn't so much sexually morbid as I was sexually frustrated.

"When the paramedics initially got there, Armentrout was still alive, still talking."

I stepped back, interested. "What did he say?"

"He said, 'Find her.'"

"Find who? An estranged wife, a daughter?"

As an orphan—my mother passed away when I was three and my father, we were pretty sure, was Satan—I had a particular soft spot for bringing families back together. Granted, I had been forced to stake my own half sister with a trident, but she was a seriously evil fallen angel and besides, she'd totally started it.

I considered being the one to reunite the memory of old Lance Armentrout to a long-lost daughter, or deliver some sort of years-old letter of love and apology to his estranged wife. It would be nice to be the bearer of good news for a change.

Alex looked away and I pressed harder. "Well, who was he looking for?"

Alex shook his head, blue, icy eyes intent on me as he handed me a scrap of paper sealed in a clear plastic evidence bag. I looked down at the paper; its edges were curled, licked by fire, but the words were clearly legible. A cold stripe of needling fear made its way down the back of my neck as the words swam before my eyes, then burned themselves into my brain: *Sophie Lawson, Underworld Detection Agency, San Francisco, California.*

Find her.

TWO

I tried to swallow, but my throat was a desert. "That's my business card."

Alex nodded. "I realize that. You're certain you don't know Lance Armentrout? Maybe from the UDA, or you guys ran into each other at some point?"

I sat gently on the edge of Alex's visitor's chair. "No. I told you I don't know him."

Alex's leather chair groaned as he leaned way back in it and crossed his arms in front of his chest. "So you have absolutely no idea why this man would have your business card in his hand or why we would tell the paramedics to find you? Why he would mention you as his *last* words?"

"Are you—are you interrogating me?" I felt anger flick at the base of my spine. "Am I a suspect or something?"

"Should you be?"

My mouth dropped open and now the flicker of anger was a full-on inferno. I stood, balancing against the desk as I leaned toward Alex. "Look, I know things aren't always great between us, but are you seriously suspecting me of torching a vampire? Have you forgotten? My best friend is a vampire, her obnoxious nephew is a vampire. And my manager! If my plan were to start killing vampires, don't you think I'd start with Vlad? At least then maybe I could get my couch back."

Alex stood, patting the air in that universal calm-down sign that only made my anger boil harder. "I was just being thorough, Lawson. I had to ask."

He didn't actually apologize and my anger didn't dissolve.

"Well, you can officially take me off your suspect list. Unless you don't believe me. Should I take a polygraph or something?" I flung an arm out, veins up. "Do you want to take a DNA sample? Go ahead."

Alex rolled his eyes, and I continued needling him with my red-hot glare.

"Lawson, it was a couple of questions."

"And I gave you a couple of answers."

I saw the muscle jump in Alex's jaw. "Why did he have your business card?"

"I work for the Underworld Detection Agency, Alex. Vampires are our main clients. Maybe he was on his way to see me."

"Yeah, but you front the Fallen Angel Division. Why would he want to see you? What was so important that his last words were 'find her'?"

A tiny tremor of anxiety danced up my spine. A lot of people have wanted to "find me" in the past. Generally, to kill me, bleed me dry, or stuff me into some sort of swirling vortex of Hell. I was a lightning rod for the stupid and mysterious, but this was one instance that clearly had a logical explanation. At least that's what I was telling myself as I tried to muster up my anger again, hoping it would douse out that niggling anxiety.

"Should I take this down to Sampson now, or can it wait until Monday?"

"Lawson . . ."

I looked at Alex and cocked a brow. "It's not a big deal, Alex."

"I think this could be something serious. I think this is something we need to pay attention to."

"I'm not worried. I'm done freaking out about everything."

Alex covered his mouth with his hand while he studied me. I could see him trying not to laugh, and I considered giving him a reality smack upside the head. I couldn't believe less than ten minutes ago I had been seriously considering getting naked (again) with him.

Finally, he went on.

"That's commendable. But Lawson, I think this really might be something you should start to freak out about. A man was burned alive and he had your business card in his hand. He begged the paramedics to find you."

Anger roiled through me—anger, tinged with the smallest bit of hurt.

"What's it matter to you how I react? Are you asking for my help on this case?"

"No, but—"

"But nothing then. I can take care of myself, Alex. I'm a big girl." I snatched the folder from him and turned on my heel, using every ounce of willpower that I had not to dart, running and crying, from the room.

I was new to this taking-care-of-myself, being-a-big-girl kind of thing.

I was barely over the threshold when I felt Alex's hand close on my elbow, his grasp gentle but firm.

"Lawson." His voice was soft and when I turned, so were his eyes.

"What?"

"Just because we're not, you know, together—it doesn't mean that I don't care about you. It doesn't mean that I don't still . . ."

He let his words trail off and every silent second that passed was an eternity, my eyes on his, neither of us willing to give in. I heard his voice in my mind, saw that image that I had studied from every angle every moment of the last few months:

I choose you, Alex. I want to be with you.

The muscle in his jaw jumped, and his lips were set in a hard, thin line. "Do us both a favor, Lawson, and don't."

A wave of nausea rolled through me and I shrugged his hand off my arm, steeling myself.

Alex Grace wasn't going to break my heart again.

"I'll be sure to consider the fact that you 'don't still' while I deliver this to Sampson."

I was out in the hallway then, making a beeline through uniformed officers who stared at me with slight concern as the tears rolled down my cheeks. By the time I pressed through the double doors and out into the faint San Francisco sunlight, I was breathing deeply, commending myself on not turning into a puddle of pitiful goo—bawling outright in front of a patrol officer leading a drunk to the tank notwithstanding.

My heart was thumping and my sadness was twisting around to sheer anger. *First he considers me a suspect, then he decides that I'm in some kind of danger?*

I was fuming by the time I hit Market and Fourth streets so I had to buy myself a cool-your-jets ice cream. I was loading it with sprinkles and cookie crumbles when a fire engine went sailing by outside, its siren so loud that the ice cream shop's windows shook. The woman behind the counter stopped wiping and looked at me. "That's the third one today."

"The third fire engine?"

She nodded. "The third fire. The other two engines went cruising that-away," she pointed her grayish rag in the opposite direction the most recent engine had gone. "Looked like they were going a hundred miles an hour or more." She pursed her lips and dropped the rag back on the counter. "Sure hope they got there in time."

I stepped a little closer. "Three fires?" I repeated. "Are you sure?"

"It was on the news and everything. The new fire marshal with the accent? He thinks they was all arson." She shook her head, clucking her tongue. "People seem to be just plum going crazy."

I fished my cell phone out of my purse and speed dialed Will Sherman. It went directly to voice mail, directly to his accented voice telling me, "You've reached Fire Marshal Sherman. If this is urgent, hang up and dial . . ."

* * *

I drove home chasing cheery songs on the radio—"Walking on Sunshine" on KOSF, "Accidentally in Love" on KFOG, but the slew of fire engines and the flambéed Lance Armentrout itched at the base of my skull.

Fire happens, I told myself. *There were always fires in the cities. And people occasionally self-combusted . . .* right?

My mind was a mass of bouncy tunes and flaming hellfires by the time I pulled around the corner to my apartment building. I lived in a squat, three-story place that bore all the beautiful architectural nuances of old San Francisco: hand-laid black and white tiles outlining a solid slab of marble in the front vestibule, intricate ceiling moldings, hand-tinned backsplashes. In keeping with times of 1905, the place also boasted a deathtrap-slash-elevator, poor heating, and windows that could snap and behead you at any moment.

But it had parking.

I sunk my key into the lock, hearing the jingle of ChaCha's collar as she threw herself at the door, yipping and growling. With the door closed, she was a fearsome predator, the weight of her well-muscled dog body thumping against the wood as she clawed and snarled. When I flung open the door she was still yipping and snarling—four and a half pounds of terrifying, flouncy beige fur and teeth the size of Tic Tacs. She popped up on her popsicle-stick back legs when she saw me, patting at the air with her front paws, her little pink tongue hanging out the side of her mouth. I dropped my shoulder bag and scooped her up.

"Hey, girl! You're a good little attack dog, aren't you? Yes, you are! Mama's going to spend some quality time with you, yes, she is!"

I clicked on the television and rifled through the fridge for something chocolate covered or at the very least, not rotten. I settled on a sort-of-yellow banana and was popping open a Fresca when a stern-faced newscaster broke onto the screen.

I instinctually went to the remote, but froze, arm extended, when the little box to the left of the anchor's face showed an animated picture of a fire truck, emblazoned with the word ARSON. I turned up the volume instead.

"Firefighters were called out three times today to fight flames in downtown San Francisco. Authorities were alerted to the first one at about ten o'clock this morning with an anonymous nine-one-one call."

"Nine-one-one, what's your emergency?"

The screen went blue, yellow words populating it as the crackling recording went on.

Heavy breathing. *"Fire."*

"I'm sorry, what was your emergency?"

"Fire."

"There's a fire? Sir, did you say fire? Where? What's your location?" The dispatcher's voice was direct and quick as the responder breathed heavily on the other end of the phone. *"Sir, are you in a structure that is currently on fire?"*

"They'll burn. Everyone will burn."

"Is there a safe way to exit? I have your location as one-

eleven Harrison Street. Can you tell me if you have access to a door or a window? Can you feel the door or window?"

There was another muffled word, but it was drowned out by the wailing sound of approaching fire engines.

"Firefighters are on their way to help you right now. Sir? Sir?"

There was the fumbling of a receiver, and then the line went dead. I sucked in a breath, a cold shudder whipping through me. The camera flipped back to the newscaster at her desk, her eyebrows knitted together sympathetically.

"The burning building was the old home of the Leonard Textile Mill. Though the nine-one-one call was shown to have originated inside that building, firefighters found no bodies inside the blaze, but they did find paraphernalia that led them to believe this fire was not accidental.

Firefighters are still working to contain the fire on Fulton and Golden Gate Avenue, which has grown to five-alarm. The earliest fire, called in at seven-twenty-five this morning from the Sunset neighborhood, was contained, but authorities have confirmed that none of the five occupants survived."

The television flicked to a picture of a single-family home pulled down to the studs, the wood wavy and black. The detritus of the home was scattered knee deep as a fireman waded through the remains with a clipboard. As the camera continued to pan, I could see little bits of someone's life—a bright red boot now licked by soot and partially melted, framed photos, the glass warped and yellowed, the once-smiling subjects grotesque and stained black.

"We will update you with more information as it comes in. For KNTV news, this is Patty Chan."

I muted the television, a heavy feeling of dread settling in the pit of my stomach. First Lance Armentrout, and now two buildings and a residence in quick succession . . . That familiar anxiety flared up again and I tried to quash it down.

Fires happened. People died. It was unfortunate, but not supernatural. I kept repeating the mantra, but I wasn't sure who I was trying to convince. The old me—the me of about three weeks ago—would have jumped to screaming conclusions that there was a fire-breathing dragon or a witch gone hellfire crazy on the loose. I would have thrown on my yoga pants and sucked down a Fresca, then gone screaming across the hall to rouse Will—my Guardian; we'll get back to that—or back down to the police station to get Alex while packing a crossbow and dragon bait into my bra.

But the new me was taking the fires and Armentrout for what they were—whatever it was that they were. Coincidences? San Francisco *is* speckled through with pre-twenty-first-century electricity and an inordinate amount of solid wood buildings. The general shift of the super magnetic field that hovered around the city? That's a thing, right? Global warming? I wasn't exactly sure, but I wasn't about to go ridiculously nerve-wracked on a dime again, either.

Though San Francisco is, at its core, a supernatural town, inhabited by all manner of demons as they mix with their human counterparts, it is also layered by the pathetically normal: grocery stores, religious zealots, dim sum. Not everything is brimstone and graveyard dirt. Of course, your garden-variety breathing San Franciscans have no idea that they're sharing a Muni seat with a decaying zombie corpse or that the local coffee shop serves the undead after dark. I've seen people look a troll right in the face and acknowledge nothing but the fact that he's only three feet tall—and let me tell you, that's not the first thing that hits you when you see a troll. It's the stench. The mossy, blue-cheese-left-out-in-Hell kind of smell.

And before you go saying that San Franciscans are crazy, envelope-pushing, leftist tree huggers and it's no wonder we cohabitate with the undead, you should know that you're doing it, too. The undead are everywhere, separated from our human vision by that thin, magical veil and the completely human rationale that there is no way the guy bussing the table at the local Chili's is a centaur. It's sort of a mythical hand-in-hand kind of thing.

I, however, had the aforementioned honorable distinction of seeing through that magical veil whether I wanted to or not. So when a three-foot troll dressed in a velour track suit and smelling like the devil's dung heap hit on me, I could see every one of his snaggleteeth and smell that horrifying scent that clings to my hair and clothing for hours after our encounter, like some sort of unholy bon-fire smoke.

And, since the supernatural super-vision also comes with the power to be completely unaffected by magic, I'd never be turned into a toad or charred by a pissed-off witch's thunderbolt, but I couldn't ever experience the beautiful incantation that puts a six-foot wall between me and that oversexed troll.

So I couldn't sing or dance, but I could see through supernatural veils and avoid magic and it had really never been more than a giant pain in my ass—except, of course, that my special abilities allowed me to enter the underworld and take a full-time job at the UDA. Even with the occasional death threats and sexual harassment via troll, running the Fallen Angels Division of the Underworld Detection Agency was as cush a job a chick with a BA in English could get. The dental care was superb (gotta love those vampire staff members), and I got paid vacation, weekends off, and the world's largest stash of fake sugar and non-dairy creamer since the majority of my coworkers took their blood red.

I supposed I owed a debt of gratitude for my abilities to my deceased mother, who had been a seer, and my absent father, who was probably Satan. Not Satan in the couldn't-you-at-least-pay-child-support kind of way, but Satan in the Prince of Darkness, Lucifer, Legion kind of way.

It was probably a good thing that he hadn't been around for the father-daughter dance in junior high.

After my mother's death, when I was a toddler, my grandmother hadn't talked much about my father, leading me to fantasize that he was some CIA super spy with a James Bond suit and George Clooney hair who would come and swoop in to find me one day. He would pepper me with apologies for never making contact, but it was all for my own good as he was such a wanted man from all the evil plots he'd foiled while I was being stuffed in my locker by the mean girls at Mercy High. We would run off together and live in a chalet in some part of the world where chalets were prevalent, and we would drink cocoa and he would tell me how he'd cried when he'd missed my eighth birthday, but he'd had to protect the prime minister of Dubai and there really was no safe way to send an American Girl doll at the time.

I fantasized much less about my father as I grew older, but I'd still found it a stomach-lurching shock when I'd realized that Dad's digs were probably more charcoal than chalet and that my direct bloodline contained a tendency toward belly fat, high cholesterol, and soul-stealing eternal torture.

I was pacing the apartment, pretending to be completely cool and unaffected when Nina pushed open the front door. She broke into an instant grin when she saw me, her tiny fangs pressing over the Corvette red of her lipstick.

"There's the little scamp who took off two hours early and didn't even bother to come get me."

"Sampson gave me the rest of the day off."

Nina kicked off a complicated-looking pair of Jimmy Choos and pulled a blood bag from her Plymouth-sized Marc Jacobs purse. She massaged the pouch for a beat before piercing it with one angled fang. "So, what did you do with two hours' worth of freedom? I'd shop. Or get a massage—you know, if I could."

Truthfully, there wasn't any real reason that she couldn't—except possibly that her cool, bloodless, breathless, marble-hard torso might make it a little rough for any living masseuse to get the knots out.

Nina glanced at the television and her face fell. "Please don't tell me you squandered your time watching marriage-to-murder stories on Lifetime?"

"Thanks for the vote of confidence, best friend."

She grinned, her teeth tinged a heady pink. "Tell me I'm wrong."

"You are. I had to stop into Alex's office." I took my time, letting the words come out slowly. Nina's eyes grew with every syllable.

"You saw Alex? How was he? How were you? Did you tell him you were dating someone?"

"I'm not dating anyone."

She sucked the last of the bag and massaged the bit of plasma at the bottom, tipping her head to slide it down her throat. "He doesn't need to know that. He just needs to know that you've moved on."

"Oh." I waved at the air. "I've totally moved on. Totally."

Nina gawked at me.

"Well, I'm no longer wearing sweatpants, okay? But we didn't talk about any of that. There was an incident."

The lock on the front door tumbled, and Vlad walked in, a backpack slung over one shoulder.

"What?" he asked as we stared up at him.

"Nothing, Count Chocula. Sophie was just telling me about an incident."

Vlad's face remained unchanged. "There's been an incident?"

"Nothing major," I said, eyeing Nina. "Just something Alex was a little concerned about. But I told him there was nothing to worry about." I shrugged, even though my anxiety seemed to inch up every time I thought about Lance Armentrout.

"Oh, God," Vlad moaned. "Is this another chapter in the Sophie Lawson/Alex Grace love story? Let me guess: you told him you loved him, someone dropped dead, now he won't call you back."

"Vlad, that's not nice. Besides, I think we're on Will now, right? She slept with Will last time."

Vlad rolled his eyes. "So hard to keep track."

"Do you guys want to hear this or not? And it's not about me and Alex. Or me and Will. It's about a dead guy."

"It's always a dead guy with you two. Or three," Vlad said, dumping his backpack and heading toward the kitchen,

I started telling Nina about my run-in with Alex, about Lance D. Armentrout, the barbecued vampire. Nina just sat there, gaping at me. "What?" I asked her.

"What? What do you mean, what? You just lay it all out there and that's it?"

I popped open my second Fresca. "What were you expecting?"

"Crying! Screaming! You to hide under the covers watching *Bandslam* while you mainlined chocolate marshmallow Pinwheels. What is this?"

"This? This is my Zen."

Nina leaned back, crossed her arms in front of her chest, and eyed me, the depth of her coal-black pupils shooting a chill right through me. "By this time you're usually hysterical, having slept with Alex or Will or possibly both while claiming that you love—no, hate—either or both."

"I don't fall into bed every time. That's just your favorite part to focus on."

"But you panic. And then there's always a run on marshmallow Pinwheels and soothsaying cantaloupe."

"You're right. That's my usual M.O. Obsessive panic, rash decisions, supernatural fruit. But you know what I figured out, Neens? We're going to be okay. We're always okay. We kick down a couple of doors, get into a few scrapes, but we always save the day. The five of us. As long as we're together—"

"Oh God," Vlad moaned from his spot at the kitchen table. "Is this the one where we have to sing? I'm not singing."

"No one's singing, Vlad." I stood up, the eighties sitcom we're-going-to-have-a-moment music playing in my head. "Everyone says they're going to start the apocalypse, but no one ever does it. It's not like starting a car. It's not like any idiot on the street or in a robe or lighting a candle can do it. If it ever happens, we'll have plenty of warning. And we can handle anything that comes our way until then." I looked at my friends. "Together."

Nina nodded, pleased. "Huh. I kind of like this kinder, gentler Sophie."

I sat down, slung my arm over the back of my chair, and kicked my feet onto the coffee table. "I prefer to think of it as the cooler, kick-assier Sophie."

"I think you mean more kick-ass."

I glared at Vlad. "More kick-assier Sophie is totally going to kick your sorry ass, Vlad."

He looked up, cocked a wicked eyebrow, and grinned. "Noted."

Nina shuddered. "Still. The guy was burned alive? I hate stories that have fire in them—blech!"

There are only three ways to kill a vampire: the Hollywood stake-to-the-heart (which is a lot more difficult than modern media would lead us to believe, I'm told), a full-scale beheading, or death by fire. And while very few things ever rattled my ever-living roommate, fire was one of them. Polyester was another, but other than me lighting a warehouse full of pants on fire once, one had nothing to do with the other.

I watched Nina swallow. "Do you think whoever lit up this Armentrout guy knew he was a vampire?"

Vlad sat down next to us, looking at me intently. "Is Alex working on this? Are you?"

"No." I shrugged. "You guys, I told you it was no big deal. This happened almost a week ago and not a single other body has turned up."

"I don't like this," Vlad said, shaking his head.

"I don't either, but I don't think we should be panicking."

"No. I don't like you sitting here, being so calm."

"Maybe I've learned a few things in my years of demon slaying and Vessel of Souls-being."

In addition to the roots of my family tree being Hell-adjacent and my penchant for attracting the worst and most evil in society, I also functioned as a kind of supernatural Tupperware. The Vessel of Souls is a non-tangible entity where souls not yet ready for Heaven or Hell are stored. A bunch of Holier-than-thou monks thought it would be nothing but shits and giggles to hide that entity in Satan's pug-nosed kid. On a day-to-day basis it really didn't affect me much, but in the grand scheme of things, it made my father (should he ever truly know I am the Vessel) want to kill and/or possess me, and kept the fallen angel I pined for (one Alex Grace, *natch*) in an eternal state of Earth-walking limbo.

"Grammar not being one of those learned things," Vlad said.

"As lovely as this is, I'm pretty confident that everything is under control." I stood up, but neither Nina nor Vlad moved.

"I told you, you guys—there is nothing to worry about. Unfortunately, crime is up everywhere. All crime, not just supernatural." I forced a chuckle. "What? Are you expecting the apocalypse?"

Vlad shook his head slowly. "No one expects the apocalypse."

THREE

I snorted at Vlad and was reveling in the sunshiny warmth of my newfound lack of crazy when we heard the thumping on the stairs.

"What the hell is that?" Vlad wanted to know.

I pulled open the door. "Sounds like someone is dragging a body. Oh my God, Will!"

Will Sherman looked as if he'd used the last of his strength just to crest the landing. His dark eyes were downcast, his hair dirtied with soot. There was a wide gash across his cheek, but it wasn't fresh. The blood had already congealed in some spots, was drying to a burnt rust color in others. He looked up when he saw me, his lips parting delicately as he flashed a weak smile. He gave me a two-finger salute.

"Consider yourself saved."

Normally, I would have come back with some sort of smart remark about him finally doing his job. When he wasn't rushing into burning infernos as a firefighter, he was my Guardian—not in the until-you're-eighteen or until-you-stop-being-a-nutter kind of way. It was more in the saving-you-from-ancient-evil-and-mortal-danger kind of way. And he's usually pretty good at it.

Unfortunately, I'm pretty great at plopping myself right back into mortal danger, ancient or otherwise.

I stepped in front of Will, his arm around my shoulders just before he fell. He trudged along, half helping while I walked him into the apartment. I gestured for Vlad to give up the couch and was expecting a growl in return, but his coal-black eyes were big as he took Will in.

"What happened to him?"

"The fires," I said as Will pitched onto the couch. "At least I'm assuming so, right, Will?"

But Will was already stretched out, blanketing our crumb-covered couch with soot. His eyes were closed and his breathing was shallow, but steady.

"I'm going to get something to put on that cut."

I couldn't have been gone more than a minute—we generally don't bother to put the medical kit away—but when I returned Will was sitting up slightly and Nina was sitting on the chair-and-a-half across from him, her face drawn as she leaned in. Vlad had taken the other chair, and for the first time, possibly ever, he looked interested, which I'd thought was physiologically impossible for a six-teen-year-old, regardless of how many years he'd been sixteen.

I broke up the little caucus. "What's going on? What happened, Will?"

"The fires," Nina said authoritatively. "He worked all night."

I fished through the medical kit, looking for something to clean Will's wound. "I thought there were only three fires this morning?"

Will pulled away as I dabbed Mercurochrome on his cheek. "They've been happening all night. Not huge ones, but enough to keep us in our boots."

I examined my handiwork before extracting a handful of butterfly bandages from the kit. "So how did you get this cut? Fire kick your ass?" I grinned, hoping to inject a little humor into cocktail-hour surgery.

Will's hand closed around my wrist. "About that, love."

Will had been born and raised in Chester, England, and in situations that didn't include blood and soot, his smooth British accent made me swoon.

Yes, I know. There's Alex and there's Will. Like I said, we'll get to that.

I let out a breath. "What?"

"These weren't your normal, garden-variety fires."

"What? Why?"

"Arson. All of them."

I shrugged, not understanding. "So there's a serial arsonist on the loose."

Will sucked in a breath. "Every one of the fires has been burning hotter than any other fire on record. We haven't been able to find an accelerant or point of origin. There's nothing."

Vlad looked up. "Then how do you know they

were arson? I mean, other than the idea that it's pretty weird to have multiple spontaneous combustions in the same city on the same day."

Will shifted and pulled a tiny hippopotamus from his pocket.

"That's a hippo. Unless it's also a junior pyromaniac, I can't exactly see what that proves."

Vlad came by and snatched up the little hippo. "It's a jump drive, brain trust."

I rolled my eyes and grabbed Vlad's laptop, handing it to him.

He scowled. "Use your own laptop. I'm in the middle of a game."

I yanked the hippo and glared at him. "You should start saving your games, brain trust."

I pushed the hippo bottom into the USB port and we all watched Vlad's *BloodLust* game—a fearsome-looking vamp a la Bela Lugosi—freezing on the screen, little animated drops of blood falling from his mouth, pausing in midair. A new screen popped up, black and white and grainy. The camera holder was walking quickly, as sirens and chaos wailed in the background. There were people crying and the rush of water spraying.

"Where is this from?" I asked.

"The fire. The most recent one. It's from the body cam on my uniform."

The camera finally settled on a building, huge flashes of white fire roaring through the windows.

I squinted. "What is that?"

Will leaned over and turned the volume up on the laptop. The camera focus became a little sharper and the shape standing in front of the house was a man, arms raised in a sloppy V, head thrown back. He was shouting something incoherent and seemed to be stomping or dancing. I could feel myself pale.

"Mentally ill? Terrorist?"

Vlad cocked his head. "He's speaking Latin."

"*In voco te Satana! Et educam vos de igne! Flamma tibi fortitudinem,*" Nina repeated. She took a miniscule step back. "He's calling Satan."

"He wants him to come through the fire. The flame will bring him strength, right?" Will said.

I looked at the drawn, studious faces of three of my dearest friends and felt like the village idiot. It wasn't that my Latin was rusty—it was more that it was completely nonexistent.

"You speak Latin, too, Will?"

"Don't look so shocked, love."

"Oh, you probably had to learn it as a Guardian, though, right?"

"I had to learn it in primary just like every other kid in England."

I threaded my arms in front of my chest and nodded nonchalantly. "Yeah, sure. Us too."

Nina turned to me, her mouth so wide open the knife-sharp tips of her fangs were visible. "It doesn't matter where he learned Latin, Soph. Are you hearing this? Is this the guy who lit the fire?"

Will nodded, raking a hand through his hair. "Gerry Ford. The homeless guy, not the president. Said he set the fire because the devil told him to."

I snorted. "Typical nutter."

Will, Vlad, and Nina all turned to me, faces serious.

"His Latin was impeccable."

"The incantation . . ." Nina shivered.

"What? This guy is a crazy. They're all over the place. If they're not screaming for Jesus or The Gap or a shot on Google Maps, they're screaming about Satan, right?"

Will reached out and poked a key and the video started over again.

"When he says 'the flame shall give you strength,' look in that window right there." He pointed to the screen and slowed down the video, the man's speech stretching out. If it didn't sound devil-like before, it certainly did now. When he got to the phrase, "*Flamma tibi fortitudinem,*" the flame in the window doubled in size, leapt from the window with a whooshing roar, and began raining flaming bits of detritus down to the ground. A piece of the flaming debris fell into the man's outstretched hand and he pulled his palm toward him, fascinated. Even with the grainy output, I could see the flame dancing in his eyes, illuminating the weird smile on his lips.

"Sir, sir, you're on fire! Let me help you!"

I could barely make out Will's accent behind the respirator as he yelled at Gerald Ford. When Will's gloved hands came into view, moving closer and closer to the man with the flame, Gerald looked directly into the camera, his eyes fearful but wild. He pulled his burning hand into his chest and I could see his skin crackling and bubbling as the fire engulfed each finger, then rose up his sleeve.

Bile itched at the back of my throat. "Turn it off, please."

Will looked at me with pity in his eyes, but shook his head. "In just a second. You need to see this."

Gerald Ford approached the camera—which meant he approached Will—the fire crackling up his arm and singeing the edges of his longish hair. His face was completely serene.

"The fire lives," Ford said in a delighted whisper. "The fire lives and so does he. You don't have much time, Will Sherman, and neither does she."

Breath choked in my throat and my eyelids felt as though they were glued open as the man crossed his arms in front of his chest and caught the rest of his clothing on fire. The flames rose and swallowed him, licking across his chest and his arms, moving toward his throat. Finally, they were at his chin, the flickering firelight reflecting in his wide-open eyes, illuminating the grotesque smile on his melting face.

I heaved and clapped a hand over my mouth. Nina handed me a glass of water and I sipped, grateful for her sympathy until she used her vampire strength to shove my head between my knees.

"Nina!"

"Just breathe, Sophie, honey. It'll be okay."

I pushed myself up to sitting again and glared at her, then looked at Will. "Why did you show us this?"

"Because that guy was talking about you," Vlad said as though it were the clearest thing in the world.

"Uh, no, I don't think so."

"Sophie, he knew who I was. He knew my name," Will said.

I felt a surge of vague hysteria and just as quickly stamped it back down. "You were wearing your uniform. Your name is right on your jacket, right there. And it's on your helmet!"

"My last name is on both of those things. Not my first name. And no reference to any kind of bird, let alone you, love."

I knew exactly what Gerald Ford meant. I know exactly *who* he meant. But I wasn't ready to let go of my cool new sense of not-freaking-out-ness just yet so I tried to play the logic card.

"San Francisco is a small place and you're out patrolling a lot. You talk to everyone. It's totally possible that you talked to Gerald once and he remembered you."

Will nodded. "True. And what do you make of the bloke setting himself on fire?"

"Crystal meth."

I had no idea whether or not crystal meth would turn someone into a human torch, but given that the alternative explanations were that my father had turned a homeless guy into an inflammable minion of Hell, or a homeless guy just decided to up and smoke himself for hellish glory, it didn't seem that far-fetched.

Nina swallowed. "I hate to tell you this, Soph, but—"

I held up a silencing hand. "Don't. I have a couple hours off work for the first time in I don't know how long, and horrible camera video aside, I would like to have at least a tiny sliver of enjoyment. Just an hour or two."

I could feel the sweat beading along my hairline

and upper lip while Nina, Vlad, and Will looked at me, each with a mixture of incredulity and sympathy in their expressions.

Honestly, I wasn't sure what was worse.

As I'd spent most of my adult life running from crisis to murderer to sadistic police officer, I knew how bad the video, the fires, and Lance Armentrout were. And what was far worse was the gnawing, warning ache at the pit of my stomach telling me that this case—these circumstances—would make everything I had faced in the past look like pure child's play.

"Please?"

My blood was already humming at a frenetic pace, but I was damn determined to keep a bit of normalcy in my early weekend. Will was exhausted and sooty and looked like the most beautiful calendar fireman in all of humanity, but he wasn't hurt. The fire had been contained, and it was a balmy and unreal sixty-six degrees outside my apartment window. I was pretty sure the entire world was going to come crashing down anyway, so I figured I deserved a few minutes of what passed as sunshine out here on the coast.

"I'm going to take ChaCha for a W-A-L-K."

Everyone stared at me, but no one spoke. I took that as a sign of agreement and stood up.

My little dog couldn't tell me when she had to pee and spent forty-five minutes each night fighting with a sock, but she knew how to spell "walk." She immediately tore into the living room and popped up on her hind legs, jumping around like a circus poodle.

The expression on Will's face was skeptical so I put a hand on his shoulder. "We're just going to the park and back."

He heaved himself up. "Just give me five minutes to change."

I shook my head. "Appreciate the sentiment, but I don't need an escort."

I looked to Vlad and Nina to back me up, but they were both staring at me, wide-eyed.

"Soph, I'm not sure going out alone is such a good idea."

I forced a smile and pointed to ChaCha. "I won't be alone."

"Right," Will said. "You'll be with your attack mop."

Vlad shook his head in disbelief as I scooped ChaCha up. "Something bad is simmering, Sophie."

"Yeah, well, call me if Armageddon breaks out while I'm out scooping poop."

FOUR

I clipped on ChaCha's rhinestone-studded leash—no easy feat, since she was jumping and yapping like a prisoner just set free—and grabbed her doggie diaper bag. I couldn't match my shirt to my skirt, but my pooch was outfitted with an entirely color-coordinated wardrobe, thanks to her auntie Nina, who practically ripped my throat out when I "forced" ChaCha into a blue nylon collar once.

I zipped into a windbreaker and mashed my Giants cap over my hair. It was still in its reality-show-marathon mess, so I pulled the hat down lower, shoving every bit of hair I could find underneath. A few red tendrils still poked out, but none of them were snarled or caked with chocolate, so I figured I was good to go.

The great thing about parks in San Francisco is that they are situated by, and basically hidden by, urban sprawl, so each postage-stamp-sized lot appears to be a lush, emerald jewel among hobos and hipsters. The closer we got, the spazzier

ChaCha got, her brown marble eyes bulging as she yanked against her leash, her tiny toenails clawing at the sidewalk as she struggled to gain an inch. I let her run the second we reached the small dog enclosure and she sped off, her feet barely hitting the ground as she pranced like a show pony through a collection of butt-sniffing dogs twice her size. When she came nose-to-nose with a miniature schnauzer, I thought for sure she'd turn tail and run, but she sucked herself up, making her body look minutely larger but no more fearsome. She bared her teeth and the schnauzer backed up slowly before trotting off to join a pack of beagles along the back fence.

"That little thing has some guts."

I blinked at the woman standing next to me. She was a full head taller than I am, her jet-black hair cut in a severe pageboy that ended at her chin. When she smiled, her eyes—a combination of midnight blue and violet—seemed to glitter.

"Yeah." Warmth bloomed on my cheeks. I may be absolutely adept at quieting a screaming banshee, but making small talk with the warm blooded isn't my strong point. "She's mine. She thinks she's a bull mastiff."

The woman nodded. "If only we could all be that confident, right?"

I smiled, suddenly feeling a lot less like a single-syllabled idiot. "Which one is yours?"

The woman gestured to a pile of beagles and mutts as they vied for a soccer ball glistening with slobber. "In there."

I was about to ask which dog when ChaCha's spastic barking cut through the calm of the park.

"Hey, could someone get this dog?"

A balding man in a Members Only jacket was shielding his dog as ChaCha inched forward, her spastic barking as terrifying as a pop song. I jogged over and snatched her up.

"I'm sorry, sir. She really is harmless. She's never bitten another dog or anything, she just likes to assert—"

But the man was crouching down, scratching his pooch under the neck while he murmured baby talk in its big, floppy ear. Finally he turned to me and pointed. "That dog is a nuisance. She should be leashed at all times. I could file a complaint."

I didn't have time to answer nor sic my tiny terror on him as the man marched forward, nose in the air, brushing by me with the faint scent of Drakkar Noir and dog slobber.

"Well, ChaCha, do you see where your aggressive behavior has gotten you?"

She did the air doggie prance in my arms, then struggled to climb up and give me a face-moisturizing kiss.

"Love you, too, you little monster. Ready to go home?"

ChaCha and I took the long way, crossing the park but giving the dog enclosures a wide berth. The sun was fading and the fog had rolled in, giving the early autumn air a cold bite and making the bushes and trees loom larger as people left the park in droves. I could see the woman with the pageboy crossing the street. She pulled her coat up tight, flipping her collar up to her ears.

I heard a low growl behind me. ChaCha immediately stiffened, the hair along the back of her neck bristling. She bared her teeth but stayed silent, her body pressing against my chest.

"It's okay, ChaCha baby. There are lots of dogs here. They're not going to hurt you. Mama won't let them hurt you."

I nuzzled into her warm, caramel-colored fur but she stayed stiff.

I heard the crackle of leaves behind me and then that deep, low growl again. My heart started to beat a tiny bit faster, and I tightened my grip on my dog as I slowly turned around.

I had never seen eyes like that before. Black, as though the iris covered everything. Flat, but focused, as though there were one thing—and one thing only—on his mind. The dog's black lips curled up, exposing incisors that looked as sharp as any vampire's, and he growled again. Only this time, it seemed to come in stereo.

"Good boy," I said, my voice shaking. "Good, good boy." I glanced over the dog's head. "Where is your person?"

The dog took another step toward me, his eyes focused on my throat.

My heart thudded and heat raced up my spine. *What were you supposed to do to quell an angry dog— run? Not run?*

I didn't have time to decide because the dog—a hard-muscled, fearsome-looking cross between a Rottweiler and a raging bull—charged, his jaws snapping, his short red-black fur glistening like scales on a fish.

ChaCha yipped and I spun, kicking dirt and leaves behind me as I covered ground, gripping my dog to my chest as my heart slammed against my rib cage. The dog barked, a throaty, deep roar that tore through the fog and terrified me. There was more barking, more than one dog could do, and as I hit the sidewalk, his paws thundered behind me.

The dog lunged and snapped, catching the edge of my scarf in his mouth and pulling with the force of a tow truck. I felt my knees buckle as the soft fabric tightened around my throat and I clawed at my neck, trying to release the noose.

The dog pulled and growled and barked.

I steadied myself and felt the nip of his teeth as he caught the back of my calf, teeth cutting like barbed wire right through my pant leg, scraping against my skin. It seemed like the dog was everywhere.

Finally, I found the edge of the scarf and wound my way free, catching a glance at the snarling face of the dog as he lunged closer. But it wasn't the same dog. This one had a narrow, almost pointed face, with a thin muzzle that made his teeth look that much bigger. In a split second I heard another bark, another snarl, but the dog's jaws were clamped tight.

A pack of dogs?

I kept running, my thighs burning, the hand that held ChaCha soaking from my sweaty palm, but I managed to glance back.

One dog. One thick, well-muscled body. Red

black fur stretched across a back that seemed as wide as a horse. Snarling, snapping jaws just at my waist—at my hip, at my flailing right hand.

One dog. Three heads.

If I weren't so terrified of even one rabid dog's teeth sinking into my flesh, I would worry about the three-headed monstrosity vaulting toward ChaCha and me.

I started to scream, and I could feel ChaCha's tiny body quivering against me. The dog seemed to be gaining on me and for the first time—probably in history—there wasn't a single person on the street willing to help. There wasn't a single other person out at all.

I flew off the curb, darting toward the door to my apartment, but the dog used the curb as a springboard. I felt his front paws on me first, his sharp nails digging into the flesh just below my shoulders, dragging long ribbons down my back. There was a head on either side of me, different colors, different breeds, but both with the same dark eyes. I had thought they were all black before, but now I could clearly see red pupils, bright like laser sights.

The head on my right was arching forward, the sinewy muscles of his neck bulging as his jaws snapped toward ChaCha. Her terrified tremble went through my whole body and her eyes were on me—trusting at first, then in a split second, resigned.

I didn't think. I shifted ChaCha and flung my arm, my elbow bashing warm snout. I felt the puncture of my skin as the other dog's teeth dug in. I felt my flesh clinging as he tried to pull it from the bone. The second and third heads must have smelled blood because they were whipping toward my gaping wound—and that's when it happened.

ChaCha.

She sprung out of my arms, a rocket of fluff and rhinestones, and went for the dog head closest to her. There was a growl, then a shriek, and I was set free. I shot toward the front door, my bloodied skin feeling icy as I ran.

"ChaCha!" I screamed for her as I slapped open the glass door to the apartment vestibule. She didn't come.

Ten paces back, the three-headed dog was glaring at me—six eyes with laser sights and bared teeth, this time dripping with blood. One of its enormous paws stepped forward a half foot, and I could see ChaCha's collar discarded on the pavement in front of it. The few rhinestones that weren't shrouded in blood winked in the light.

A cry lodged in my chest. I couldn't breathe. The torn skin on my shoulder burned and throbbed, but I didn't care. ChaCha was dead. ChaCha had lunged at a dog a dozen times her size to save me.

My heart was breaking.

I dropped to my knees, holding my head in my hands. Everyone—everything—I loved was in constant danger or ultimately destroyed because of me. The dog was after me. Where had it come from?

I vaguely heard footsteps coming down the stairs to my left, but I had no strength left in my body. I wanted to curl up there on the scuffed tile floor and every other tenant could just step over me—which is what the boots that caused the footfalls did.

I looked up, my face wet, snot running over my upper lip, and Will was right in front of me in a fresh T-shirt and jeans. His face crashed and he rushed toward me. "What happened? I knew I shouldn't have let you out alone."

I tried to shove him off me. "You didn't 'let' me out. I'm not a dog." My voice cracked on the last word and a new round of tears started to fall. "ChaCha . . ."

Will stood up and edged a hip against the door.

"No, don't, there's a—"

But he ignored me, cracking the door open about six inches.

And ChaCha darted in.

I lost my breath, my heart swelling. "ChaCha!"

She jumped right onto my lap, doing her little foot-to-foot dance, licking the tears from my face.

"What are you doing, letting that little mod out there all alone?"

I ignored Will and instead held ChaCha at arm's length, examining her for gaping wounds or missing limbs. Except for a tiny notch at the tip of her ear and a clutch of blood-matted fur by her chin, she was fine. I hugged her to me, thanking her profusely.

Will, still standing, shifted his weight. "I was the one who opened the door."

I pushed myself up and Will's eyes went wide all over again.

"What the hell happened to you, love?"

My hair must have shifted, showing more of the bite mark on my shoulder.

"Dog bite."

"From what kind of a dog? A giraffe?"

"A giraffe is not a dog, Will."

"And a dog that could bite you on the shoulder—short as you may be—is not a dog. Were you lying down or something?"

I sucked in a deep breath, still snuggling ChaCha against my chest. "It was a big dog. A mythical dog. A three-headed dog."

"Run that by me again, love."

"A big—"

"I got the big. I got the mythical. But three-headed? You're telling me there's a three-headed werewolf"—Will turned toward the glass door—"out there?" He very gently pushed my hair over my other shoulder and touched the bite mark. "He got you. Does that mean you're a—you're a—" I could see the terror in his eyes.

"A werewolf? I'm very touched by your concern, but I'm not turning into a werewolf."

"Whew! Thank God! I know our deal is that I only have to guard you from the fallen angel things, but I'm pretty sure getting you turned into a werewolf won't go into my gold-star file."

I put my one hand on my hip. "Thank you so much, oh, white knight. First of all, there were no werewolves. Second of all, it was a dog. A three-headed dog. Like Cerberus."

"Well, multiple heads or not on your Rin Tin Tin, we should get that bite cleaned up." He stepped closer. "Doesn't look like you'll need any stitches."

I jerked away. "Three heads. I saw it."

Will laced his arm through mine, and as annoyed as I was with him, I let him lead me to my third-floor apartment. We had just stepped out of the elevator when my front door opened and Vlad poked his great white head out. I saw him sniff, his eyes lighting up.

"Who's bleeding?"

It's nice to be welcomed home by a roommate. It's less nice when you're welcomed home because you smell like the vampire equivalent of a steak dinner.

Vlad's face fell when he saw me. "Oh, it's you."

Will and I stepped into the house, and I rolled my eyes. "Even if it weren't me, you could smell but not taste, you know."

Vlad shrugged and slunk back to his computer.

"Sophie Lawson, what have you gotten yourself into now?" Nina pressed her fingers to her forehead. "I swear I'm not going to let you out alone anymore unless you're fully engulfed in bubble wrap and a helmet."

"She was bitten by a dog," Will said, making a beeline for our medical kit.

I yanked open the fridge and plied ChaCha with a half-pound of roast beef before flopping down on the couch. My adrenaline was starting to wear off, and I was beginning to feel the sting and ache of my run-in with the dog.

"It wasn't just a dog, Neens."

"That's right. It was multi-headed," Will reported as he came back with the kit.

Vlad's dark eyes appeared over his computer screen. "Multi-headed?"

"Three-headed."

Vlad and Nina exchanged looks while Will handed me a wet washcloth and went to work on my shoulder.

No one spoke for a beat.

I wiped the cool washcloth over my brow and broke the silence. "It's obvious what's going on here."

Will, Vlad, and Nina all swung to face me.

"The gates of Hell have been opened and Cerberus was sent to find and kill me."

Nina arched a brow. "Cerberus? He had a name?"

"Cerberus is the three-headed dog that guards the gates of Hades, according to Greek mythology."

"You're jumping to conclusions, Soph. It was just a dog."

"I didn't jump to any conclusions. Conclusions came snarling and snapping at me in a murderous rage that may or may not have been rabid. With three"—I held up my fingers again—"heads."

"The whole thing happened pretty fast, love, and I know you were frightened. Are you sure it just didn't seem like the dog was multi-meloned?"

"I saw what I saw."

"A three-headed dog," Vlad confirmed. "You know what that means."

I narrowed my eyes, daring him to say it. He silently mouthed the word, *Armageddon*.

"Okay, so you're telling me that a three-headed

dog chased you from the dog park, and ChaCha"—
Nina pointed to my heroic pooch, who was now
sprawled out on the floor, giving her lady bits a
good licking—"all four and a half pounds of her,
came to your rescue."

I nodded.

"From a three-headed dog."

I looked at Will and Vlad for confirmation or
support, but got nothing. "I don't see why this is so
hard to believe. I've been chased by werewolves,
witches—hell, Neens, you're a vampire."

"But Campos—or whatever the crap you called
him—is a creature in Greek mythology. And he's
the guardian of *Hell*."

"Maybe the bloke got fired? Doing some work on
the side?"

Vlad huffed. "I think we're all forgetting Occam's
razor here." He looked at all three of us, then
rolled his eyes when no one agreed. "You know, the
simplest explanation is generally the right one?"

I crossed my arms in front of my chest. "So what's
the simplest explanation, Vlad? We're hanging on
the precipice of the end of the world?"

"Of course not. I was just messing with you. It's
obvious you were hallucinating." He offered me an
apologetic frown and patted me gently on my good
shoulder. "It was bound to happen. Your grip on reality was tenuous at best."

I slapped his hand away. "I was not hallucinating!
Did I hallucinate this?" I swung so my back—
scratched, shredded—was visible. "And this?" I
jerked a thumb toward the now bandaged wound
on my shoulder. "Clearly a dog bite."

"A dog," Vlad stressed.

"It was one dog," I challenged back. "Three heads."

Will snapped the emergency kit closed and looked at me. "You doing okay? Want to get a bite or a lager before?"

"Before what?"

"Before we go looking for a three-headed dog."

I sped into my bedroom, threw on my best pair of mythical-dog-chasing pants, and sucked in a hard breath.

Cerberus was a three-headed dog. The guardian of the gates of Hell. I slunk down on my bed and pressed my eyes shut, trying to call up the scene in my head. I saw his huge paws closing the distance between us. Smelled the salty stench of dog breath as his jaws snapped shut just behind my left ear. I heard the sound of my flesh puncturing as his incisors sunk in, then the overwhelming penny scent of my own blood. But had it just been a dog?

I opened my eyes and blinked at myself in the mirror. What happened to the non-jumping-to-conclusions, cooler, more Zen Sophie Lawson?

It was just a dog, I told myself.

It was just a dog.

Once I got my breathing under control, I stepped into the living room, where Nina and Will were in the kitchen, Nina rifling through the freezer while Vlad looked on contemptuously between text messages.

"We're not going to look for the dog," I said with as much authority as I could muster.

Will blinked at me. "Why's that, love?"

The bandage over my bite mark itched. "Maybe

I was wrong. Maybe it was just a regular dog, you know? I could have just—I mean, I've had a lot on my mind so maybe I was just . . ."

Nina turned to face me, a kind-of-proud grin splitting across her face. "A kinder, gentler Sophie."

"I thought she was more kick-assier," Vlad grumbled.

The doorbell rang and while my hackles went up, a grin split across Will's face.

"Pizza's here."

My head was swimming and I pinched the bridge of my nose, trying to straighten up.

"The guardian of the gates of Hell has escaped and you're ordering pizza?"

Will tipped the pizza guy and immediately helped himself to a slice, gesturing toward the TV. "And watching a game. It's not Arsenal, but at least it's football."

I stared at him, hands on my hips, for a quick beat before I relented and helped myself to a slice.

"And by the way," he continued, "we're going after that dog. Got any beer?"

The bite of pizza I had already taken was like wet sand in my mouth. "Will, I told you—maybe I was wrong."

"You know you're not. Anyone else I would doubt, but because it's you . . ."

He let the word trail off and I felt steam rising in my gut. "Because it's me? Like, because I'm such a klutz? Or because I'm the kind of person that dogs and people want to kill on a regular basis because I'm such a jerk? What is it, Will? Come on. Out with it."

Will went from leaning toward me to shrinking back. "Is it your time of the month or something, love?"

I slammed my pizza slice back into the box and fumed. "That's your response? I was almost killed by a three-headed dog today. A three-headed dog that almost ripped the throat out of my little teeny baby and you ask if I'm on my period?"

Will finished his slice and wiped his hands on his jeans. When he was done chewing, he glanced at me with an exasperated expression. "I believe that you were chased by a three-headed dog because you're the Vessel of Souls and I am your Guardian. Your klutziness and general jerkiness did not factor into my statement. And it's obvious by your delightful demeanor that your hormones are up to par." He offered a Styrofoam container to me. "Hot wing?"

I grumbled, but took the container of hot wings.

"So much for going Zen, huh?" Vlad called from his place behind his computer screen.

I flipped Vlad off, pulled two bottles of beer from the kitchen, and flopped down next to Will on the couch. I offered him a bottle. He opened both of ours with his keychain bottle opener and cheers-ed me.

I took a long pull on my beer.

I really wanted to remain calm. I really wanted to be nonchalant and believe that the three-headed dog was a figment of my imagination or that I had mistakenly eaten a handful of hallucinogenic mushrooms.

Two more monster-sized swigs and I was no calmer.

"So?" I said finally.

Will turned and looked at me as if surprised that I was still there. I snatched up the remote and turned off the game.

"Oy!" he cried.

"We need a plan, Will. Do you really think we're just going to run outside, shake a box of Milk-Bones and hope Cerberus comes running?"

"You didn't need to turn off the game."

I pinned him with a glare. "You're supposed to be my Guardian. So"—I gestured toward him—"guard!"

"I've been a great Guardian. You've haven't died yet now, have you?"

I rolled my eyes.

"Even if we can attract Cerberus, what then? He doesn't talk."

"We can get the pooch to lead us to someone who does."

Bat wings jabbed in my stomach and I sucked in a shaky breath. Cornering a mythical dog—even a multi-meloned one, as Will put it—was one thing, but letting that dog lead us to . . .

My father's image flashed in my mind and my heartbeat sped up. If this dog really was Cerberus, the Hell hound, then that meant—could that mean—? I stepped backward, my whole body breaking into a cold sweat.

Will cocked his head, the gold flecks in his eyes dancing as he studied me. "What's wrong?"

I swallowed heavily. "Maybe I was wrong. Maybe

it wasn't—maybe it wasn't a three-headed dog, you know? It was really fast and I was scared so it could have been—it could have been just me."

"You're back to second-guessing yourself now?"

"Well, really, what are the odds?"

A tiny smile played on Will's lips. "What are the odds, says the woman who holds all the departed souls of the universe?"

"I just—I don't know if I'm ready for this, Will."

"Ready for what, love? We don't have any idea what's going on yet."

I looked at Will and he stared back at me. I knew I didn't have to say a single word for him to know everything I was feeling. Was Cerberus really after me? Had my father really sent him? And if so—why? Why now?

Suddenly, my skin felt too tight. "I just—I don't know if—"

Will took both my hands in his and led me around the couch, giving me a soft shove down so that I was sitting. My breath was coming quick and tight now, and in one fell swoop he pushed my head between my legs.

"This isn't really helping," I said to our filthy carpet.

"Breathe slowly, or deeply or something."

I sat up and glared at him. "Don't you have to have paramedic training?"

He shrugged. "I don't know what to do about mythical panic attacks." He paused for a beat before breaking out into an enormous, annoying grin.

"What?"

"Feeling better now, aren't you?"

I flopped backward on the couch, rubbing little circles at my temples with my index fingers. "Okay, what do we do? How do we go about finding this thing? I don't think there's any chance we could just head down to the nearest Kinkos and run off a few lost-dog fliers, huh?"

"'Have you seen my three-headed dog?' I suppose it would get people's attention."

"People are crazy about their—" I felt my brows furrow. "That's weird."

"What's that, love? Being attacked by a Hell hound on Fulton Avenue?"

"Remember when I told you about the woman that I met? Right before the run-in with poochie?"

Will nodded.

"She said that her dog was playing with a group of other dogs at the park. She kind of just vaguely pointed when I asked which one was hers."

"And was one of them him?"

"No." I swung my head and turned to face Will. "That's the thing. Right before I heard Cerberus behind me, I saw the woman. She was walking up Hayes, leaving the park, but she didn't have a dog with her. She didn't have anyone with her."

"Do you think she was with Cerberus?"

"Maybe she was with him, or maybe she just told him to sic me." I shook my head. "I don't know, though. He came out of nowhere. But, anything is possible."

Will gently touched the gauze that was puckered around the bite mark on my shoulder. "Anything is around here."

I felt myself draw into Will's sweet, comforting

eyes even as the wound burned underneath his fingertips. "Maybe some meat?"

Will blinked.

"Excuse me?"

I pulled away, trying to break the moment. "Maybe we should get some meat. That will help bring out the dog, right?" I crossed into the kitchen and began rifling through the fridge. Behind me, Will raked a hand through his hair, the movement reflected in the stainless steel oven.

"If a Hell hound eats meat. I was thinking more small children."

In my imagination, our refrigerator is always stocked with healthful snacks like yogurt and fruit, and maybe the occasional lone cupcake or flaky custard tart. In actuality, our fridge is one part science experiment, two parts phlebotomy storage. Tonight there were three Styrofoam take-out containers stacked one on top of the other—though I can't remember the last time I ate out—a half-can of chocolate frosting, something that was a peach and now might be an avocado, and Nina's neat stack of blood bags, alphabetized from A to O. There was also a handful of condiments and a box of baking soda that had come with the fridge.

"I'm not sure anything here would attract a dog."

"You don't have any steak or anything in the freezer? Some bacon or something?"

"I gave it to ChaCha. Wait!" I snapped. "I've got burgers."

"Great. I'm going to grab my coat and some rope in case we have to wrestle the bugger. You warm up a few of those burgers, really get the meat smell going. Maybe we can hold them out of the car window or something."

I nodded, impressed. "Look at you with a plan."

Will closed the front door and I got to work frying up four burger patties, flopping the finished products onto a paper plate. I grabbed half a roll of paper towels and met him in the hallway, where he was coiling a length of rope over one shoulder, Indiana Jones style. His eyebrows dove down when he saw me.

"What do you have?"

"Meat." I held the plate up closer for him to inspect.

He wrinkled his nose. "Doesn't smell like meat."

"It's vegan."

"What?"

"They're veggie burgers. But they look and taste just like real meat."

"In what dimension?"

I rolled my eyes. "Are we going to do this or not?"

"Come on. One three-headed dog who hopefully has a taste for soy and cardboard, coming up."

FIVE

Will and I were silent as he started the car and pulled out into the cool night. I balanced the bait plate on my lap, sitting up straight, my eyes darting toward the dark crevices of every building we passed, straining to see into the hulking shadows cast by parked cars.

"I don't see him."

Will turned toward the park and nudged me. "Roll down the window."

"Oh, right. The dog will be attracted to the smell."

"I don't care about the dog. I don't want that noxious odor seeping into Nigella's interior."

Nigella was Will's beloved car. She was a broken-down Porsche from the seventies that sported a maroon and rust paint job and deep bucket seats lined in the most horrendous Pepto pink and white leather. As far as I was concerned, Nigella had two wheels in the scrap metal pile and the other two on a banana peel, but Will protested, certain he would restore her to her former glory. He hadn't done so much as put up an air-freshener cone. But, she ran, and wasn't spray-painted across the hood with graffiti that said VAMPIRE, so she was one up on my car.

I picked up one of the glossy veggie patties between my forefinger and thumb and hung it, and my head, out the window.

"Uh, here, doggie. Here, pup." I whistled. "Here, boy."

"Throw the burger."

"What?"

"Crumble it up and throw a bit of the burger. Maybe it'll lure him out."

I sighed as Will slowed to a crawl near the corner where Cerberus had started to follow me. "Here, doggie."

I crumpled up the faux burger and tossed pieces of it toward the sidewalk, the grayish pieces falling with a greasy smack on the concrete.

"This isn't working, Will. There's no one out there."

Will leaned his head out his open window. "Here, pup. Here, dog. I've got some delicious, delicious Vessel of Souls just waiting for you to take a bite!"

"Thanks a lot."

"It's just a ruse, love. I would never feed you to a three-headed dog, you know that."

I slunk back into my seat. "We're going to have to get out of the car. Hey." I pointed. "Over there. There's a spot."

We strolled down to the dog park in silence, me carrying my plate of veggie burgers, Will whistling, rustling bushes as he passed them.

"Which way did the lady with no dog go?" Will asked once we'd crossed into the park.

"I met her here. We were talking right here and the dogs were playing over there. At least, the dog she pointed out as being hers was playing over there."

"Did you notice anything different about her? Hooves, scales, face on the back of her head?"

I cocked an eyebrow. "Do you think I wouldn't have noticed any of that? She looked normal. Completely normal."

"Except that she is the owner of a Hell hound."

"We don't know that for sure. It's just a hunch." I picked up another patty and swung it. "Hell dog! Come on, Hell dog! Uncle Will wants to wrestle with you!" I chucked the thing and heard the sickening slap as it hit the hard-packed dirt. "I don't even know what we're doing out here. If the dog comes after us, we're going to be running away from it."

"You might be running away."

"Either way, we won't be able to follow it anywhere."

"Maybe it has a collar."

I shot Will a look.

"It's worth a shot. He's got three necks to wear it on."

We stepped out of the car. I took a huge gulp of the sea-tinged air, loving the way it chilled my lungs the whole way down. If we weren't on the hunt for some sort of underworld demon, it would qualify as a perfectly pleasant night.

"Let's try down by the dog park. We can just retrace your steps. Maybe poochie is still around."

Though the cars shot by with blinding headlights and lights were on at the gas station, stores, and homes lining the park, the park itself rested in a tiny pocket of darkness. The surrounding lights just shadowed the mature trees, making them look ominous and menacing. I tightened my windbreaker and tossed a veggie patty in front of us.

"Here doggy, doggy."

We waited in silence, me standing there with my plate of burgers, Will with arms crossed in front of his chest.

"Maybe this wasn't such a good idea."

I tossed the last burger. "You think?"

A car horn wailed in the distance, but once it stopped, we both heard it—the shifting sound of feet pushing through the dried leaves on the ground. Will grabbed me by the elbow and we crouched down, hiding behind a thick bush.

I couldn't see anything immediately, but there was definitely someone—or something—moving through the brush. The footfalls were measured, deliberate.

"That's not a dog," I whispered to Will.

He pressed his index finger in front of his lips, then mouthed, *Wait*. I did, while he slowly rose to his full height and crept, silently, away from the bush.

I've never been good at doing what I was told or keeping myself out of harm's way, but this time, I really wish I would have. Will was a half step in front of me when I heard the slice of knife through air.

There was a shriek and something heavy bowled into me. I hit the ground in slow motion, hearing the crunch of every bone as my body made contact with the earth. My lungs seemed to constrict and fold in on themselves, and I was desperate for breath, my lips feeling chapped and huge as I sucked frantically, unable to breathe.

My head hit the hard-packed dirt last and stars shot in front of my eyes. Electricity burned through me, and the city sounds were drowned out, replaced by a frenzied buzzing in my ears, a din so sharp it rattled through my teeth.

"Will!" I was finally able to eke out his name, but he didn't answer me. I clawed at the ground, ignoring the screaming pain in my body, pressing myself to turn, to try my best to crawl toward where Will was.

I saw the man in front of Will. He was dressed all in black, but there was something about his clothes, something that didn't look right. He didn't look like an average city thug.

He and Will were equally matched in height and weight, but the man jabbed at Will with a long, slick blade that reflected the pale light of the moon.

Definitely not an average city thug.

"Will!" My voice had gained strength. The attacker's attention snapped away from Will and he focused on me as if just realizing I was there. He was wearing a black mask that went down past his nose, his eyes piercing and sharp behind the two narrowed slits in the mask. His lips curled up into a grotesque smile that shot ice water down my spine.

"You." It was a growl more than a word and

suddenly the man was lunging toward me. It all happened in painfully slow motion: his arm reaching out, his fisted hand gathering the fabric at my chest—the way he lifted me as if I didn't weigh a thing. I blinked and he slammed me up against a tree, the back of my head snapping against the rough bark. Leaves shimmied down all around us as though we were happy picnickers and not strangers in the midst of the fight of our lives.

I kicked out and made contact, my left foot getting him right in the abdomen. It seemed to surprise him for a half second, just long enough for me to reach forward and scratch at the man's eyes.

I saw Will come up behind him, his arm snaking around the man's neck. What happened next I will never be able to forget, the blazing, bloody millisecond etched in my brain forever: Will's grip tightened. The man let me go. I saw his hand go for his jacket. I saw it disappear. I saw it reemerge, saw the paper-thin edge of a dagger as he turned and sliced Will across the gut.

"Will!"

I crumbled to my knees, crawling through the dirt toward him. Somewhere, in the back of my mind, I knew the sticky wetness that was pooling around my fingers was blood—Will's blood—but I refused to let myself think about it. I vaguely heard the sound of leaves crunching and then the thud of footsteps as the masked man ran away.

"Will! Will!" I said, crawling up next to him.

He looked uncomfortably calm, his complexion waxy. "Sophie," he whispered.

"I'm here, Will. I'm here."

"I need you."

I felt the tears pouring in heavy sheets over my cheeks. "I'm here, Will. I'm here for you."

He took a long, shuddering breath and a tiny triangle of pink tongue darted out of his mouth. He winced, then stared up at the moon.

"No, Will, no." I swung my head. "Stay here. You can't die. You cannot die! I can't do this alone—I can't do this without you! You're going to be fine. You're going to be fine."

My eyes immediately went to where his hands were, pressed against his belly. His fingers were slick with blood, and I felt the bile burn up the back of my throat. "Oh, Will."

"Cell phone."

"Yes!" I was digging around for my phone when I heard the sirens. A police car was fronting a fire truck and an ambulance, tearing down the street in our direction. The colored lights flashing on the darkened buildings around us was the most beautiful thing I've ever seen and I flew to my feet, jumping up and down, flagging them down.

"Hey."

I went back down to my knees. "Will, they're on their way. The police, and an ambulance. You're going to be okay."

"I know." He shifted and gave a little cough that exposed his teeth. They were bathed in blood and I looked away, winced. "It'll take a hell of a lot more than a little stab to take me out."

I nodded, wanting to laugh, but this was no "little stab." The cut went from the bottom of Will's right rib in a perfect slice to his right hip. The blade made a clean cut through his T-shirt, through his skin and layers of flesh. More blood, so dark in the moonlight that it looked black, pulsed from the wound each time Will took a breath—each time his heart pounded.

I blinked back tears as he pressed against his gut, his blood covering his hands and digging into his fingernails. He rasped.

"Will," I said. "Oh, Will."

"I need you to take this. Hide it." Slowly, painfully, he rolled up on one side, exposing a dagger with a weird, rounded blade.

"Is that what—I didn't see—"

The weapon that I had seen sink into Will had looked like a normal dagger. Straight blade. Plain, utilitarian hilt. Nothing stand-out about it. This knife that Will was trying to press into my hands was elbow-to-wrist in size, with that strange, curved blade.

"Where did this come from? The blade that got you was—"

"I know. I pulled this from his belt before I went down."

Close up, I could see that there was something etched on the blade, tiny symbols carved in a swirl from tip to hilt. The gold continued to the quillon, which rolled up, their edges seemingly as sharp as the blade. At the base of the hilt was a cross, also done in gold. I stared down at it. Looking down at the knife in my hand the cross was right side up, but if I were to point the blade down, the cross was upside down.

"An upside-down cross," I whispered, feeling my stomach shift. "Evil. Satan—"

Will wagged his head, a nearly imperceptible move from side to side. His voice was barely a whisper. "Bring it to Alex."

"Is it yours?"

Will worked hard to focus on me. "Hide it until you can get it to Alex. You have to bring it to him. He'll know what to do with it."

I edged the knife away and slid the cold, dirty blade underneath my sweatshirt. I knew that if Will was suggesting I do anything with Alex, then this knife was something big—something huge. On a normal basis, Will and Alex wouldn't share a bagel, let alone the weapon of a—I felt the sob choking in my throat—possible murderer.

After the paramedics loaded Will into the ambulance—and he gripped my hand, reminding me that I had to go find Alex—I jogged back to my apartment, clutching the dagger in my rolled up sweatshirt. My T-shirt was sweat soaked and my teeth were chattering; by the time I made it home I was certain I smelled like veggie burgers and despair.

Nina sat bolt upright when I walked in. "I take it you found your Hell hound."

"No." All I could do was swing my head. My lips felt chapped, my throat bone dry. Nina handed me a glass of water, and I drank gratefully, then pushed my bundled sweatshirt onto the table.

Vlad looked up from his laptop, gesturing

toward the sweatshirt with his chin. "What's that?" His nostril flicked. "And whose blood?"

I looked down at my hands and my breath caught. I hadn't realized that I was covered in Will's blood. I started to sob. "It's Will's. Oh, God, Nina, someone attacked Will. He was stabbed!" I fell against my best friend and cried until I started to hiccup.

Nina held on to me, awkwardly patting my back and rhythmically murmuring, "There, there." She let me gather myself together before she dragged me down to a chair and gaped. "What do you mean someone stabbed Will?"

I sucked in a deep, steadying breath. "Someone attacked us while we were out looking for the dog. Will saved me, but the guy, the guy—" A wave of nausea roiled through me. "The guy stabbed him."

"Is he okay?" She sprang up from her chair. "What are we doing here? We need to go to the hospital."

I took Nina's hand. "No, he told me not to. He told me—"

"To bring this to Alex?" I hadn't noticed that Vlad had deserted his spot at the table and unwrapped the dagger from my sweatshirt. He was holding it just inches from his face, seemingly mesmerized by the thin, sharp blade.

"How did you know that?" I asked.

He turned the dagger over and over in his pale hands, fingering the fine etchings in the handle. "Because it's the sword of the Grigori."

Nina and I glanced at each other, blank faced, and then at Vlad.

"Who is the Grigori?"

"Not who," Vlad said, leaning over his laptop, his fingers flying over the keys. "What."

He turned the laptop to face us, and Nina and I leaned over, nearly cheek to cheek—mine hot, hers ice cold.

"The Watchers," I whispered, fascinated. "So they're not exactly fallen angels."

"But they are evil," Vlad said.

"Evil? It says right here they taught their human counterparts how to make metal weapons and cosmetics. The race that created MAC can't be all bad." Nina batted her heavily mascarra'd lashes.

"I don't get it," I said, pushing the laptop closed. "Why would the Grigori be after Will?"

"They're not after Will, Sophie. They're after you."

There was something in the way Vlad said it, his voice edged with a severe finality, that made a fist of terror grip my heart.

"Because I'm the Vessel."

Vlad nodded.

"So, the fallen angels want to kill me and now so do the Grigori." I opened the laptop up again, in a panic, and began reading. Finally, I pointed, my body breaking out in a cold sweat. "There! There! It says there was a flood and they were all wiped out. Right? So maybe all but that guy. Or, or, maybe he's not even really one of them, maybe he just got the sword, you know, at a garage sale. And this is all a huge, funny coincidence that we'll laugh about. Ha, ha, ha." I forced a loud, high-pitched laugh that came out sounding more psychotic than confident. "Right?"

"There were two hundred original Grigori. Some of them mated with human women and created the Nephilim, but some of them didn't. They were left to walk 'the Valleys of the Earth'"—Vlad made air quotes—"until Judgment Day."

"But if they were cast out of Heaven and made to wander around . . ." Nina began.

"They were ripe for the picking. They turned even darker. They want the Vessel of Souls for themselves," I said.

"Or for the person they're working for."

I sat down with a hard thump. "Let me guess. For Satan? Dear old dad strikes again."

I wanted to hyperventilate. I wanted to scream. I wanted to gut myself and dig out whatever the hell the Vessel of Souls was with a soup spoon and pass it off to anyone who wanted it, anyone who could guarantee that Will would make it home alive.

"I have to call the hospital."

I slammed the door to my bedroom and dialed the hospital, then paced while they put me on hold. The computer voice told me that my call was important, and would be answered in three minutes. And maybe it was—but every second that passed dragged on and on and I was growing more certain that Will was splayed out on some emergency room table, dying.

"Screw this."

I grabbed my jacket and the Grigori dagger and cut through the living room.

"Where are you going?" Nina wanted to know.

"I'm going to check on Will. Then I'm going to take out what's left of the goddamned Grigori."

SIX

I must have driven with blinders on because I made it to the hospital in record time. I don't know if I stopped for any lights or, hell, if I even stayed on the road, but me and my car made it in once piece so I considered that a plus. I dialed my phone as I crossed the parking lot.

"Grace?"

"Alex? It's me. You need to come down to San Francisco General right now."

"Lawson?" His voice grew tight. "Are you okay?"

"It's the Grigori."

Alex was silent for a long beat before he breathed out an almost disbelieving, "Shit." Then, "I'm on my way."

A stout nurse with her lips set in a deep frown led me into Will's room. The curtains were drawn and only a pale light above the bed was on, giving Will a terrifyingly corpse-like look.

"You've only got ten minutes," Nurse Frown said. "Ten minutes."

I could see Will's eyes moving behind his lids. Then his eyelashes fluttered delicately and my whole body tensed. He looked so incredibly fragile—every inch of him, even the ones that weren't covered in bandages or hooked up to tubes. His breath was a steady in-out, his chest rising and falling, but every second I expected it to stop, expected the sick joke that had been this night to continue on and steal Will away from me.

"Will?" I whispered.

His lips broke. "Soph?" His voice was soft and hoarse, something akin to a whisper, and it broke my heart.

"Oh, God, Will, are you okay? How are you?"

"Been better." He smiled, then winced.

"Don't try and move. Just—did they say—did they—"

He opened his eyes and blinked at me. "Did they say that I should start saying my good-byes? Nah. You're not getting rid of me that easily."

I let out the breath I hadn't known I was holding, and the tears rushed over my cheeks. "Will, I'm so sorry—this whole thing is my fault! If I hadn't made you come look for Cerberus—" I fisted my hands, feeling the tight skin of my palm split as my fingernails dug in. "If you hadn't met me, none of this would ever have happened!"

"It happens, love. I'm your Guardian. This"—he gestured vaguely to the enormous bandage strapped over his stomach and chest—"is part of the job."

"It's because of me!"

"Yes, of course it is."

I stopped crying abruptly. "That's a terrible thing to say."

"I'm just agreeing with you."

"If you weren't my Guardian . . ."

"But I am."

He edged his hand out of the blankets and gripped me by the wrist. His eyes, his face—everything—went deeply serious. "Did you get the dagger to Alex?"

I reached for my shoulder bag and pulled the thing out. "This?"

"Good Lord, love, put that back. Don't they have security around here?"

"Not as much as you'd think. I know about the sword, Will. I know about the Grigori."

I waited for him to reel back in stunned amazement. Or to hang his head, ashamed that I had uncovered the secret of the warriors he was guarding me from.

"That's good. With me out"—again, he tried to move, his breath coming in shallow huffs—"for a bit, you're an even bigger target."

There was a soft knock on the door, and then Alex poked his head in. I was about to say something when I noticed Nurse Frown coming in on his heels. "You've got two minutes." She jerked her chin toward Will. "He needs his rest."

She shot withering glances, first one to me, then one to Alex, before stomping out the door.

Alex's gaze swept to Will. A slight flicker of emotion went through his eyes and my heart broke a little more.

"Tell me what you know about the Grigori," Alex said.

Will opened his mouth and I stepped forward, placing a hand gently over the bandage on his chest. "You don't talk. Rest."

I filled Alex in on our attack, first giving a brief overview of my run-in with the three-headed dog. Alex opened his mouth to respond, but Nurse Frown stuck her head in a second time. "Say good night. He's discharging tomorrow so y'all can come get him then and talk all you want. But visiting hours are over," she said, punctuating the word "over" with a scowl.

"We're leaving."

Alex followed Nurse Frown out the door, but I paused, looking down at Will. Though he was shirtless, his shoulder muscles and biceps slim but bulging, he looked so vulnerable. The tears started again, and Will lolled his head to the side, then back again.

"Oh, Sophie, geez."

"I'm sorry, Will," I said, snatching a tissue from the box on his nightstand. "This is all my fault."

He huffed. "This is my job. And if you're going to sit here and pine for me for the rest of your life, well"—a smile cracked across his face—"that's okay. But not right now." He waved toward the door. "You need to get a move on. Even if you have to do it with angel boy over there."

I stood, silent, until Will's eyes narrowed.

"Go! I'll be fine."

I said a hasty good-bye, then joined Alex in the

hall. Once the door closed behind me, I looked over at Alex. He was staring at the doors, jaw set hard.

"So you know about the Grigori, too?" I asked him.

He nodded slowly, chewing the inside of his cheek. "We've met."

"Did you know they were coming after me?"

"I knew they would eventually."

I swallowed the lump in my throat, feeling the first white-hot flames of anger. I don't know why, but Alex's admission was like a betrayal. "How come you never said anything to me?"

He turned to me, his blue eyes clouded, his lips held in a tight expression I didn't understand. "Because I never believed it would come to this."

"This?" I asked with a shrug.

I watched Alex's Adam's apple as he swallowed. "Armageddon."

I pranced to keep up with Alex as he made a beeline through the parking lot. "Armageddon? What are you talking about? Things like this—things like this happen all the time. I mean, Ophelia came back and she brought an army of fallen angels after me and that wasn't Armageddon, that was, well, that was just a really shitty week. Why is this any different?"

Alex stopped and sucked in a sharp breath. "The man who was burnt to death."

"Lance Armentrout?" I asked, confused.

"Have you been following the news?"

I wanted to say that I had, wanted to sound like I did something other than tune in to marathons on HGTV and Lifetime. But Alex knew me better than that.

"There have been three suspicious fires in the last two days."

"Well, yeah, I know that." I gestured back toward the hospital. "Will told us. He even showed us a crazy video where a homeless guy was screaming."

Alex straightened. "What was he screaming?"

I took a deep breath, knowing that I was proving Alex's point—whatever it was—for him.

"He was screaming in Latin. He was—" I stared down at my sneakers on the mist-dusted concrete. "He was calling on Satan."

Alex nodded. "Strength of the flame."

A stripe of fear shot up the back of my neck. "How did you know that?"

"Because that's what happened at both of the other fires, too."

My breath caught. "What does it mean?"

"Fires, Cerberus, the Grigori?"

"Yeah. What—what's happening?"

"Look, Lawson, we're no longer dealing with someone trying to summon the devil. We're not dealing with someone fiddling around with spells or potions, trying to open the gates of Hell."

"How do you know that?"

His eyes were fierce and they pinned mine. "Because the gates of Hell have been blown wide open."

I blinked. "I—I have no idea what you're talking about."

"First of all, do you still have the sword?"

I patted my shoulder bag. "Uh-huh."

"They let you bring that into the hospital?"

"Yeah, security is not what it used to be. Why does it matter?"

"We need to get rid of it. He's going to come back for it and if he doesn't, another member of the Grigori will."

"Okay." I nodded, gripping the straps of my shoulder bag more tightly. "We should go to the wharf. We can drop it into the bay. Or maybe we can burn it? You know, melt it down?"

Alex shook his head. "It's not that easy. The Grigori swords aren't made from standard materials."

"Okay, well, what are they made from? I'm sure we could burn or bury or drown just about any kind of metal."

"It's not of this world."

I cocked a brow and then blew out a defeated sigh. "Of course it's not. Because that would be too easy." I yanked the thing out of my bag. "So what the hell are we supposed to do with you?"

"Jesus, Lawson, put that thing away!" Alex was on me in a flash, stuffing the sword back into my bag, looking around like we'd just done an illicit drug deal.

"Geez, sorry, I didn't know. Does it have a tracker on it or something? GPS?" I shrugged the bag off my shoulder and held it at arm's length. "Because if that's the case I'm not carrying—"

"Relax, okay?" Again Alex's eyes darted from side to side. "There is no GPS on the thing, but first of all, it's a weapon—a dangerous weapon. You shouldn't just be whipping it out and flaunting it."

I frowned, then narrowed my eyes. "I didn't whip or flaunt."

Alex went on, ignoring me completely. "Second of all, it is a mythical sword and it has powers."

"Powers?" I could feel my eyebrows go up, could feel a little zing of intrigue shoot through my nervous system. I immediately imagined myself in slick black leather, my shoulder-length hair suddenly long and flowy, my A-cup boobs a solid C. I was wielding the Grigori sword over my head and people—jerks from high school and people who cut me off in traffic, mostly—were cowering in front of me.

"Lawson?"

I snapped back to attention. "So you were saying something about powers?"

"Just keep the thing hidden until I can figure something out, okay? Actually, you know what? Give it to me." He held out his palm.

"I can keep it. I can stash a sword. I'm not a complete idiot."

He cocked his head. It wasn't entirely an admission of doubt, but it wasn't a glowing expression of support, either. I sighed.

"Carefully," Alex said as I opened my purse.

I dug out the sword, finding it blade first. "Crap!"

I stuck my now-bleeding finger into my mouth, and Alex reached into my bag, yanked the sword out by the handle, and shook off the wad of Kleenex that was stuck to it. He popped his trunk and buried the thing inside.

"That should be okay for a while."

I put my hands on my hips and we stared at each other for a beat. "So, now what?"

He clapped a hand against the back of his neck and sighed. "I'm not exactly sure. I don't think we should go hunting for the Grigori without more information."

"So we research?"

Alex nodded, and I worried my bottom lip, my feet rooted to my spot on the concrete.

"What?" he asked.

"You said the Grigori and Cerberus and the fires—you said that meant the gates of Hell were blown open."

Alex nodded.

"Why? Who would do that?"

"I don't know, Lawson."

I nodded then, looking over Alex's shoulder at the twinkling lights of the city beyond. The view almost made me forget that we were standing in a hospital parking lot—and that we were talking about Hell.

Alex put an index finger under my chin and guided me to face him. "What do you really want to ask me?"

I edged my chin front him. "Nothing. That was it."

He crossed his arms in front of his chest, and a smile played on his lips. It was a grin I had seen for years—that I had grown to love and despise and love again and now it was stuck somewhere in between.

"We've known each other for a long time, Lawson."

I sucked in a breath, feeling the cool air rush over my lips, then down my throat, itching at the giant lump that had grown there. "Do you think my father could have opened the gates? Do you think it's him—do you think he wants to start a war?"

Alex's eyes were a deep, glistening blue with a clarity—and an uncertainty—I'd never seen before. "For you, Lawson, for the whole of humanity, I hope to God not."

A tremor went through me and the world around me looked bleak—and fragile. Behind Alex, a hunched woman pulled a cart filled with groceries behind her. A Muni bus huffed to a stop and three girls in private-school uniforms got out, giggling and shrieking over their cell phones. A cop came out of the police department, eyes heavy, desperation etched into his face.

Alex took a step closer to me, and it was the first time his fingers brushed over mine all over again. Sparks shot through my body and everything about it—about him—felt wrong but necessary, like his energy charged mine. He cupped my cheek with one palm and I closed my eyes, leaning into his touch, wondering what it would have been like if we were regular people, just two people falling for each other—not on the eve of Armageddon, not in the face of perilous doom, not with full knowledge that our time together, because of what he was and what I am, was finite.

"I—I don't know if I can do this, Alex. I don't know if I can take much more."

His arms slid around me, encircling my waist and pulling me toward him. I breathed in his familiar, cut-grass and cocoa scent, felt the warmth emanate from the crook of his neck where I settled my head.

His palms were flat at the small of my back and I felt safe and comfortable and *home*.

"You don't have to, Lawson. You don't have to do this—anything—alone. I'm here."

The Underworld Detection Agency is thirty-five floors underground. I've never actually stopped at any of the interim floors between the police station and the Agency, but I've been told it's nothing but old files, crap, and mole people. Anyway, the point I'm trying to get at is that we are underground—deep underground. So when I heard the telltale growl of tectonic plates shifting, the sound that every native Californian recognizes immediately, it was deafening where I was standing and I immediately crouched, gripping the two arms of a waiting room chair while all manner of demon and other scattered. The ground underneath me undulated in large waves while the carpet seemed to vibrate, shooting itchy little shock waves through the soles of my shoes.

"It's just an earthquake, people," Nina said, filing her nails while perched on a stool. The rattling of the earth stopped for a few seconds—long enough for Nina to glare as if daring the earth to continue to shake and possibly interrupt her manicure a second time—before it set to rattling again.

A couple of trolls stepped under the coffee table, little troll hands gripping the pressboard edges of our cheap IKEA furniture. A zombie started to systematically fall apart as his stiff limbs refused to roll with the earth. Nina continued filing, but I noticed she had hooked her Via Spiga peep-toe booties behind the legs of her stool, her thigh muscles tight as she held on. I instinctively heard my second-grade teacher's voice ring through my head: *Duck and cover!* I dropped to my knees, crawling across the waiting room, looking for someplace to cover. I went for the coffee table, but the trolls growled at me. I could have fit under one of the waiting room chairs if I hadn't eaten those last five or six dozen boxes of chocolate marshmallow Pinwheels. I made my way to a doorframe and stood there triumphantly as magazines jiggled off tables and the spider plant I had been forced to repot due to similar—though vampire, not natural—disasters fell and broke.

And just as quickly as the growl started and the shaking tore through the place, it stopped. Everything was plunged into an immediate, eerie silence for a beat before we heard the car alarms, the barking dogs, and the sirens.

"Wow," Nina said, popping off her stool. "That was a good one. Kind of like 1906." She grinned, a wide, toothy smile, ultra-white fangs gleaming. "You can't take your eyes off them, can you?"

She was talking about her teeth and I had to agree. "Yeah. The pulsing blue is mesmerizing." I turned. "Everyone okay in here?"

Everyone was creeping out of their duck-and-cover spaces, and I considered laying into them about letting the only person who could die—whose life could actually *end* should she be clobbered by a falling desk or grandfather clock—fend for herself in the duck-but un-coverable open space of the waiting room. But one look at the pale, nervous faces of the trolls and the sad zombie, shoulder stumps reaching uselessly for arms that were flopping on the industrial-grade carpet, and I decided against it.

"That was quite the shaker," Vlad said, coming down the hallway. He was grinning too, though his fangs had not gone through the Crest 3D White treatment (probably against VERM policy) and weren't quite as blinding. He waggled his brows. "Someone's awake down there."

Sampson came down the hall next, a few other employees trailing him, everyone looking in on everyone else to make sure there were no (more) lost limbs or lives.

"Are you okay, Sophie?" It was Lorraine, our resident Gestalt witch and Kale's mentor. Her honey-colored hair was pushed back, over her forehead. Her eyebrows were drawn and her blue-green eyes looked concerned. It warmed me.

"I'm okay, Lorraine, thanks."

She nodded curtly, and I noticed everyone else was staring at me, wide-eyed, studiously. "I-I'm okay everyone," I said, self-consciousness washing over me in pink-tinged waves.

"Oh, good."

"That's good."

I heard the murmuring and a few stepped forward to pat me on the back or touch my arm gingerly, and I was basking in the warmth of this weird, horned, extended *family* that cared, that gave a damn whether I lived or died.

And then, the elevator dinged.

Alex was standing there and it was like the first time I'd ever seen him: his shoulders were thrown back, chin hitched, one lock of wavy hair impishly falling over his forehead. His chest looked impossibly broad, Greek-God like, and when his badge winked from his hip, I felt my mouth water.

Once again, I was: *Sophie Lawson, turned on in the face of disaster.*

Alex's icy eyes cut across the waiting room until he saw me. I saw him suck in a breath, and I was ready to shimmy out of my panties—all the demons cared *and* Alex, too—when the other elevator dinged.

We all waited, no one breathing, until the doors slid open.

Then I had to pick my jaw up off the floor.

Will was in the second elevator, leaning against the back wall and looking relaxed and comfortably cool, as though he were in an Abercrombie ad just awaiting his scantily clad co-model. His hazel eyes were slightly hooded in that "hey, baby, I'm holding a kitten" kind of way that made my heart bloom and ignited something low in my belly. Between the two of them I was a pile of supercharged horny goo while the whole of the world trembled on the precipice of holy hell.

As I clamped my knees together and gritted my teeth, I was fairly certain that my inappropriate sex drive was half the reason the city was vaulting toward our brimstony demise.

Both Alex and Will stepped out at the same time, each with a set of eyes fixed on me for a brief second before they glanced at each other. Then each seemed to get an inch taller. Suddenly, chests were puffed out and, I'm not entirely sure, but I'm fairly certain that arms were flexed. I would have paused to scrutinize further, but both made a beeline for me, talking at the same time.

"Wanted to make sure—"

"—you were okay down here."

They stopped talking at the same time, too, glared at each other, then swung to face me and my army of Underworld associates.

"We're all okay here," I said, feeling suddenly overwhelmed with domestic love and nearly throwing my arms around the armless zombie and the troll who had kicked me out from under the coffee table.

"Things aren't okay up there," Alex said, jaw tense, eyes fierce.

"I'm going to suit up. It's chaos out there," Will agreed.

"Will, you're injured. You can't go to work."

He shrugged and I felt a wave of respect for his dedication and annoyance for his stupid hardheadedness. I glanced behind me and saw everyone rapt.

"Well, guys"—I was so appreciating the plural there—"I really appreciate you coming down to check on me, but I'm safe and—"

"I wasn't coming to check on you," Alex said, then paused. "I mean, I'm glad you're okay but—"

"I think what angel boy is trying to say is that this isn't about you." Will's eyes coasted over me and to the group formed around me. "It's about them."

"Don't call me Angel Boy," Alex growled.

I frowned. "Hey, wait. What do you mean it's about them?"

"Something's coming, Lawson." The muscle along Alex's jaw jumped, and I knew he was tense, clenching his teeth against saying what he really wanted—or needed—to say.

Will gave Alex a cursory glance and then looked back at me. "I think it's already here."

"I know. We all know. Will was stabbed. It's the Grigori. And the gates of Hell."

For a group of demons that barely shared a breath between them, the collective air that got sucked in behind me was deafening. I turned to look, and every eye was wide and terror stricken. Mouths hung open.

"Figure of speech?" I said hopefully, trying to wipe the abject fear from the faces of those who usually terrified. No one moved, and I turned back to Alex and Will.

The guys exchanged a glance and a heavy black stone sunk in my gut. There was more. I opened my mouth and then shut it, completely unsure of what this entire encounter meant, but expert enough to know it was bad. Really, really bad.

Will's cell phone chirped a strident ring that nearly yelled "emergency," and Alex's went soon after.

Will grabbed both of my arms. "Stay here until I come back for you."

Alex nudged Will slightly, his eyes settling on mine for a split second before they went over my head. I turned, seeing Sampson striding down the hall.

"Sampson."

Both Will and Alex both strode for the elevator and popped in the same one. I vaguely wondered who would make it to the upper world alive. I turned and clapped my hands once. "So, that was weird. Earthquake, them, sorry about that."

But nobody moved.

SEVEN

"Should we get back to work? Sampson?"

Sampson swallowed hard, sucking in a long, deep breath. "Can you come with me, Sophie?"

I blinked and everyone peeled away silently—even Nina. I tried to catch her eye, to silently question, but either she didn't see me or she was purposely avoiding me. But it couldn't be that, because Nina was my best friend. Wasn't she?

With his hand on my elbow, Sampson led me to his office. He offered me the guest chair and went around to his desk, sitting, staring at me in silence.

"What is it? No offense, but you're kind of scaring me with all this." I gestured to the look of consternation on his face, to the way his lips were pulled downward at the corners.

"This isn't easy to say, Sophie."

I straightened, pricks of heat walking up my spine. "What isn't easy to say?"

Sampson seemed to sag, sinking back in his chair. "You know, I never had children of my own."

I nodded nervously.

"I didn't want them to carry this burden that I've been saddled with."

"You know they might not—it doesn't always work that way." My voice was small and my head was churning. What was Sampson trying to get at? I knew all this already.

"I know. But having you here, especially after your grandmother made me promise to take good care of you, I kind of feel like I have a daughter in you."

A lump was rising in my throat, and I tried to swallow it down. I wasn't sure if I was on the verge of tears because I'd always thought of Sampson like a father, or because no one says "I've always thought of you like a daughter" unless it's a college graduation or you're about to die.

And I graduated college a long time ago.

"But we both know I'm not your father, Sophie. You do have a father."

"I have a man who added his genetic material to my mother's to make me, yes. But he's no father."

Sampson nodded, taking that in. "Nonetheless, he's your father."

I stood, suddenly agitated. I wanted to scream. I wanted to run from the building. I wanted to hop a plane to Tahiti where no one would talk to me in this weird, ominous commentary that said nothing but meant something I didn't want to know.

"What's going on, Sampson? Just tell me. I'm not a little girl. And hell, I've faced, like, everything. Real murderers, mythical murderers, bat-shit-crazy high school students. Why is everyone looking at me like I'm about to die or burst into flames at any moment? It's really fucking unnerving."

"It's him."

"Him who? What the hell? Why can't people just say what they mean? 'It's Harry, Sophie.' 'It's Jack, Sophie.' Why 'him'? What is everyone trying to keep secret?"

Sampson nodded slightly, the motion nearly imperceptible. "You're right. It's Lucas Szabo."

I sat down hard, feeling like I had been punched in the stomach. "Lucas Szabo?"

Yes, I had known my father was involved. Whispers of "Satan" and "the devil" had been everywhere, casually tossed out in the last two days. But that name—hearing it, molding my lips around it and squeezing out the sound—hit a place so deeply buried in my psyche that I never wanted to revisit it. Lucas was my father, the one who, four days after my birth, abandoned me and my mother, and who, when I was nearly three, caused my mother to take her own life. He was a horrible, spiteful man, but for some twisted and masochistic reason, I had always wanted him to notice me, to want to come back to be with me, to approve of me, his daughter. I knew, intellectually, that could never happen because I knew who Lucas Szabo really was.

My father is Satan.

It strikes a chill down my spine whenever I think about it—which I try to make as little as possible. He had raised another daughter, my half-sister Ophelia. And even though she was evil and cuckoo bananas crazy, he had raised her and loved her and kept her with him—when he had abandoned me.

I know that Hell is no place for a child. And frankly, I've never been totally sure of what my father does or what, exactly, being the devil entails. I mean, I was the one swallowing souls, so really, what else was there? I guessed he was in charge of heinous eternities and sharpening pitchforks and all, but I had never dwelled on it. My father didn't want to have anything to do with me, so even if I wanted to, it wasn't like he was grooming me to take over the family business or anything. Which I would be terrible at, truth be told. I'm a total softie. I hate serial killers and axe murderers and people who say "supposably" as much as the next person, but damning someone to Hell? That seems a little heavy handed. And actually being the devil? Well, frankly, I look awful in red. Like a big stewed lobster.

"Do you understand, Sophie?"

I shook myself out of my head. "I'm sorry, what?"

Sampson blew out a sigh, but his lips turned up into a twinge of a smile. "Always Sophie. What I said was there has been a prophecy, a foretelling, whatever you want to call it. Are you aware of this?"

I squirmed. "Like the Mayan 2012 thing? Or the Nostradamus thing? Or is there another thing?"

"Armageddon, apocalypse—it's been called a lot of things."

I batted at the air and crossed my legs. "Of course I've heard of all that end-of-the-world stuff. I've seen every zombie/apocalypse movie ever made. And I swear, the way the zombies down here react, you'd think they really believe they're next in line to take over. Who are we kidding, right? Zombies are going to overthrow us. With what? Half of them can't keep track of their own limbs to save their . . . lives."

I knew that wasn't what Sampson meant. I know because when I'm wrong and I don't want to face reality or the craptasm that is *my* reality, I babble.

"Satan has been calling people in."

"Okay."

"Just like the good, his people can roam free. They are allowed to do as much destruction as they like."

"Allowed?"

"Well, by his standards."

I nodded. "Because everyone has free will."

Sampson bobbed his head. "That's the spin he puts on it."

"So I don't understand. I know he's my—" I wanted to say "sperm donor," but it didn't seem appropriate in the shadow of Sampson's Boss of the Year trophy. "I know he's my father, but why does he want to see me? Why now? Why is he"—I pantomimed shaking the earth—"doing all this?"

"Well, Sophie—"

I cocked an eyebrow. "Don't tell me. The devil works in mysterious ways?"

Sampson gave me a look, and I blew out an exasperated sigh. "It's been said in all the stories, prophecies, whatever you want to call them that one day the devil will come back and call on all his sons"—his eyes cut to me—"or daughters, as it were, and his family will rise up to overtake the good of humanity."

"I'm not answering that call. I'm not rising up.

I am good. I mean, sure, I've sampled a few grapes before buying and yes, I admit it, I did cut that tag off my mattress under penalty of law, but that hardly equates to me being rooted in evil or joining the uprising against, you know, you guys."

Sampson looked down at his hands. "I'm hardly good, Sophie."

"Regardless, I have no intention of going into the family business. So what am I supposed to do?"

Sampson clapped a hand over his mouth and stroked his chin. "A lot of people could potentially be in danger."

"Prophecy, prophecy." I nodded.

"A lot of our people."

My eyebrows went up. "Our people? Underworld people? Our people eat my people for breakfast. Or they would if it wouldn't cause their insurance premiums to skyrocket."

"Sophie, I care about you. I love you, you know that. But you can't be here."

Sampson didn't move, didn't flinch, but it felt like he had kicked me in the chest.

"What are you saying, Sampson?"

He pushed back from his chair, stood, and started to pace. "I promised your grandmother that I would always protect you."

"Yeah, we covered that."

"But I have a duty to protect the demons of the Underworld, too."

I pumped my head. "Yeah, yeah."

"You being here—and Lucas, with this, with"—the words seemed to choke in his throat—"you, is putting everyone down here in danger."

My body temperature bottomed out. I could feel the icy cold seeping into my hands and feet, swirling through my veins. "Oh."

"It's not permanent, of course. Certainly not. You're still a very important part of the Underworld Detection Agency, Sophie, and you always will be. You are a part of this family—"

"But I just can't be here."

The obvious pain in Sampson's face should have moved me, but it didn't. "So I give everything I have to the Underworld Detection Agency—to everyone here—and now that I might be the one who needs help . . ."

"You have to understand where I'm coming from, Sophie."

I held up a silencing hand. "I get it. You have a duty to protect everyone. The good of one versus the good of the many. I know, I've seen that *Star Trek* episode."

"Sophie, please. We're not abandoning you. We would never abandon you. We're all here—"

I stood, numb. "But I can't be."

"It's just that we don't know what to expect with you father. He's a trickster. And I can't, in good conscience, risk—"

"Sampson, I understand."

He dropped his head. "I'm sorry, Sophie."

I stood up silently, without looking at Sampson, and walked back to my office. I had planned on avoiding the stares of everyone around me, but I didn't have to. Once they saw me coming, everyone averted their eyes, turned their backs on me, pretended to be busy with anything else.

I had gone from a glowing cocoon of two-man love to being the loneliest person on the planet in a matter of moments.

I stayed in my office and organized and reorganized papers until I was sure just about everyone had left the building. I kept the radio on, my computer speakers on low as newscasters broadcast minute-by-minute updates on the quakes—which streets had buckled, which blocks still didn't have power, how many people had been freed from the rubble.

Sampson's words kept coming back to me, and each time they did I turned the volume up a little bit more so that the scientists and seismologists that the radio station kept patching in could explain that earthquakes happened because of shifting tectonic plates and heat and not because a piddly red-headed woman had Satan's calling card running through her veins.

There were fires and there were tragedies. That didn't always spell the end of the world—at least that's what I kept telling myself as I rode up the elevator, listening to the soothing sounds of Jon Secada Muzak.

"Oh. Hey."

Alex was standing in the police station vestibule, but he was dressed in full SWAT gear and my knees started to shake faster than the earth did. He looked rugged with a five o'clock shadow and dirt streaked over one cheek, his hair plastered back with sweat and grit. He was dressed in all black, his short sleeves straining against his thick, round biceps, showing just the tip end of his feather tattoo. His black-gloved hands were fisted at his sides and even though he had an assault rifle slung across his slim-fitting bullet-proof vest and a six-inch knife strapped to his thigh, I had the overwhelming and unsafe urge to rush him, to throw my arms around him and hiccup-cry until he promised me that no one was abandoning me, that he would always be with me.

Instead, I shifted my weight and cleared my throat, biting back those threatening tears. "You look pretty. Tough. You look pretty tough," I said, with all the grace of a blubbering idiot.

He wiped a piece of grit from his chin with the back of his hand, and if I hadn't been served such a heartbreaking blow by my so-called "family" downstairs, I would have tripped over my panties falling head over heels, once again, for Alex.

"You shouldn't have taken the elevator."

It wasn't exactly the sexy, comforting line I had imagined, but the fact that SWAT Alex was talking to me still sent a delighted shiver through me. I realized that the only thing I was in real danger of was becoming a jiggly pool of lady goo.

"Sorry," was my sexy rejoin.

"Anyone else down there?"

I shook my head. "Why are you dressed like that? You're a detective."

"It's a state of emergency. The city was hit pretty severely by the quake. Power lines are down, windows were shattered on Market. There's widespread looting. I'm SWAT trained so I was patrolling. People get pretty awful when they think they can take advantage of someone else's misfortune. Is there a reason you're staring at me?"

He patted his chest with his gloved hands, and I clamped my knees together tightly.

"No. I was just listening intently to what you had to say. Why did you come back here if it's so bad out there?"

"Things are beginning to go back to normal. Power is being restored. And you weren't answering either of your phones. Nina said she'd left you back at the office."

There was a wash of crimson under the dirt streak on Alex's cheeks.

"You came to save me."

He rolled his eyes. "I came to check on you. If anyone is going to be able to save herself, it's going to be you. Come on."

He threw an arm around my shoulders and steered me toward the door.

"I must be moving up in the world. Usually you would ask how I was responsible for the disaster in progress."

"Yeah, well, I thought this one was probably out of your realm of expertise."

Alex pushed open the door for me, and we both scanned the city in the fading twilight. We weren't staring at the city I lived in; we were staring at the smoky, ruined set of some disaster film. Cars were abandoned in intersections. A piece of street had buckled and split down the center. A Muni bus sat empty, doors wide open, gaping front windows like hollow, sightless eyes. The humming pulse of San Francisco—horns honking, cable cars ringing, the general chatter of *life* in the city—had been snuffed out, and the silence was unnerving.

I shivered. "This is weird."

"I'll give you a ride."

"That's okay—I drove today." I pointed to my little Honda, which looked like it had been fished out of the bowels of the earth post-quake. Most of the spray-painted VAMPIRE graffiti had worn off, and I had fixed the back window with a good dose of duct tape. It wasn't much to look at, but it moved. Mostly.

"I'd feel better if you let me drive you."

Normally this kind of chauvinism would grate on me because I like to think I'm a feminist, but after the whole puddle of goo in the face of G.I. Joe Alex, I wasn't even going to bother.

The streetlights were out along all the avenues so it was slow going.

"So when you were out . . . patrolling," I started, pinching the skin on my upper lip. "Did anything interesting come up about the quake?"

Alex glanced at me as he took a corner. "What are you talking about?"

I glanced around the empty car as if there were spies everywhere. "Do you think this was a regular earthquake or was it something more . . . supernatural?"

He guided the car down a street that was completely dark, the gaping black windows of each still house looking ominous and foreboding. I pulled my jacket tighter over my shoulder and shifted in my car seat.

"Remember that house over there?" Alex asked, gesturing with his chin.

I squinted to make out the boxy house. "Yeah.

That was where we saw the werewolf." I smiled. "Good bloodthirsty times. You still didn't answer my question."

"It was an earthquake, Lawson. If you're asking if the road split and the devil came tap-dancing up, I'm going to have to say no. It was just an earthquake."

I picked at a piece of dried rice stuck to my pants. "But the gates of Hell . . . and Sampson just fired me."

Alex's brows rose. "He fired you?"

"No exactly fired, fired. But he said that I should make myself scarce until all of this is figured out."

"What does he mean by 'all of this'?"

"Armageddon, I'm assuming. Isn't that what you're thinking?"

"Look, Lawson, I know I told you about Armentrout. And I know I was the one who told you there might be more to it than you think. But . . ." Alex shook his head. "I just have a hard time buying that this"—he jutted his chin out the windshield—"is . . . that. But then again . . ."

"But then again what?"

"You know what they say about the devil."

"No, not really."

"He's a trickster."

I rolled my eyes. "Trickster? Sampson said the same thing. So, is this Satan or a ten-year-old boy?"

"He's into ruses, games."

"I pose my question again. I don't know if I should be quaking in my proverbial boots or picking up a stash of lollipops and sling shots."

"There's the feisty Lawson I know."

I waited for him to say, "and love," but it never came. I shifted in my seat and reminded myself I had bigger fish to fry. "Have you heard anything?"

"Haven't been on the fallen angel website lately. Didn't see any apocalyptic tweets."

He shot me that sexy half smile, and I couldn't help but smile back. Alex had the uncanny ability to put me at ease, even when he was the one I was always putting into danger.

"Like I said, I'm halfway convinced that if—and that's a very big, very I'm-not-totally-convinced *if*—we are dealing with Armageddon, the apocalypse, whatever, that it has nothing to do with Satan. It's probably some *Dennis the Menace* shit like it always is."

"And you've fallen for Satan's greatest ruse."

I felt my eyebrows dive down. "What's that?"

"Convincing the world he doesn't exist."

We drove in silence for several blocks, Alex negotiating the police tape and destruction outside, me chewing the inside of my lip and trying to focus on something soft and light like kittens or cotton candy.

It wasn't working.

"What?" Alex finally asked.

I looked down at my hands. "Nothing." Pause. "Hey. Can I ask you a question?"

"Do I have to answer it?"

"Let me ask it and you can decide."

"Deal."

I did my best to make out his profile in the dim cab. "You used to always be searching . . ." I cleared my throat. "For a way to go back."

Alex was officially a fallen angel, but he lacked

the cold black heart of the real baddies. He wasn't welcome to go back to grace and he didn't want to go to the seventh level where the truly fallen live. So he was earthbound—which meant he was never really anywhere.

He gave me a quick glance and went back to studying the road. "I think about it every day. I don't know why, since it's useless."

Again, he shot me a quick look and then looked away. We both knew what he meant—for him to return to grace, he would have to return the Vessel of Souls that he had stolen and subsequently lost. For him to retrieve the Vessel of Souls, he would have to kill me. As murder is a mortal sin, he would be cast back down to Hell. His life cycle was pretty much a theological catch-22 and as the blasted Vessel placeholder, I couldn't help but feel a little guilty.

"I'm sorry. I didn't mean to bring it up. I just . . . was wondering."

I went back to staring out the passenger-side window. Alex snaked an arm across the seat back and laced his fingers in my hair. His touch was soft, the movement intimate. My heart ached for him and I blinked away tears. I knew what it was like not to fit anywhere. I didn't know what it was like to have a place to go, but no means to ever get there.

I was sitting on the grass, my skirt spread over my knees. I could feel the way the grass pricked at my palms when I reclined, could feel the slight moisture of the earth against my hands. It was bright—a perfect day, really—and I squinted as the yellow-white sunlight streaked off the ripples of the lake in front of me. I could hear slight murmuring and laughter punctuated by the sound of honking geese. And the laughter again . . . I realized it was coming from me, from my own mouth, as I watched my mother and father facing each other, holding hands and spinning—the way little children do. Just spinning round and round, my mother with her head thrown back, her lips bright red arches as she laughed. My father spun her, laughing too, but his smile didn't reach his eyes the way hers did.

Suddenly, I was cold. I could feel the bay chill and moisture in the air and I scratched at my bare shoulders as though there were a sweater there. My fingernails were digging into my flesh, dragging angry red lines that burned. I watched, fascinated, as my skin split and dots of blue-red blood bubbled up. The cold was everywhere now and everything was getting louder—the geese honking, then car tires squealing. The crashing sound of windows breaking, a rumble from the bottom of my feet. I knew that buildings were tumbling and my hands went to the grass, grabbing uselessly at blades that broke off. The world was spinning out of control, and when I looked to my parents, their joyous, egg-shaped arc had gone crazy. I was mesmerized by my mother's bare feet, by the tiny, frantic steps she took, her toes first on the lush green grass, then stepping among shards of broken bottles and glass.

"Mom!" I tried to reach out, but I was rooted to the earth and my voice was lost in the swirl of wind from their movement. "Dad!" I tried again, and this time my voice was thick and strong. My father stopped, snapping to attention, his eyes—an inky, ominous black—laser focused on mine. I watched my parents' fingers loosen; then his slipped out of hers. She was still reaching, clawing, desperate for him to save her, but he wouldn't. He stared at me with a tiny, whimsical smile while his hands fell listlessly to his sides and my mother went on spinning—dangerously, wildly out of control. She called for me, but I didn't answer. I flinched when the water came.

And suddenly, she was gone.

I looked down at my palms and they were red, blood red. I studied the viscous liquid as it oozed through my fingers in steady, velvety sheets.

There was a hand in front of me.

EIGHT

"Come on, Sophie. There's nothing else to do here. It's time for us to go."

I blinked up at my father, then at his out-stretched hand. I didn't remember thinking it or doing it, but my hand slid into his and he laced our fingers together, the blood—*my mother's blood?*—making a sucking sound when our palms met.

I walked with him, neither of us speaking, until we reached the edge of the lake. Everything inside me froze up, clenched, pulled in. I know my lips were moving. I could hear the sound, far away, but still there.

No, no, no, please, don't make me—

But I—the image of me in the dream—didn't so much as pause or flinch. I watched myself step into the water, my bare feet instantly covered by the murk, my father stepping in beside me. He had on his shoes, his pressed, slate-colored work slacks, but he didn't seem to notice. He kept hold of my hand and we walked on, the water rising up over my calves, over my knees. It was at my waist, at my chest, just under my nose, then over my head, but I kept walking, breathing, calm, until there was only blackness in front of me.

"Huuuuuuhhhhh!" I took an enormous, gulping breath of air and sat bolt upright, tossing ChaCha from a deep, doggie sleep onto the floor. I was clawing at my throat, trying to remember how to breathe while blood pulsed through every vein in my body, thundered through my ears, and thudded in my skull. I was sweating and freezing at the same time, trying to shake off the murky lake water—but there was none there.

I looked around my bedroom, stunned, certain that I had been at the lake and then lured here. I could even still feel the blood on my—

"What the heck is going on here?"

Nina flew through the bedroom door and landed a hairbreadth away from me, the cool air wafting from her skin making me shiver even more. I clenched my jaw to keep my teeth from chattering.

"Are you okay? Soph?" She sat back on her haunches, her eyes impossibly wide and darker than I'd ever seen, and snapped in front of my face. "Soph! SOPHIE!"

Vlad was in the doorway, reclining against the frame, arms crossed in front of his chest. His legs were crossed, but his expression didn't have the calm, unaffected look that he had perfected. He actually looked—fascinated.

Nina snapped again. "Sophie?"

"I'm sorry," I said. "I'm sorry." I looked from Vlad to Nina. "I—I just had a bad dream, I guess." I looked down at my palms again, certain there would be some trace of . . . something there, but they were clean.

Vlad flicked on the lights. "You were breathing hard."

"And screaming." Nina threw her arms around me, yanking me to her marble chest and nearly knocking out the breath that I had just managed to catch. "Oh my God, I was so worried. I thought you were hyperventilating or having a heart attack or—"

"Having sex," Vlad finished.

Nina pinned him with a glare and then turned back to me. "I did not think you were having sex." Her face softened. "I thought someone may have been attacking you. Or some*thing*."

I stiffened instantly and licked my lips. "Someone after me? You know of someone coming after me?"

Good God, I thought. *The last thing I need is someone* else *after me.*

"No, just the usual." Nina smiled helpfully and my comfort level rose not at all. "Do you want to tell me what the dream was about?"

Vlad harrumphed and left the room while Nina scooched up next to me and slid her legs under my blankets. I sighed, my whole body feeling like tightly coiled knots. I propped my pillows up.

"It wasn't all that creepy—like I wasn't being chased or anything, but it was scary."

I don't know why I was keeping the truth from Nina—my very best friend, the girl who has trusted me with her afterlife and whom I've trusted with my *this* life—but for some reason I felt like if I were to say how badly the dream terrified me, it might let it out, make it happen all over again.

"So what happened?"

I was biting my thumbnail, looking off into space, trying to erase the image of my blood-soaked palms, of my father reaching out a hand to me. I'd taken it. I'd taken my father's hand and abandoned my mother.

My heart started to thud.

"I dreamed about my parents."

Nina sat up a little straighter. "Your parents, as in plural? Mom and Dad?"

I swallowed hard and nodded. "Uh-huh. It was like my dad—my dad killed my mom."

Nina's gaze was sympathetic and she took one of my hands. "Honey, you know that your father did kill your mother."

It was something horrible that I had learned a few years ago—although I'm not sure it was anymore horrible than thinking that my mother had committed suicide for most of my life. I'd learned that I was there, just a baby, when the noose had gone around my mother's neck. I'd learned that the swaying feet that I would see now and again in dreams, in snatches of errant thought, were my mother's. I had sat there and watched her. I had sat there and watched my father put the noose around her neck—*hadn't I?* Not everything was clear, but even considering the memory shot the same cold stripe of fear down my spine.

"I know, but this time—in the dream, at least— she was happy, first. They were laughing. She must have felt safe." I could feel the hot prick of tears behind my eyes. "She must have trusted him."

I felt Nina squeeze my hand, but she just looked away, not saying anything.

"She split from him and spun away, and her blood—her blood was on my hands."

Nina looked back at me then, sympathetically before she cocked an eyebrow and slipped into her regular, wry Nina-face.

"You had blood on your hands? Her blood? Way to beat the obvious horse with the obvious stick, Sophie's conscience."

I laughed despite my complete discomfort. "So my self-conscience is trying to tell me that I feel responsible for my mother's death? I don't know why I needed to dream that. I've felt that way every moment I'm awake."

"Driving the point home?"

I shrugged, still uneasy, but feeling slightly better.

"Anything else happen in the dream?"

That was when it hit me—like a burning arrow, searing through my flesh. "My dad. I took his hand and I went with him."

Nina's eyes widened. "Like, to Hell?"

"No, to Cleveland. It was a dream! We walked into a lake. With our clothes on. My dad didn't even care that his suit was getting wet." A giggle tore through me, slightly maniacal, as I imagined me in my skirt, holding hands with a man who looked like a cross between Walt Disney and every bad red devil Halloween costume ever made. We were stepping into a lake and walking down into the water, chatting about the weather and the

Giants, not bothering to notice that the water was creeping up over our chins.

"Not that I ever like dreaming of—of him—but . . ." I shook my head. "It was just a stupid dream."

Nina was quiet, her eyes wide, her entire body stiff. She still held my hand and her grip was steel.

"Ow! Neens!"

"What?" She blinked furiously and stared down at her hand, then let me slide mine out.

I shook my aching hand, letting the circulation come back. "You're very comforting when you're not trying to rip off my limbs."

She glanced at my flapping hand absently, then quickly scooched out of my bed. "I'm sorry, Soph, I didn't mean to—" She pointed, then took a step back. "You should probably go back to sleep. We have to work tomorrow." She turned and headed for the door, slapping the lights off in the process.

"Night, Soph."

Her voice sounded hollow in the darkness.

I tried to fall back to sleep. I counted sheep, ducks, and the number of times I'd seen Kristen Stewart smile, but I was still wired like a carnival sign in the dead of summer. The dream with my father seemed to sizzle into my periphery each time I closed my eyes, and even though I had dreamed of him before, there was something about this particular dream, something about the way my hand had slipped so easily into his, something about the way I'd instinctually trusted him and never looked back on my mother's fallen body.

By the time my cell phone chirped I was knee-deep

in *Freud's Dream Theory* and suicidal as the dream apparently meant I wanted to have sex with my father or that I had more than a passing fascination with walk-in vaginas. I snapped up the phone and pressed it to my ear.

"Hello?"

It only chirped again, and I pulled it away and swiped at the screen, the little icon of a police light flashing and bouncing, alerting me that something had come across the police scanner.

Yes, there's an app for that.

I listened to the recorded message, my stomach starting to burn as the scant details were meted out: double homicide. Marina District. Fire. Suspicious circumstances.

I immediately dialed Alex and was met by his gruff voice mail commanding me to leave a message. Instead, I yanked on my most authoritative yoga pants and sped out the door, guiding my let's-hope-no-one-blows-up-this-one Honda Civic down the grid of city streets until the blue and red police lights bounced off my front windshield.

I coasted my car to a stop amongst the first-responder vehicles and clicked off the police scanner, tucking my cell into my back pocket. The fog was thinning, but a heavy drizzle was taking its place, obscuring the red and blue police cruiser lights into wild swirls of color against the gray.

A few officers I recognized from the police station were milling about with notepads and pens poised as they talked to neighbors who peered around them, trying to catch a glimpse through the open front door. I cut around them and met Officer

Romero at the base of the front porch as he tossed a thick roll of yellow crime scene tape to a pup officer who couldn't have been more than nineteen years old.

"Romero, what's going—?"

His eyes flicked over mine, then settled on my forehead as he held out a hand. "I'm sorry, Sophie. This is an active crime scene. I'm going to have to ask you to stay back."

"It's an active crime scene, which is why I'm going to have to go in there." I leaned closer to him and dropped my voice. "I think we can both agree it's one of mine."

Romero actually stepped away from me, putting an inch of distance between us that may well have been a mile.

"You're going to have to stay back."

"Romero!"

His gaze was steadily avoiding mine, and when I saw a snippet of Alex cross in front of the house's enormous bay window, I rolled up on my toes and yelled.

"Alex! Alex it's me!"

I saw Alex's head cock, and in a minute he was standing in the doorway, pulling off a pair of latex gloves. Romero was standing as solid as the Statue of Liberty so I waited for Alex to come to me, to tell Romero off and pull me inside.

"Hey, Lawson. What are you doing here?"

I gaped. "What do you mean what am I doing here? I think the question is what am I *not* doing here."

Alex's eyebrows smashed together. "Come again?"

I gripped Alex by the arm and pulled him into a

semi-private corner. "Why did I have to hear about this on the police scanner? This should be my case, Alex. You know it. It's got Underworld written all over it."

He threaded his arms in front of his chest. "And tell me how you got to that conclusion."

"I could show you if you'd just let me in there," I hissed. "Seriously, I don't get you, Alex. Three days ago you practically clobber me with the Lance Armentrout thing, and suddenly you don't want me anywhere near a case that is so obviously mine."

"Correct me if I'm wrong, Lawson, but aren't I the detective and you're the liaison? The one who doesn't have cases?"

I rolled my eyes. "You know what I mean. Do you want me out of this partnership? If that's the case, just say the word because remember, Alex, you came to me. You came and asked for my help."

"Lawson . . ."

"Don't Lawson me. Answer the question."

The rain had started to strengthen, and the patter of the drops seemed to roar in my ears. Alex looked at me and looked away, then pinched the bridge of his nose. "It's not that."

"Then what is it?"

"Just come on."

I should be an old pro at crime scenes—this one wasn't my first and with my luck and penchant for seeking out the dead, nearly dead, and in-the-midst-of-dying, it wouldn't be my last. We stopped at the front porch and pulled on latex gloves and booties. Then Alex looked over his shoulder at me, his ice-blue eyes grave.

"You ready?"

I batted at the air in an attempt at nonchalance even though my heart was thudding against my rib cage and my stomach was already starting to roil as the foul stench of death wafted through the open door.

Death has an oily, bitter smell that assaults the nostrils and lodges itself as a noxious olfactory memory, an imprint that one can't shake, no matter how hard she tries. It hit me with a breath-pulling wallop this time, and my eyes started to water as I followed Alex over the threshold.

"The body isn't fresh?"

"Bodies."

My mouth filled with the metallic saliva that comes before vomiting, and I braced myself against the doorway, taking one last, refreshing gulp of the fog-tinged San Francisco air.

I expected Alex to shoot me his I-told-you-so look, but his eyes were soft, his touch softer as he rested his hand on my arm. I steeled myself and stepped back into the house, my eyes immediately burning from the smoke I hadn't known was there.

I coughed. "Smoke?"

"Yeah. The . . ." Alex pursed his lips and swallowed, and I knew that even he was having a hard time with this crime scene. "The bodies were burned."

I immediately thought of Lance Armentrout, the image of his burned and broken body flashing in my mind, his charcoaled, outstretched fingers clutching *my* business card.

Is that what Alex didn't want me to see here?

The foyer and dining room of the house were so perfect they looked staged. A brush palm flourished in one corner, its bright green foliage lying delicately over the cocoa brown of an overstuffed leather couch. There was a matching coffee table and a selection of cream-colored accent pillows, the whole effect lending the room an airy, Cuban feeling. I could see where the room would have been inviting, once, before the stench of death swallowed everything.

"They're upstairs. The Culversons. Gerry Anne, forty-one, husband—"

"Kenneth, forty-three," I finished, reading over his shoulder.

Alex glanced at me, eyebrows raised, but I just shook my head, anxiety humming through me as we walked.

I followed Alex up the steps, walking close enough that I could smell the cut-grass scent of his cologne, the fresh, soapy smell of his hair. But death still crept in.

We passed a bedroom and I glanced in, stopping when I noticed an officer and a plainclothes detective crouched at the end of a child's bed. A little boy was sitting on the bed, legs out straight in front of him, his back nestled into the pillows. Tears popped into my eyes, and when the boy nodded, then smiled, I felt like laughing, like rushing into the room and scooping him up in my arms and taking him away from this horrible scene, this stench of death. The boy—who couldn't have been more than nine or ten—unhanded the teddy bear he was clutching and waved at me, a peculiar finger wave, more apt for an adult than a child. I waved back.

"The little boy—he was spared?" I whispered into the back of Alex's neck.

Alex turned on a breath. His eyes cut into the room and then back to me. "It was his parents. As you can see, the boy was unharmed."

I tried to swallow over the knot in my throat. "Does he know yet?"

"Let's just look at the crime scene first."

NINE

Alex pushed open a pair of double doors, and I sucked in a breath at what should have been the grandeur of the master bedroom. Floor-to-ceiling windows looked out over the bay, the sparkle of the Golden Gate's white lights poking through endless sheets of fog. The furnishings in the room were opulent but efficient, and the ceilings ran high enough for me to fit all three stories of my squat apartment building inside. We were in the sitting room, I realized as Alex walked with purpose through the beautiful area and turned a corner into the sleeping quarters.

And that's when it hit me. The smell. Full force. Not just death, but the fetid stench of decaying flesh. The pungent scent of fear. And that smoky, choking smell of a fire just burned out.

"Oh my God."

I can't describe the feeling that overtook me. It was fire down my spine. My stomach gone to liquid. My eyes held open in terror even though I desperately, painfully wanted to close them.

But somewhere inside I knew it wouldn't matter because the image in front of me would be imprinted in my mind forever.

Even though it was well charred, I could make out the curved edges of a king-size bed. The headboard and footboard were pockmarked with black buds of fire and weeping stripes of soot. The once-white bedclothes were edged with a muted grey where the fire hadn't reached, but in the center they were ripped clean, the mattress devoured by flame leaving only the black entrails of half-melted springs.

And then there were the bodies—what was left of them.

A man and a woman were entwined, the blackened remains of her fingers gripping at his shoulder. Their mouths were gaping open, stark white teeth looking freakishly out of place against what used to be—I guessed—the taut, young skin of faces screaming in terror. The fire centered heavily between the two and decimated their torsos, their faces.

"There was an accelerant used here," Alex said, using the back of his pen to point to the ruined bodies. "You can see where it dripped here and here and this is the line it ran."

I nodded blankly, begging my mind to focus on anything other than the utter destruction in front of me, but there was nothing else to focus on. Blood arced across a window, a stark trail of red mixing with the muted colors on the other side of the glass. It was on the bed, too, most of it lost to the blackness of the soot, but some of it, like the red velvet trail on the woman's unburned foot was there, another ridiculous-looking punch of color in the palette of blacks and grays. Just under the woman's foot—her toenails painted a sweet, bubblegum pink—was a thin replica of a baseball bat.

It, too, had been untouched by the flame, but it was scarred nonetheless. One whole end of the thing was covered with a viscous layer of blood mixed with hair and what I knew—with a pulsing, aching beat of my heart—was skin.

"They were beaten and then set on fire?" I couldn't recognize the sound of my own voice, but I knew it was me because Alex turned around, eyebrows up.

"That's what it looked like."

"Premeditated?"

"We can't tell yet."

I leaned in. "Do you know much about the family yet? Are they"—I lowered my voice to a hoarse whisper—"human?"

"Yeah."

"Nothing para?"

Alex shrugged. "Normal as you and me."

Neither Alex nor I was anywhere near normal, but it didn't seem the time to point it out.

"Do you have anything on the son?" I asked.

Alex shook his head and I was immediately thinking of the small child in the other room, sitting on the bed, innocently clutching his fat, fuzzy teddy bear.

"The little boy. He was . . ." I gulped down a sob. "He was here when it happened?"

His voice was raspy. "Yeah."

"So he was spared? Did the—animal—who did this not know? Was he spared on purpose? God, Alex, we need to be working on this right now." I dug in my back pocket for my cell phone, my finger hovering over Sampson's name when Alex grabbed my wrist and led me out of the room.

"You don't want me to call Sampson? Alex, this guy—this—this whoever or *what*ever did this is going to strike again. This isn't a one-off. This brutality? This looks like the making of a ser—"

"We know who the perpetrator is, Lawson."

I sputtered. "We do? Who? Did you catch him in the act—or . . ." I glanced back to the ruined bodies and immediately tried to shake the image out of my head. "I want to be in on the questioning. At least on the two-way. This asshole has to answer for a lot. He orphaned a child."

I couldn't hold back anymore. My voice broke on the word and tears raced over my cheeks, tickled the end of my nose. I was crying, bawling even, hard, body-wracking sobs that turned into hiccups and hysteria. Suddenly, Alex's arms were around me, tight, confining me, and I fell into their comfort. I listened to his heartbeat, steady against my erratic one. He let me cry for minutes or hours until I had cried myself out.

I shook off his embrace and used the heel of my hand to swipe at my cheeks. "I'm sorry. I'm sorry—that was really unprofessional of me."

"That's all right," Alex said. "Are you okay?"

I did that fingertip-under-the eye thing as though

I were wearing mascara rather than Chapstick and chocolate Pinwheel.

"I just feel so bad for that kid. What's his name?"

"Oliver."

"Oliver." I felt the word in my mouth, round and sweet tasting. "What is going to happen to Oliver now? Does he have family, someone to take him in?"

I watched Alex's Adam's apple bob as he swallowed. "He has someplace to go. He's the perpetrator."

I couldn't breathe. I must have heard wrong. "I'm sorry. Who is the perpetrator?"

Alex took my arm again and I followed him down the stairs. When we passed Oliver's room it was dark, the bed made up with a cheery patchwork quilt featuring a red, white, and blue sailboat, the teddy bear he was clutching so fiercely lying upside down on the floor, forgotten.

"Oliver. The kid."

"That's insane. He can't be more than nine or ten years old."

"Eight, actually."

I yanked my arm from Alex's hold and stopped at the edge of the foyer, pushing Alex into the nearest room—a den painted dark green with an enormous desk spotted with black and white family photos. Oliver, and the smiling man and woman on either side of him, at the beach, at Disneyland, looking every inch the normal American family. Not the decimated, tortured one I had just encountered.

"Who told you that the kid did it?" I hissed, suddenly strangely protective of Oliver.

"Lawson, I'm as stunned as you are. But it's true. The bat, the trajectory, everything. It was Oliver."

"I don't believe that. Someone is trying to set him up. Who would set up a child?" I snapped. "Obviously the guy who burned up Armentrout." I began to pace. "But what could his angle be?"

"There's no angle, Lawson." I could hear the exhaustion in Alex's voice, but it only bolstered me.

"Who told you that this kid, this little boy is responsible for beating his parents and then burning them in their own bed? Who told you this?"

Alex waited a beat before speaking. "Oliver did."

I shook my head. "No. No. He's—he's *eight*."

He shook his hand, squeezing the back of his neck—a move he only did when he was overwhelmed. "They're getting younger and younger every time."

"Oliver told you he did this?"

"The neighbor saw the smoke and called nine-one-one. He broke into the house and found Oliver there"—Alex jutted his chin toward the kitchen table—"eating milk and cookies."

There was an abandoned milk glass at the kitchen table, a napkin underneath, cookie crumbs littering the glossy wood of the tabletop.

"Did he tell the neighbor someone was in the house? Did he even know his parents were—" I couldn't bring myself to say "on fire." I couldn't bring myself to say "dead" in this house where everything looked happy-family perfect but death clung to everything.

"According to the neighbor, Oliver smiled and welcomed"—Alex checked his little notebook—"Effron Salazar into the house. Oliver told him his mommy and daddy were upstairs and then offered Effron a cookie."

"That doesn't sound like a child that just murdered and set fire to his parents."

"Effron told Oliver they had to get out of the house because there was smoke. He told the boy to run outside to Mrs. Salazar and that he would go up to get Oliver's parents. At which time Oliver continued eating his cookie and told Effron not to bother because, quote, 'they're already dead.'"

I thought of the little boy sitting on the bed, the joyful little finger wave.

"No . . ."

"Effron reportedly asked Oliver how he knew that, and the kid said, 'Because I killed them.'"

I was doubled over then, dry heaving. My stomach started to spasm and tears dribbled from my clenched tight eyes. "No."

"That's what Lewinsky took down."

I sat down hard on the desk chair and shoved my head between my legs, gulping huge gusts of air. Alex disappeared for a second and returned with a glass of water, filled to the brim.

"Where'd you get this?" I asked, referring to my empty cup.

"Kitchen's right there."

"Oh, God. Crime scene. You can't do that." I gagged. "I just drank dead people's water."

"It's not like they were swimming in it."

"I don't want anything muddying up the crime

scene. Nothing. We have to find out who actually did this. It wasn't Oliver."

Alex looked at me, open-mouthed.

"It wasn't the kid," I snapped. "I don't believe your account. It's hearsay anyway. And what is that? Third-person hearsay? Fourth-person, if you count you to me."

"Do you think I would make this up? To you?"

I stood up, glad when my legs held me. "Where is this Salazar guy? Where is he? I want to talk to him."

"He's outside in one of the ambulances. Being treated for smoke inhalation."

I shoved past Alex, maybe a little bit harder than I meant to, and made a beeline for the front door, snapping off my latex gloves and booties in the process. One of the ambulances had its back doors splayed open, and a heavyset man was framed in the yellow light. His chest was bare and a technician pressed a stethoscope against it while the man breathed slowly through an oxygen mask.

"Salazar?" I barked

The technician looked at me and frowned, holding up a hand stop-sign style. But Salazar straightened and gently pushed the man aside.

"Yeah," he said, pulling the mask aside.

I was at a loss then, not actually sure what I had come careening out here for. My tough-chick bravado had been swallowed up by the surprise of actually creating a plan and then successfully carrying it out.

"Uh." I jutted out a hand. "I'm Sophie Lawson. I'm with the San Francisco Police Department."

It wasn't a total lie. I was, in fact, here, on the premises, with the San Francisco Police Department.

Salazar took a long, deep breath from the ventilator and nodded. "I already talked to that guy," he said, waving his arm vaguely.

"Did you know Oliver and his family before the incident?"

Salazar nodded. "We've lived here for twenty-two years. The Culversons have been here for six. We've known . . ." Salazar looked away, then thumbed at the tears that pulled in his eyes. "We've known little Oliver since he was tiny."

I sat gently next to Salazar on the ambulance tailgate. "And you saw him, Oliver, tonight? You saw him first?"

Salazar nodded and a ripple of something—cold, fear, maybe—wracked his whole body. He pressed the mask against his mouth and nose, and I listened to the serpentine hiss of his breath as he sucked in. His voice sounded very small. "Yes."

"And he told you . . ."

"I already told this to the police. Please, I don't want to repeat it. Not again."

The look in this man's milky eyes shot aching cracks through my heart. He looked like a kindly old grandfather, and the weight of the evening was pressing on him, so thick and so solid it was nearly tangible even to me. "I'm sorry, sir. You and Oliver were pretty close then?"

He nodded and a tear slid silently down his cheek. "But he wasn't like that. Not like he was tonight. He was . . . cold. He was empty."

Salazar started to shake, and I pulled a thick wool

blanket from the ambulance and rested it over his shoulders. He eyed me, his gaze suddenly steady and remarkably sharp. "Something happened to Oliver, Ms. Lawson. He's—he's not right anymore."

When I left Salazar with his heavy blanket and oxygen mask, I was numb. The wind had kicked up, and the fog had riddled it with the kind of cold wet that sinks into your bones and settles a deep ache everywhere. My hair slapped against my cheeks, and I knew that life was going on all around me. I knew that lights were flashing and people were calling out orders and car doors were slamming, but I couldn't hear any of it. The only thing I heard besides the pulsing beat of my own heart were Mr. Salazar's parting words: "He's not right anymore."

TEN

"He's not right anymore," Nina said the words slowly, carefully, as she balanced the business end of a wet nail polish brush over her big toe and our carpet. "That kind of seems like the understatement of the year, doesn't it? I mean the kid just beat and incinerated his parents. 'Not right' doesn't even being to cover how seriously not right the little socio is."

I balanced my chin in my hand, mesmerized by the bubble of lavender paint beading on the end of her nail polish brush. "It doesn't seem right."

Nina swiped the polish over one nail. "Of course it doesn't seem right. This is real life. This is San Francisco. This is not the opening montage of *Halloween*, parts one through eight."

"He smiled at me, Neens. He smiled and he waved. He was clutching a teddy bear and he just looked so innocent and peaceful."

"You mean he wasn't foaming at the mouth and gnawing on a neck bone like all the other serial killers you meet."

"He's a *kid*, Nina. An eight-year-old *kid*."

Nina swiped the paint over her pinky toe, dropped the brush into the bottle, and attempted to blow on her wet toes. "Let me tell you a little story. Back in, 1951, I think—yeah, it must have been fifty-one because the UDA-V bylaw didn't go into effect until fifty-three. Or four."

"The kid is going to be an adult by the time you get to the point."

Nina rolled her eyes and slid the nail polish jar across the coffee table to me. "Anyway. There was this rash of murders—horrible, horrible things. Schoolgirls, mainly. Pretty little things with young, pink complexions and bright, wide-open eyes. And their throats were torn clean out."

My stomach lurched. "That's horrible."

"Of course it is. They were these lovely maidens, six of them, if I remember correctly, cheerleaders, too, if I'm not mistaken. They were strewn all through the French Quarter. That was why I was back in New Orleans."

I sat up straighter. "You never told me you did any investigative work before me."

She shrugged. "I thought my skills spoke for themselves."

I thought of the time Nina dressed me in a black evening gown and cashmere gloves when I asked her for burglar wear and decided to stay quiet. I brushed a lavender streak across my thumbnail. "So you had a previous incarnation as a paranormal investigator."

"Do you want to hear this story or not?"

"I'm not entirely sure. Does it have a point?"

Nina's nostrils flared and her voice went tight. "Six lovely girls, throats torn clean out, left all over town. In the city's best date spots as a matter of fact. It was tragic and the crime scene was horrific. Scattered remains, very little blood . . ."

Despite my stomach threatening escape, my interest was piqued. "Vampire?"

"Indeed. A very young one. An attractive, sweet-faced boy."

"I really don't see what this has to do with anything. Oliver is clearly not a vampire."

"And you wouldn't think that Vlad was the type of boy to rip out the throats of six teenage girls."

"What?" My stomach was truly starting to revolt, and I swigged a tiny sip of my half-flat Fresca, hoping what remained of the carbonation would settle it. "Vlad did that?"

"Yeah. I did what?"

Vlad stepped out of Nina's room looking red-eyed and disheveled as though he had just woken up. Which was weird because vampires never slept.

Nina wrinkled her nose. "What were you doing in my closet? If you say something disgusting I'm going rip your head off."

Vlad let out a sound like a rapidly deflating balloon and held out his cell phone. "I was texting Kale. Don't be so gross. Why were you talking about me?"

"I was telling Sophie that you don't look like a rabid killer, but, well, you kind of are."

Vlad's eyes went wide and there was—shame?—in them. "That was a long time ago, Sophie. And God, Nina, you said you wouldn't tell! I was just a kid!"

"Sophie's family, Vlad. And I was just using your criminally bad behavior to illustrate a point."

"Which is?" I asked, still caught.

"That even someone who looks as soft and dough-like like our little Vladykins here, can make a few seriously bad decisions."

"I didn't know my own strength yet."

"He is an eight-year-old boy, Nina!"

"I was sixteen."

I pinched the bridge of my nose. "Not you, Vlad. Oliver. This kid. This case tonight. This kid killed his parents."

"Meh." Vlad shrugged.

"I'm so glad you two can be so cavalier about human life, but the rest of us can't. I have one life. And I consider it pretty precious. As do most of the other breathers I know. That's why murder is a serious crime and it's not something routinely committed by little boys who still sleep with teddy bears under sailboat sheets!"

"Okay, okay." Nina patted the air and pulled me to sit next to her. "I can see this is obviously bothering you a lot. What can we do?"

I looked from Nina to Vlad, pausing on the sweet-faced little death machine who was currently kicking off his shoes, unceremoniously dropping them—and a limp pair of socks—in a pile in the center of the living room. He looked so harmless, so unassuming—so annoyingly regular, leaving messes and being completely oblivious to the fact there was a hamper thirty feet away.

"Did you really do what Nina said, Vlad?"

Vlad suddenly focused very hard on balling up

his socks and using them to swish an arc across the toes of his black boots. Just when I thought he wasn't going to answer me, his head bobbed slightly, almost imperceptibly, and his broad shoulders seemed to sag.

"It was a long time ago."

Nina leaned close to me, resting her head on the pillow between us. "It's not always easy . . . when we start. That was before UDA was established. Part of why it was established."

The pitiful look on Vlad's face was fleeting, and in a half second, his expression was back to vast indifference.

"But Oliver is just a child," I said softly. "He's not—he's just a kid. A little kid."

"'The lion shall lay with the lamb and a little child shall lead them,'" Vlad said.

"What?"

"Apocalypse. Armageddon. End of times. 'The lion shall lay with the lamb and a little child shall lead them.' Isn't that in the Bible?"

A leaden rock sat in my gut and fear pricked the back of my neck. I recognized the phrase— vaguely—but hearing it come out of Vlad's mouth made it all the more chilling. My lip started to tremble. "Wh-what are you saying?"

"This kid set fire to his parents. And there have been other signs, everywhere."

"Like what?" Nina spat.

"Earthquake?"

Nina snorted. "If it were Armageddon every time an earthquake hit the Bay Area, we would have been Satan's minions years ago."

I glanced at Nina. Vlad glanced at Nina.

"You know what I mean!"

I gulped. "Yesterday? The earthquake?"

"But it's not like we're living in Iowa. We're living in San Francisco. We're filthy with quakes. So the earth shook a little. Any reports of brimstone vapors of the fires of Hell coming up through the Union Square? No. You've got nothing"

"We've got the three-headed dog," Vlad said. "You said it yourself: he's the guardian of the gates of Hell."

I surreptitiously pulled the collar of my shirt over my bandage. "Who I may or may not have seen. And there are supposed to be horsemen." I wracked my brain for every other Apocalypse-type reference I had ever heard in my brief stint in Bible school. "And fish boiled in blood and—and—stones falling from the sky."

Nina grimaced. "And we're supposed to be the evil ones?"

Vlad remained uncharacteristically silent, and goose bumps shot up along my spine, then radiated outward until they were covering every inch of me. I shivered and pulled my hands into my sweatshirt. "Nothing to say to that?"

Vlad ignored me and went back to typing on his computer. I was about to tell him that it was rude, even for him, to go tech in the middle of a conversation, but he turned the screen to face me and sat back in his chair, not even attempting to hide the enormously smug smile splitting across his face.

I leaned in, examining the four aging men on the screen. They were standing in a line, one under the other on descending steps, their traffic-cone orange shirts pressed, black rope detailing on their chest pockets and cufflinks.

"What am I looking at?"

Vlad scrolled down a little further and a newspaper heading popped up.

"*Four horsemen to be parade grand marshals,*" I read.

I crossed my arms in front of my chest and eyed Vlad. "Really, Vlad? This is a team of geriatric horse wranglers from Bend, Oregon."

"The four horsemen are mentioned in the Bible. Did you expect them to be a bunch of teenagers? And they're coming. It says it right here." Vlad jabbed an index finger toward the screen. "They're coming from Bend to grand marshal the parade after the Slow Foods conference."

"They're coming from *Bend, Oregon,* Vlad. Not Hell. And they're coming to lead a parade. Not the world into a fire and brimstony war of the ultimate good and evil."

Vlad rolled his eyes. "Well, they're not going to say they're coming to bring on Armageddon, now are they?"

I gave Nina my "Do you believe this guy?" stare, but she shot me back her own and it leaned more toward "He does have a point." I felt myself shiver, ridiculously.

"Coincidence," I said. And then, correcting myself, "Stupid coincidence."

"Okay, how about this." Vlad pulled a *Metro* newspaper off the counter and thrust it at me.

"Great, the Rolling Stones are in town. Another farewell tour?"

"No," Vlad clarified, handing Nina the paper. "Would you do the honors, Auntie Nina?"

She raised her eyebrows but took the paper anyway. "Uh, 'the Rolling Stones enter concert at AT&T Park with an eye catcher.'" She murmured a few more unremarkable lines about the fourth annual farewell tour and then paused. "They sky-dived into the concert," she said slowly.

"So?"

Nina looked at me, her eyes huge and dark. "Stones. Falling from the sky."

There was a beat of tense silence as we all stared at each other, eyes wide. The silence was only broken when Vlad started howling, his laughter popping in the quiet room.

"You should have seen your stupid faces," he said between breath-stealing giggles. "You were like, you were like—" He went on to imitate Nina and me with a glazed-eyed, slack jawed look before he doubled over again, snorting this time. "You guys are so lame!"

"You were making this all up?" Nina said sharply. "You're such an ass, Vlad!"

He paused long enough to gauge how serious—and how pissed—we were. Then he went back to chortling like a goddamned hyena, and I felt the heat, the adrenaline, those pinpricks of body-alerting fear whoosh out of me. Vlad stopped laughing long enough to point at me. "Armageddon! It's Armageddon!" he screamed while I wondered how far I could ram a wooden soup spoon into his heart.

* * *

I don't know how long I laid there that night, staring at the ceiling, but I remembered the shadows changing from a faint pale blue to dark outlines of angry black and soothing back again once the sun started rising.

My mind was a constant churn of the sweet, innocent face of Oliver Culverson, the resolute terror in the eyes of Effron Salazar, and Sampson, eyes focused hard on me when he mentioned my father—maybe he really meant that I should find him. The thought of that terrified me, and I padded to the bathroom and spent post-daybreak hours waiting for it to be an acceptable time to call someone and popping Tums by the handful.

At a quarter to seven I was burping up orange-flavored chalk and in desperate need of a Valium. I dialed Alex, ready to fire back when he complained about the early hour.

"I'm surprised it took you this long," he said, his voice raspy—and sexy—with sleep. "The boy started talking."

I swallowed hard, the action suddenly taking all my concentration. "And he said he didn't do it."

It was silent for a beat, and then I heard Alex suck in a breath. "No. No, he took full responsibility, again."

"No." I shook my head, knowing that Alex couldn't see me. "I don't buy it."

"He had details, Lawson."

"Because he was there, Alex."

"No. He had details that even an onlooker couldn't know. He was the murderer, Lawson. He murdered his parents and set fire to their bodies."

I felt like I had been kicked in the stomach. I worked in an industry and lived in a city where crime, albeit unfortunate, was commonplace. Horrible stories came up in the papers, and I had waded through my own horrible crime scenes—broken, decimated bodies laid out at angles no healthy human would ever be able to mimic. Rooms where the walls seemed to be bleeding. Flesh torn and puckered by knives, by teeth, by whatever could be considered a weapon enough to cause pain and destruction. I was getting used to them—at least as used to as anyone could expect. But I don't think that I'll ever be able to "get used to" any crime that involved children—whether they were the victims or the perpetrators.

"But he's only eight years old," I heard myself whisper.

"I know."

"Did he say anything else? Did he say why?"

I could hear Alex suck in a shallow breath. "He said, 'The devil made me do it.'"

As it was probably the most inappropriate thing possible to do after an admission like this, I giggled.

"Lawson!"

"I'm sorry!" And I truly was. But I had one of those bizarre conditions that made me do emotionally inappropriate things at exceptionally bad times. Seriously. Ask me about my libido at the next murder scene.

"I know it's not funny. I know it's horrible, but I just get this mental picture of the little guy dressed up like the Penguin saying, 'The devil made me do it.'"

Alex didn't respond, and I was finally able to

control my egregious laughter. "So, the devil made him do it?"

"The kid was serious. He said he was supposed to send a message from his new friend who turned out to be the devil."

"Turned out to be the devil?" I asked. "He didn't know that before?"

Alex went on as if he hadn't heard me. "He said he met the man—an adult male—in front of his house when he was out with his nanny. Apparently, the kid spent twenty minutes talking to this guy. He said the man was there waiting for him, outside, every day last week. He gave him candy, ice cream . . ."

I shuddered. "This man is some kind of predator. No wonder why he thinks it was the devil. Outside his own home, a guy approaches him and forced him to do evil. Was the kid able to describe the man?"

Alex cleared his throat. "Actually he had a name. Lucas Szabo."

I opened my mouth and tried to speak, but all my breath was gone. "He actually said Lucas?"

"Lucas Szabo. Out of the mouths of babes."

"Murderous, arsonist babes," I said, the tears rolling down my face.

My whole body started to tremble, and I rooted the soles of my feet onto the floor, fisted my hands, working against the involuntary current. "So my father—Lucas—befriends this kid and forces him to do this?" I could feel all the color draining from my face, could feel the wobbly, uneasy feeling in my head. I pressed my palm to my forehead, pushing as hard as I could. "Oh my God."

"The kid didn't say he was forced."

"He said the devil *made* him do it."

"Let's just say he didn't seem too upset about the order."

I swallowed, a myriad of emotions coursing through me. What was my father doing? I worked to swallow the growing lump in my throat as I thought of little Oliver Culverson, alone somewhere in the seventy-two-hour psych hold, waiting for my father to rescue him, to reward him. But I knew that Oliver would sit there. People would wonder what his parents did wrong, and my father would abandon him just like he had abandoned me.

"I want to talk to him."

ELEVEN

I dumped half a can of Alpo into ChaCha's rhinestone dish and she danced around it like it was caviar or donuts, then I grabbed my keys and was out the door in record time—in time enough to ram chest to chest into Will.

He shrank back, folding at the waist, pressing his palm against his wound.

"Oh, Will, oh my God, I'm so sorry."

He batted at the air and attempted a deep breath, his voice strained. "Hey, no problem. Doc said the best way to get better was to have people slam into me repeatedly. Where you off to in such a mad hurry?"

I bit my bottom lip, unsure of what to say.

"Look, love, I appreciate the secret, but the sky is falling and this is no time for you to be all 'I am woman, hear me growl.'"

"Roar."

"What?"

"Roar," I said again. "It's, 'I am woman, hear me roar.'"

He shrugged. "You can make whatever sound you want, love, but I'm partial to a growl." He waggled his brows.

"So you *are* feeling better."

"Well enough to come with you."

"You don't even know where I'm going."

"Doesn't matter," Will said, pulling his keys from his jeans pocket. "I'm your Guardian."

"What if I'm going to buy tampons?" I asked.

"Doesn't matter," he said again. "I'm protecting, not carrying."

"Come on," I groaned.

I filled Will in on my and Alex's conversation on the drive over. We were at the station, staring through the observation window, when Alex approached, his eyes clear and sharp but narrowing when he noticed Will by my side.

"What are you doing here?" Alex asked.

"And thank you for having me." Will gave a shallow bow. "There was a fire," he said dryly, making sure that his SFFD department badge was visible. "So technically, the welfare of a fire survivor is within my jurisdiction."

Alex's eye cut to mine. "You sure you want to do this?"

I nodded, not sure at all.

"I know what he said about—about Lucas, but before that: was he—were there signs?" I asked.

I know that both Alex and Will knew what I meant: the MacDonald triad. Sometimes called the

Evil Three or the rule of three, the MacDonald triad were the three most common traits of sociopaths—chronic bedwetting in late childhood, animal abuse, and arson. In cases where children have perpetrated such atrocities, often the triad was in their past, a misread—or ignored—early warning sign of the extreme danger to come.

But Alex swung his head. "By all accounts Oliver was a great kid. Honor roll, soccer team, Sunday school. He was a happy, popular kid who showed no signs of anger or violence. Everyone who knows him agrees this is something completely out of character for him."

"I want to go in now."

Alex and Will exchanged a glance, a rare, joint acknowledgment of silent agreement. If I hadn't thought Armageddon was on its way before, I was pretty sure of it now, since those two were vinegar and water.

"I'm coming with you."

They spoke in unison and I blinked, stunned. "No. I'm going in alone. Alex, you've got stuff to do and so do you, Will. I can handle this."

Frankly, I had no idea whether or not I could handle dealing with this angel-faced child who, according to two men I mostly respected, could be a tiny nugget of evil incarnate. But I was going to try. I didn't wait for Will or Alex to answer me. I shoved past them both, steeled myself, and opened the door to the observation room.

Oliver looked up when I stepped in, and smiled.

A great, big, friendly kid smile. It wasn't creepy at all.

He was dressed in a Social Services-issued gray sweat suit with a zip-up hoodie that was at least three sizes too big, a plain white T-shirt, and a pair of sweatpants that were rolled around the waist, and rolled again at the ankles, making fat donuts of fabric around his socks. I was happy to see that he was wearing plain kid sneakers, the kind of shoe that fit kid feet, not cloven hoofs.

I considered that a big, positive checkmark in the "not evil incarnate" column.

Oliver was sitting at a kid-sized table in a kid-sized chair with a piece of paper in front of him. He was coloring something that could have been the beginning of a cheery sun and rainbow scene or the fiery gates of Hell. He dropped the red crayon he was holding when I walked in the room, and his grin widened when I pulled the mini chair next to him and attempted to sit in a remotely ladylike position.

I wasn't particularly great with kids—and wasn't even as a kid. I have no cousins or siblings (except for the one I shish-kebabed and she seriously deserved it), and when I'd grown up it was mainly just my grandmother and me. I'd gone to school and had a few acquaintances there, but when you're weird—or when you offhandedly mention that you know for a fact that pixies cheat at cards—you tend to get branded as the kid that no one wants to play with. Or be field trip bus buddies with. Or lab partners, hall monitors, or summer camp friends with. Thus, I'd spent the bulk of my childhood years refilling the bridge mix at Grandma's weekly mah-

jongg games and shopping for school clothes at
Misha's Mystical Clothing Mart and Cauldron Em-
porium with a fashion-forward shape-shifter named
Juan. Or Aretha.

I put all of that out of my mind and attempted to
talk to Oliver the way social workers talked to all
the scarred children on the various *Law & Order*
iterations.

"Hi, Oliver. My name is Sophie."

Oliver glanced at me with his hot-chocolate eyes,
his grin still wide and, up close, toothless. He was a
darling little boy and everything inside me raged
against my father for using this tiny little vessel, who
smelled of strawberry shampoo and waxy crayon, as
an instrument of evil.

"I know your name," Oliver said, picking up a
crayon. "He said you'd be here."

A chill ran through me.

"He said?" My heart started to thud. I looked up
toward the enormous glass window that ran hori-
zontal across the front wall and Alex gave me a
thumbs-up.

"Oh! You mean Detective Grace."

Oliver dropped his crayon with a tight little snap.
"Not him, silly." He picked a yellow crayon from the
pile in front of him and started coloring, bright,
brilliant slashes across the page. "Lucas."

My heart dropped into my socks. "What did
you say?"

But the little boy was onto something else now,
scribbling a sea of orange over the yellow as he
hummed something that sounded a little like a
hymn. Having heard very few church hymns—

unless you count "Jesus, Take the Wheel"—I tried to take a couple of deep breaths while I convinced myself that I was totally projecting my neurosis and daddy issues on this sweet, little evil child.

"Oliver? You said a name before—what was that name?"

Oliver very deliberately set down his crayon, careful to line it up with the others. Then he turned to me, his pale lips pressed in a serene smile. He stared at me in silence for a beat, then scooted to the edge of his chair. I thought he was going to bolt until he reached out one hand and cradled my cheek. His hand was tiny, his fingers warm against my skin.

"Lucas was sorry he had to go before, but he's ready now. He can't wait to see you. He told me you were pretty. You look so much like her."

My heart lodged firmly in my throat. "Her?"

Oliver nodded, his hands leaving my face as he selected another crayon. He started coloring again, splashing bright red streaks across the page and bubbling over them so they looked almost like hearts. "Your mom."

Someone sucked all the air out of the room and ripped out all the lights. I saw the blackness, then felt like I was being shot out of my chair, zipped backward, pulled by some imaginary rope. I saw my mother's eyes, blinking first and terribly bright and behind her was Lucas, his face in a fog that quickly dissipated to show the hard planes of his bleak expression. I thought my mother was smiling at me, but it was a grimace, a tortured, silent scream on her lips as her eyes held mine. Lucas lunged at her—around her—arms outstretched toward me, and something happened. A loud clatter, a flash of light, and I was staring into my mom's eyes again, but the brightness had been replaced by a dull, lifeless sheen, her blue eyes as pale and as flat as stone. I felt a crack in my chest and my lungs burned, feeling as though they were being squeezed with an impossible force. Then Lucas's face flashed before my eyes, this time at a distance, at the schoolyard as he held Oliver's hand, leading him away from the burning building.

I blinked furiously and desperately sucked in air. The lights were on and one of the admins outside gave me a funny look as my eyes darted around the room, as if I were an animal in a cage.

"What just happened?" I clamped my hand over Oliver's. "Did you do that? Do you have some powers, kid? Some way to make me see things?"

But Oliver just smiled that serene, unnerving smile and swiveled himself back to the table. He chose another crayon, bent his head, and started coloring again.

I burst out of the observation room. "Alex, Will!"

"Will got a call from the chief. He went down to the fire station."

I was breathing hard, working to keep air in my deflated lungs.

"What's wrong?" Alex put down the stack of papers he was reading and hurried to me, concern creasing his features. "What? Lawson, what happened?"

"That kid. That kid!" I was pointing toward Oliver, panic vaulting through me with every heartbeat.

"Did he say something to you?"

The admin who had given me the weird look before was staring me and Alex down now so I grabbed the front of Alex's shirt and shoved him farther down the hallway. He glanced down at my hand fisted on his shirt and wrapped his own hand around mine.

"Lawson, what is it?"

"Your office."

I could see eyes darting toward us, cutting through the main office, eyebrows rising, but I didn't care.

I slammed the door to Alex's office, downed a cup of water from the bubbling jug, and raked my fingers through my hair.

"So, did he admit it? Did he say anything to you about the fire?"

I stopped mid-pace. "The fire?"

"The fire. The fire? The whole reason the kid is here?"

"He knew about Lucas, Alex. He knew about him."

I waited a good twenty seconds for Alex to gape, to drop his jaw, to grab his cuffs and demand we go martial law on this creepy kid's ass. But all he did was sit behind his desk, arms threaded across his chest.

"We knew that, Lawson."

I nodded. "I know. But he said it. To me! He said Lucas was 'his friend'"—I made air quotes—"and he set the fire because 'his friend'"—more air quotes—"told him to."

"Son of a bitch," he said, shaking his head. "It

looks like the devil—or someone pretending to be him—is walking the earth."

I stopped dead in my pacing tracks, feeling my jaw drop open in what I was certain was a look of pure disbelief. "What? You think there is another Lucas out there masquerading as the devil *and* my father?"

Ales sighed. "I'm trying to get to the bottom of this, Lawson. He's an eight-year-old kid who just murdered and burned his parents."

"Yes." I pumped my head. "Evil incarnate. Little evil incarnate. Isn't there something in the Bible that says, 'and a little child shall lead them'? That, that could be that kid. He's like Satan's apprentice." I top a step closer to Alex's desk and pointed to a yellow legal pad. "You should probably write that down. "A little child shall lead them."

Alex didn't pick up a pencil or break his gaze from me. "That's Isaiah 11:6."

"I knew it! So what is this? Armageddon? And didn't you get some kind of heads-up?"

Alex dropped his head in his hands in a gesture of either "You're absolutely right. All hell is about to break loose at the hand of this little Satan protégée" or "Lawson, you're out of your mind."

Alex looked up and sighed. "Lawson, you're out of your mind.

"The little child is leading a wolf, a lamb, a leopard, a fat goat, and a lion in that passage. Literally, he will be able to lead them."

"Right. Oliver Culverson, little child. Fire and mayhem, the lion. Or maybe that fat goat. Either way, shit is getting real, Alex. This is biblical."

I could see Alex biting the inside of his cheek and using all his strength to clench his lips. His shoulders quivered just the smallest bit, giving him away.

"Wait, you're laughing? How are you laughing?"

"What happened to the cool, new Sophie?"

I gestured in the general direction of Oliver Culverson. "Biblical, Alex!"

TWELVE

I stormed out of Alex's office and stopped, frozen, in front of the elevator doors. It had been less than twenty-four hours since I was expelled from the Underworld Detection Agency, and though I wanted to be haughty and over it, I felt a profound sense of longing, as if I had been evicted from my childhood home. I attempted to convince myself that what I was missing was the free and unlimited access to Post-it notes when the doors slid open.

Nina was slumped against the back wall, her shoulders sloped. Her usually pouty pink lips were pulled downward in a full-on frown so severe that even her eyelashes seemed to sag a little.

"Neens, what's wrong? You look like a pitiful little puppy."

She blinked up at me when I spoke and brightened slightly, stepping out of the elevator.

"I've been looking all over for you."

"Didn't you hear? I've been banned."

Nina's eyebrows rose a minute amount. "Banned?"

"I'm surprised Sampson didn't tell you."

Nina crossed her arms in front of her chest. "Sampson shouldn't have to tell me, Soph, you're my roommate and my best friend. You tell me everything! Even things I don't want to know."

"Hey!"

"You know what I mean: Alex, Will, Will, Alex. Blech. You're going to have to make a decision one of these days, you know. Only one of us is going to live forever."

"Is that why you were looking all over for me? To tell me that?"

Like one of those tragic masks, Nina's face fell, going directly back to the piteous look of three minutes prior.

I led her to a bench in the vestibule and cocked my head, forcing myself to look adequately concerned even though I was seriously annoyed. The whole Alex-Will thing is kind of a sticky subject for me.

"Okay, Neens. What's wrong?"

She patted my hair absently, then turned to me.

"Soph, what's my purpose here?"

I straightened. "What do you mean 'what's your purpose?' Neens, you're indispensible at UDA. The place wouldn't function without you!" I was stretching the truth into tall-tale category, but it was a time for sympathy, not accuracy.

"I know *that*, Sophie. I mean, overall. Why am I here? Why was I brought back? Was it just the sexy bloodlust of a ruined count, who couldn't resist the temptation of a twenty-nine-year-old virginal French ingénue?"

I cocked an eyebrow. "Virginal?"

"It's an expression. Anyway, you know your purpose. I mean, people are trying to kill you because of what you are, but what about me?"

I stiffened. "People are trying to kill me because what I have inside of me."

Nina patted my hand. "Oh, honey, don't sell yourself short. It's just that I wander around here for decades coming to work here, looking ridiculously adorable, but what for? I can't possibly just be part of the scenery. Can I?"

Although Nina could be—and at that very moment, was—incredibly obnoxious and a little bit self-centered, she had the uncanny ability to flash puppy dog eyes so pitiful that they made even her fangs look huggable.

"You've never been part of the scenery, Nina. You're so much more than that."

"But what do I add?"

"Uhhh . . . you . . . add fashion. You helped me to stop dressing like a blind librarian." I showed off my slightly less librarian-ish blouse, but Nina didn't brighten.

"But it didn't even stick. Look at you." Her lower lip pressed out, and even her puppy-dog eyes were starting to grate on me.

"And you help me every time there's a case or someone is trying to kill me."

She nodded slightly. "Well, yeah, that does happen a lot and I haven't let you get killed yet."

"And hey, look. Maybe you just haven't found

your purpose yet. I mean, no one does that easily. Aside from this whole thing"—I gestured to my belly, where I had always assumed the Vessel of Souls lay—"I really don't know why I'm here either. Maybe you should just start looking."

Nina sniffled. "You mean like when I was finding out what I was really good at?"

All of her past professions and hobbies marched in front of my eyes in a terrible parade of fangs, video cameras, and poorly written vampire sex scenes. As far as I knew she hadn't come across a real marketable skill set, but I wasn't ready to point that out.

"Yeah, exactly like that. You'll find your purpose."

Nina nodded, considering. "Yeah. I can try a few things out."

Although I knew the only thing worse than vain attempts at searching for purpose and meaning in life was having Nina vainly attempt to search for purpose and meaning in life, she was smiling, with a little bit of a flush in her cheeks. Granted, the flush was due to her afternoon snack of someone else's blood, but still, it made us both feel better.

You know things are bad when you are cast out of the Underworld Detection Agency and onto the streets of San Francisco and immediately miss the comfort and normalcy of an office filled with wailing banshees, drunken zombies, and trolls using all manner of excuse and stepladder to try and fondle your girlie bits. But that was exactly the way I felt the next afternoon stepping into the crosswalk, shuttled along with a crowd of sneaker-wearing secretaries and hipsters texting every step they took. Suddenly, I was out in the world and I was exposed. I didn't know the dangers; I couldn't look at someone and think, "Kishi demon—don't eat anything she offers, don't let her turn her back on you." All around me were normal-looking people in Gap clothes or slim suits and at any moment, one of them could advance on me carrying one of those crazy daggers and screaming something that sounded like "For Narnia!" as they came racing forward, stabby bits first.

It was very disconcerting.

When I finally slid into my car, my blouse was stuck to my back and a sheen of sweat had broken out over my upper lip. My heart was thundering and my stomach was a constant mass of batting butterfly wings. I jumped when someone honked driving by, I clawed at my heart when a crumpled McDonald's bag sailed on the wind and stuck to my shoe. Post panic attack, I sunk my key into the ignition and kept my eyes focused straight forward, hand on the door locks, as I raced by hordes of tourists and locals, and turned onto Larkin, slowing to find a spot in front of the San Francisco Public Library.

I stopped the car amongst the usual clatter and bang of the city sounds: the huff of a Muni bus stopping; the rush of cars, honks echoing off the high concrete buildings; the guy on the corner telling me that "Jesus saves." Once I walked into the library and the heavy door felt shut behind me, it was as if

the outside world just stopped. The library was so
silent that I was certain everyone in there was privy
to the sound of my thundering heart and my heavy,
probably-should-get-a-bit-more-cardio breathing. I
immediately slipped my hands into my purse and
switched my cell phone to off, turning a bright
lobster red when it shouted out its loud "you're
shutting me off!" protest music. Someone shushed
me. Someone else coughed.

I could see the library staff behind the checkout
counter. One woman with a nose ring and a fishnet
turtleneck smiled at me as she stamped the inside
cover of a hardcover book. I considered going over
to ask for some guidance, but strolling up and
asking, "Can you point me in the direction of Satan
and Armageddon?" seemed to be inviting trouble
on every level. Instead, I made my way to the computer system, doing my best to remain quiet and
make as little spectacle of myself as possible, which
was why my shoulder bag reached out and snagged
on a wooden chair, dragging it a good three feet
before I could untangle myself. The same kid who
shushed me before did it again. I mouthed a brief
apology and decided after I found the information
I was looking for, I would look up "holes one could
crawl into."

Finally, in front of the search computers and
facing away from the general, judgy and shoosh-y
public, I set my hands over the keys and typed:
Satan, Satan's minions, Grigori.

The entire page populated with entries.

I was relieved to see that the "evil books" portion
of the library was on one of the upper floors rather

than relegated to the basement in some scary movie knock-off. The stacks were well-lit and bathed in sunlight, making the spines—*Nebuchadnezzar's Watcher; The Rebellious; Hell on Earth*—look only slightly less terrifying. I knew that the text Will had on the Grigori mentioned the *Book of Enoch* so I went directly to it, surprised to find that it was an old set of leather-bound books rather than just a single one. When I pulled them out of the stacks, the two books on either side fell out as well and I started a spastic coughing fit at the cloud of dust they kicked up. I slid the other two back in, my nose wrinkling at the quarter-inch of dust that still stuck to the covers and littered the shelves—everywhere, except where the Books of Enoch had been.

I glanced down at the intricate patterns cut into the leather on the covers of the books; they were absolutely clean, as though they hadn't sat on the shelf long. As though someone may have accessed them very recently. A niggling of fear shot up the back of my spine, and I could feel the little hairs at the back of my neck prick up.

Who else was reading up on Armageddon?

I flipped through the pages of the *Book of Enoch I* and *II*, catching snippets of unsettling phrases referring to the Grigori as "the wakeful, the watchful ones" and "being countless soldiers of human appearance" who, in addition to rejecting "the light," showed up here on earth to introduce such fun gifts as "knives, swords, shields" and "the use of weapons for killing blows." The manuscript mentioned that they taught humans the "art of cosmetics," which cosmically may have been an issue, but wasn't one I was essentially worried about—even though it was the one that endeared Nina to the Grigori.

Also, I'd practically lived on cherry Chapstick in my teens.

I was about to put the two books back and restart my search to see if they had *Satan for Dummies* or something along the lines of *The Idiots Guide to Demon Half-Breeds* when a stack of papers that had been folded in half and shoved between the pages of one of the books floated out. I reached down to grab it, feeling the delicate, onionskin pages between my fingers. I glanced down at the hand-written title and cover image—it almost looked as though the packet were someone's term paper circa the second century BC, or some kind of hideously terrifying wedding program chock-full of grotesque images of fallen angel half-men, their human features visible but stretched in weird and scary ways. Oh, and they were naked.

"The Nephilim," I read. I traced my hand over the pencil image of blank, hollow-eyed faces looking out, and read the description underneath. "The offspring of the Watchers, or the Grigori, were dispatched to Earth to watch over the humans. Instead, the Grigori lusted after human women and defected en masse to illicitly instruct humanity and procreate among them. The offspring of this unholy union is the Nephilim."

My stomach stated to churn. I scanned further, noting that Noah's Great Flood had been called to wash away the "stain" of the Nephilim so that the earth could repopulate. I scanned over the list of fallen angels—a kind of evil family tree, if you will, pausing on Satanail. The sketch beside it made my breath catch.

It was Lucas Szabo.

The pale eyes and high cheekbones that stared out from the picture were so familiar because I saw them every day.

They were also mine.

I bore my mother's high forehead and slightly-larger-than-pixie nose, but the eyes, the cheek-bones, even the hard set of his mouth were my own.

My father was the trickster, the tempter, the head of the fallen. My mother was a human woman. That made me, their daughter, Nephilim—a stain upon the Earth. I didn't know why it had never occurred to me before.

THIRTEEN

By the time I left the library the sun was setting and the fog was rolling in, blanketing everything in a cool, misty gray. I had just gunned the engine when the rain started, big, sad drops that thumped on the hood of my car, first a slow rhythm, then growing in speed and size.

"There it is," I mumbled to myself. "A flood. It's starting again."

I pulled away from the curb, getting one of those big, I'm-feeling-sorry-for-myself lumps at the back of my throat, and by the time the rain had smoothed out again to a pitiful drizzle, I was crying in hiccupping fits as tiny rivers of rain water rushed along the street.

When I got home, I had mainly gotten ahold of myself, but with my rosy cheeks and runny nose, there was no way I could slide past Nina.

"What happened, pumpkin?" she said when she saw me, dark brows slamming together.

I waved at the air in the vain assumption that I was over being a sniveling idiot. "Oh, nothing. Just that I'm a stain upon the earth that God tried to wash away." The tears came back and I was doing that terrible silent cry with my mouth open until Nina crossed the living room and threw her arms around me, crushing me to her ice-cold chest.

"Who called you a stain?" she said in a slightly disturbing vampire-baby voice. "Who would call you that?"

I huffed and sniffled. "The-the-the Bible."

Nina pulled back, studying me. "Really?"

"My dad is Satan and my mom is regular so that makes me—"

"Nephilim," she supplied. "I hadn't thought about that."

"You know about the Nephilim?"

Nina released me and guided me to a chair at the dining table, filled a kettle with water, and dropped it onto the stove. She pulled a blood bag from the fridge and yanked open the top of the teakettle. "You mind?" she asked.

I shook my head. "No, no worries."

She dropped the blood bag into the water and turned up the stove, then leaned over, chin in hands, and looked at me. "I don't know much about the Nephilim except that they exist. And you know, the whole mixed-breed thing."

I felt my lower lip push out. "The flood was to get rid of me."

Nina rolled her eyes. "Oh my God, Soph, do you know how many times people have tried to get rid of me? How many times I've been chased by pitchfork-wielding villagers with fire? Like, a thousand."

"I know, but . . . I just thought people liked me."

"You are being ridiculous. People like you."

"Did you always know? What I am?"

Nina turned when the kettle whistled. She plucked out her blood bag, holding the plastic edge with her teeth as she dropped a tea bag and more sugar than any adult should eat in one sitting, into a mug. She topped it off with hot water and I thought she wasn't going to answer me, or was taking her time because she was going to answer me and it was going to be something horrible—like she'd taken pity on me or thought that it was only logical that the two damnedest dames in San Francisco should share a place in the city—on the third floor so as to steer clear of imminent flooding.

"Of course, Sophie. I've always known that you were a pansy-ass crybaby. For the daughter of Satan, you sure didn't get any of his fire or brimstone."

She pierced the edge of her blood bag and started sucking, the edges of her mouth twitching up as her lips and cheeks flushed.

My mouth gaped. "That's a terrible thing to say to someone who just found out they were a stain on the Earth. A *stain*, Neens! You know what people do with stains? They want to get rid of them. At all costs."

Nina sucked until the plastic bag crushed in on itself, then grinned, tossing the empty at me. "Stop being such a baby and welcome to the club of the damned."

"That's it?"

"Of course it is." Nina dragged a chair up to mine and plunked down, throwing an arm around me.

Her voice softened. "You're still the same Sophie you've always been. You're still my best friend. You're good, Sophie, you are. You have to believe that."

I sniffed, feeling the tears start again. "But I'm born of evil."

And again, Nina rolled her eyes and guffawed. "And I was made of evil." She snatched up the empty blood bag and waggled it. "This wasn't exactly a bag of Fritos."

I laughed despite my knee-deep wallow in self-pity.

"I guess we're pretty much two of a kind."

Nina smiled. "Aw, I guess we are. Love you, Soph."

I wrapped my arms around my best friend's neck. "Love you, Neens."

"Oh, what fresh hell is this?"

Vlad was standing in the living room, hands on hips, lips twisted in severe disgust.

Nina and I shared a glance and stood up, arms raised, and tackled Vlad in the death grip of all hugs.

"And Vlad is our little born-of-evil man!" I shouted.

"Who's an evil boy, huh? Who's an evil boy?"

Vlad stood statue still, the grimace carved into his face. "I hate you both," he finally muttered.

I couldn't remember the last time I had actually slept for anything longer than a few minutes. I did know, however, that it was far before the earth started trembling, houses started burning, and my countenance as a human stain was solidified in my mind. I couldn't stand staring at the skittering ceiling shadows one more minute, so I yanked on my sweatpants and my coziest Giants hoodie, slipped into my sneakers, and tiptoed out the front door. The stairs butted against the utility room, and I angled myself around it, taking the steps softly until I was up two flights. When I opened the door, the night sky was all around me.

There were two discarded chaise longues on the roof of my building, each dragged to the waist-high stone wall that surrounded the edge, and each angled so the lounge-ee could get a full view of the cityscape with the faint sound of the bay swirling beyond. I pulled my hood up and went for the longue, nearly pitching myself over the side of the building when I realized there was already someone seated.

"Oh, God!" I landed in some semblance of a defensive move, something that, I'm sure, looked like a cross between Buffy-tough and a hibernating bear.

"Sophie?" Will's accent cut my name, and I straightened, squinting.

"Will? What are you doing up here?"

He sat down, gestured toward the open chair, and pulled two beers from somewhere in the shadows. "I suspect the same thing as you are."

He was wrapped in the fuzzy yellow and red Arsenal blanket that was normally spread on his bed. I could make out his stair-step abdominal muscles as he leaned in to hand me a beer. I was slightly mesmerized by his smooth, taut skin.

"Aren't you freezing?"

Sadly, he pulled the blanket tighter across his chest. "Not really. What are you doing awake, love?"

"I asked you first."

Will crooked his arm over his head, cradling his head in one large hand as he took a long, slow pull on his beer.

"Thinking."

"About?"

"This." He waved his beer bottle, indicating the city, I supposed. "Everything in it. You?"

"Same." I took a swig. "Something's happening, Will."

Will's hand found mine in the darkness and squeezed. "I know, love. But I'm not going to let it happen to you."

A sob lodged in my chest. "I don't think you can stop it, Will. I don't think anyone can. It's my father. It's Armageddon. It's really, really bad."

The tears started to roll down my cheeks in a rushing waterfall. I hadn't realized how sad and how scared I actually was. I was used to danger—I was used to the kind of danger that was serial killers or mythical idiots on quests for ultimate powers because those were things we could stop. All of us—Alex, Will, Nina, Vlad, and me. But this . . . this was something different. A race of fallen angels worse than evil. Learning that no matter what I did, I couldn't change who I was, the evil into which I was born. I was in danger. My friends were in danger. Everything I held dear was in danger.

"It's all because of me."

Will shifted on his chaise, then held his blanket open for me. "Come 'ere, love."

I paused for a half beat, then slipped off my shoes and climbed into his blanket, into his arms. I was immediately surrounded by warmth and a comfort that was overwhelming, and my body softened to fit his.

"I'm glad you're here, Will."

He brushed his lips over the top of my head, pressing them against the part. "I would be here even if it wasn't my job, Sophie."

I edged my chin up so that I could look into Will's eyes, the gold flecks nearly hidden by shadow. "What if it really is the end of the world?"

The sound of the city, even in darkness, seemed to fade, seemed to drop into a waiting silence, and Will's lips were on mine, pressing, tasting. His tongue nudged my lips apart, and I was kissing him back, burying my hands in his hair, then slipping them down the smooth, muscular planes of his chest. When he broke our kiss, the world came crashing in and my lips were cold, stung. His hair was a disheveled mess and his voice was throaty and rich as he pinned me with an incredible stare and murmured, "If it is the end of the world, we should make every moment last."

His words sunk into me and my whole body was alive, for once, with something that wasn't terror, that wasn't ultimately devastating. My heart was pounding, slamming against my rib cage, but the ache was delicious, Will's touch sending shock waves throughout my body.

The world was ending.

My palms slid over his erect nipples, and he groaned, his hands cupping my ass.

We were losing.

I kissed him hungrily, clawing at him because I needed him closer, wanted him more than near me.

What else was there to do?

The moisture was sinking into the blanket, was settling on my skin. A cool breeze ruffled my hair, and I snuggled down deeper into bed, deeper against the warm body lying there, his breath a rhythmic rise and fall.

I sat bolt upright.

The night came crashing back. We were on the roof of our building, sharing a single chaise longue, legs pretzeled together, bodies entwined. The memory of Will's lips on mine, of his hands hot on my skin, sent fire through me.

"Will," I hissed. "Will, we need to wake up. We fell asleep, we're outside."

His eyelashes fluttered, and then he blinked. I could see his eyes scan and then focus on me, a smile breaking across his lips. I glanced down surreptitiously, glad to see I was fully clothed—if not for my own peace of mind, then for the fact that I had successfully navigated a chaotic disaster without dropping my pants.

Hey, in the face of total annihilation, you take what you can get.

Neither Nina nor Vlad was home when I came in, and for that I was slightly grateful. I was an adult and whom I went out with and whether I stayed out all night were totally my business, but it was that much easier to swallow when I didn't have to explain myself to my century-old vampire pals.

There was no note explaining where they had gone, but my cell phone was buzzing spastically, telling me I had missed three calls from Alex and a message from the UDA.

I dialed into my voice mail:

"Sophie? It's Kale. Someone called for you and it was really weird. He was really weird. He wouldn't say who he was. . . ."

My heart started to thud in my throat.

"He kind of had an accent though, and he was super-duper insistent on talking to you. Well, seeing you, actually."

A man wanted to see me.

Insisted on seeing me.

But he wouldn't leave his name.

My stomach roiled and my skin started to thrum. Was it—was he—Lucas?

I could hear Kale fumble with the phone on her end of the message.

"I thought you would be in by now. Either way, I said you would be in later today. Hope that's okay. He said he'd be by."

I was vaguely surprised that I was able to make it through the city without the streets caving in or without being attacked from all sides by someone or something brandishing a sword or a dagger, muttering something in Latin, or uttering some iteration of Satan. But then I remembered that was probably because Satan was waiting for me behind

my desk in an office I no longer worked at. Part of
me considered erasing Kale's message and hiding
under my blanket eating chocolate ice cream from
the carton while I let the UDA deal with it. But the
bigger, less-inclined-to-run-away part of me knew
that if Satan really was waiting for me, the UDA was
in trouble and I would be proving Sampson right by
letting it happen.

I considered donning an all-leather catsuit and
packing the kind of arsenal that would make the
Prince of Darkness quiver, but then I realized it had
been at least three sleeves of chocolate marshmallow Pinwheels since the last time I'd attempted
leather and my arsenal contained little more than
a stun gun, a mostly frozen snub-nosed Rossi .357,
and a four-pound dog in a rhinestone collar. Instead I dialed Alex, leaving furious, cryptic messages on his voice mail while alternately doing the
same on Will's. While I'm not completely certain
what I said, I'm pretty sure it was something to the
effect of, "My dad is at the Underworld Detection
Agency right now. There is a good chance we'll all
be in a swirling vortex of Hell by noon, but if it's
only me that goes, please feed ChaCha."

When I pulled into the police station parking lot,
my palms were sweating and I was shaking up to my
eyebrows. My head was swirling, and I was mum-
bling a series of witty, Buffy-style comebacks in between tearful reunion monologues, should my dad
just be popping in to say he'd never meant to leave
and he was so, so proud of the woman I'd become.
That last part may have been pushing it, but I was
willing to embrace my manic swing in emotion as

something positive like personal growth—not everything is about death and destruction! Right?

When I hopped into the elevator I glared at my cell phone and checked the dial tone, certain that I had lost service or fallen into a cell-signal manhole because how could neither Alex nor Will have called me back? The angst was spreading throughout my body then, but I told myself that since I didn't hear screaming or smell the fires of a thousand blazing souls in the elevator, things would be okay. I might even be overreacting. In an effort to center myself during the final descent, I hummed along to the elevator Muzak—something by Madonna that been sterilized and synthesized. When the elevator doors finally slid open, I was in a better place mentally. I figured that if my father was going to murder me, he would have done it a long time ago.

I was actually *smiling* when I walked into the waiting room. My heart was pounding against my rib cage, but every thud was like an echo—my dad! My dad! My dad!—he *must* have come to see me. He must have missed me.

My *dad*.

"Well, don't you look like the vamp who swallowed the vicar?" Vlad grinned at me, one inky-black eyebrow cocked.

"I believe the expression is the 'cat that swallowed the canary,' but yeah, I guess I do have a little bit of swallow—a little bit of—did you want something?"

His blood-flushed lips quirked into a shameless smile. "Not really. I'm just surprised to see you here is all."

I flushed red, realizing that Sampson must have told the entire staff that I was dismissed. I truly hoped he had said something to the effect of, "because she deserves a vacation!" rather than, "because her being here could possibly kill all of us."

"Kale called me. Apparently I have, or will have, a visitor shortly."

Vlad's eyebrows went up, but I didn't say anything further.

I rounded the corner and glanced into my office. The lights were off and it was obvious that my visitor hadn't yet arrived so I took the opportunity to hightail it to the ladies.

Things are going to be okay! Things are going to be okay!

I kept repeating the mantras in my head, something I had learned from a shrink or possibly Oprah or Dr. Phil. However I'd learned them, they kind of helped, and when I felt like my world was about to implode or I've been attacked in a public park, I needed all the help I could get. I ducked into the ladies' room and held my breath, scanning the stalls for pixie feet. They had their own tiny stall, but they were always using the regular and then giving you the death stare if you walked in— even though the bathroom was for all female Underworld employees. Did I mention pixies were absolute bitches? The last thing my ego needed was to be attacked by a six-inch tall sprite with sugar-cookie breath and something to prove.

Finding none, I went into a stall and did my business, when the restroom door kicked open.

"I honestly don't know how she's going to manage it."

I strained, listening over the sound of rushing water and footsteps.

"Come on, is it really that bad, really? She's always getting into scrapes and she always comes out on top."

"Sophie on top?"

My stomach dropped. I tried to see who was talking, but they were standing out of my view.

There was a little gale of laughter and I clenched my teeth. "Okay, maybe not on top, but she always survives. I'm just not sure on this one for any of us, but especially for her."

The other party clucked her tongue. "I wouldn't care normally, but even Sampson is worried with this one."

"I know. Did you see his expression during the all-hands meeting? I thought the bulging veins in his neck were going to pop out."

I felt the sweat bead on my upper lip. There had been an all-hands meeting? Where they had talked about me? I found myself holding my breath, suddenly paralyzed. Why wouldn't Sampson have at least told me about it? Had he told them—everyone—to steer clear of me? My world was crashing in, and my family—my Underworld Detection Agency family—was having meetings without me and talking about me behind my back.

My thrumming nerves turned into fury and I kicked open the stall door, skulking out. The two women talking were vampires who worked in HR. Their eyes widened when they saw me.

"Note for the future, ladies. You might want to check for feet"—I pointed—"underneath the stalls before you start talking about someone."

I felt smug and vindicated as the two just stared at me, slightly open mouthed, eyebrows jammed together in an expression of apology or sympathy. I washed my hands and reveled in their stunned silence, then threw my shoulders back and marched for the door.

One of the vampires cleared her throat and I turned, allowing her to make her heartfelt apology.

"You've got toilet paper stuck to your shoe, Sophie."

Even the righteous can't win them all.

I started when I pushed open Nina's office door and Kale was waiting for me. "Oh! Geez, Kale, you scared me."

She clapped a hand to her forehead. "Oh my goddess, Sophie, you got my message!"

I nodded curtly. "I came right in after I heard it."

I clicked the door to Nina's office shut behind us and swished Kale down the hallway with me.

"Hey," I said before she could open her mouth. "Was there an all-hands meeting today?"

Her cheeks flushed a wicked red and she looked at her shoes. "Sampson called it. It was nothing big."

"It was big enough to call in every employee except me."

"You weren't there?" Kale said, her acting horrific. "Are you sure? Maybe you just forgot."

I pinched the bridge of my nose. "Pretty sure I would have remembered going to a meeting with the entire staff."

There were so many of us that we had to move into the cafeteria for all-hands meetings and, all assembled at the standard-issue tables, we tended to look like rejects from every Halloween parade ever.

I blamed the members of the Vampire Empowerment and Restoration Movement in their frilly ascots and broaches, Vlad, a combination of Count Chocula and a Wal-Mart Lestat, leading the charge.

"Can you just tell me what Sampson talked about? Did he talk about me? Did he talk about . . ." I circled my arms, my gesture to encompass my spinning, splattering life.

Kale bit her bottom lip, her eyes going up as if she were thinking hard, as if the answer she sought were written on the office ceiling. "Not that I remember. But hey, not to change the subject, that guy that kept calling for you? He just came in. Want me to send him to your office?"

Nerves pricked up along the back of my neck, and my tiny suspicions broke out into a wild fire. This was it. This was the big moment.

"Yes. I mean, no. I'll get—no, no, yes." I cleared my throat and tried to look slightly less crazy. "Go ahead and bring him to my office, please."

Her cheeks bloomed pink. "Okay . . . because I already did."

My blood ran cold and the temperature in the waiting room seemed to plummet to match it. It was then that I realized that no one was speaking, no keyboards were clacking, no feet, hooves, or claws were slapping down the hallway. It was absolutely silent. The few people in the waiting room were statue still, wide-eyed, staring at me. A sub-demon named Aura snaked a hand out and pulled her tentacled child closer to her. Two Wendigos were holding their breaths, their chests and bellies concave with the effort.

"Did—did he say who he was this time?"

She shook her head, this time a very gentle, tense wag. "He didn't say his name. He just asked for you. He's there." She pointed, as though I needed direction. "Waiting in your office."

I blew out a sigh in an attempt to look unaffected and confident. "Okay, then I guess I'll go meet with him."

I took a few shaky steps, then whipped around, nose to nose with Kale. She stepped back an inch.

"Did he say what he wanted?" I asked.

Another mute head wag.

"And he's not a client?"

One more.

My throat immediately went dry. I wanted to ask, but the words slid out of my grasp. I wanted to ask, but I didn't want to know the answer: *The man in my office—is he Lucas Szabo?*

I stopped for a millisecond, willing my heart to go back to a regular, non-spastic beat, and talking myself into a happier place.

I started toward my office, then paused. "So, he didn't say what his name was?"

Kale wagged her head.

"And you didn't ask?"

Another head wag, this one accompanied by wide eyes. "He creeped me out, Sophie. I just—I just couldn't bring myself to talk to him. He made me feel"—she shuddered, her tiny shoulders rattling—"weird."

I nodded, silently trying to steel myself. I could handle myself. I could handle anything. And even if it was my father, so what? There was nothing he could do to me here, at the Underworld Detection Agency, where I was surrounded with friends who were like family. Friends who were like family who had clandestine meetings without me and, for all intents and purposes, had fired me.

But no, nothing fazed me.

I was *Sophie Lawson: Confidence Girl.*

Hot bile burned at the base of my throat. Because I was *Sophie Lawson: Possible Bipolar Basket Case.*

"Well, let's get this over with," I mumbled under my breath.

Kale caught up and pointed to the man standing at the door to my office.

"There he is, that's him. He's—"

I felt the jauntiness ooze right out of my step. "A monk?"

Well, that was different.

FOURTEEN

Hipster, demon, or undead, I was pretty much used to seeing every kind of fashion that retail and San Francisco could come up with.

But burlap was new. A rope belt, new. The weird pageboy with a bald middle? Super weird.

"Um, hello. I'm Sophie Lawson. And you are—"

"Abelard."

"A monk."

He knitted his fingers together, resting his hands in his lap, and looked at me with a serene smile.

"I mean, you're a monk, right? Is that the right way to refer to you? Or is it father? Brother?" I paused, biting my thumbnail. "Uncle?"

"Abelard is just fine."

"Okay, Abelard. What is it that I can do for you?"

Abelard—his round face framed by the unfortunate pageboy—blinked. Then his eyes went up to Kale, who was still standing to his left, openly gawking.

"Kale? Can you please give us a moment?"

Kale looked up at me and then back at Abelard.

"He didn't give me his intake form. I can't start the paperwork without his intake form."

Have I mentioned that the Underworld Detection Agency works with all the efficiency and modernity of the DMV office on Rural Route 9 in the Kansas backwoods? Because we do. There are forms to fill out. And then forms to fill out about the forms that were just filled out. There is even a form to fill out if you think there are too many forms. We're trying desperately to catch up with 1986 and, at the very least, get a few things digitized. Which basically means—you guessed it—more forms that get stacked between Hubba Bubba wrappers and *Cosmo* quizzes on Kale's desk.

Kale was gripping a stack of forms now, her knuckles white as her teeth worked her lower lip.

"Mr.—Abelard—can you excuse us for just one minute?"

The monk nodded—again, fingers knitted, serene smile that I didn't find off-putting at all— and I stepped around him, grabbing Kale by the elbow and leading her into the hall.

"What the heck was that about?"

"I could ask you the same thing."

I crossed my arms in front of my chest. "What are you talking about?"

"I'm talking about that." Kale's kohl-rimmed eyes darted to the back of the monk's head, every hair still as he stared at the blank wall directly in front of him. "You have a religious icon in your office. That's weird."

"It's not that weird. I work in the Fallen Angels

Division, remember? There are likely to be"—I gestured to Abelard—"those . . . guys."

"Well, he makes me feel uncomfortable." She stiffened, using her stack of forms like a shield in front of her breasts.

"Did he touch you or something?"

I thought her eyes were going to bounce right out of her head. "Oh my God, Sophie, that is so gross. I just—people like that don't usually have a lot of cause to be around people like us."

People like us.

Except I wasn't like her.

I was the only living, breathing member of the Underworld Detection Agency. Not to say that I worked alone—far from it. Our office is forever bustling with all manner of demon, deadbeat, or other, and we spent a lot of time recruiting and hiring.

It's just that all of those employees tend to be dead—or undead.

"Thank you, Kale. I can handle it from here."

Kale disappeared before I had a chance to finish my sentence. I pushed my hair behind my ears, threw my shoulders back, and pasted on a lovely, Heaven-worthy smile.

"So, Abelard, what is it I can do for you?"

His pale eyes followed me as I scooted around his chair and sank into my own. He seemed to wait until I was settled before leaning forward and dropping his voice. "I know about you."

My spine shot ramrod straight, and heat clawed at every inch of my skin. "Excuse me?"

Abelard offered that serene smile that had seemed

too oblivious and, well, *monkish,* just a few seconds
ago. Now I was narrowing my eyes and squinting,
working out if there was evil behind his smile, if I
could make it to the Taser I kept in my top right desk
drawer before he pulled out a mouthful of dragon
teeth and swallowed me whole.

"Oh, don't worry." Abelard put up his palms.
"I'm not going to hurt you."

I blew hot breath out of my nostrils. The last
person who'd said he "wouldn't hurt me" had
nearly ripped out my throat with his teeth. Granted,
he hadn't been dressed as a monk, which gave
Abelard a modicum more of trustworthiness.

"Why would you want to hurt me?"

"I said I'm not going to hurt you. But I know—I
know about you."

I blinked.

"The Vessel?"

Blink, blink, blink.

"The Vessel of Souls? You're Sophie Lawson, are
you not?"

I nodded, my tongue glued to the roof of my
mouth. I wasn't sure if it was possible, but I suddenly suspected that every damn soul that I was
hiding in my so-called Vessel had gotten out and
was river-dancing in my belly.

"How do you know that?" My voice was a hollow
whisper.

Abelard cocked his head and his smile seemed to
say, "Really? I'm a monk."

"Oh." I gestured toward his burlap robe, toward
his stylish rope belt that I thought went out with

Jesus sandals and Friar Tuck. "You know 'cause you're . . ."

"My order are the Vessel Guardians."

"The Guardians? But I have a Guardian." I ignored the voice in my head that reminded me that I had nearly gotten Will killed; that taunted I *had* a Guardian. "His name is Will. Will Sherman. You can look it up in your—in your monk tome or iPhone if you're the more modern kind of monk. Why are you here again?"

I knew I was babbling. Everything inside me implored my stupid mouth to stop talking, but it was like my entire being had suddenly been taken over by a vapid Miss America contestant who'd been asked about immigration reform.

"I mean, you're certainly welcome to be here. We are, of course, a public institution. Not *public*, public, but—"

"There is no need to be nervous, Sophie. May I call you Sophie?"

I sat there, silent, and Abelard went on.

"As you have undoubtedly noticed, there has been some unrest in the world—in this area, particularly—as of late." His pale eyes went up to me as though I was supposed to agree. "The fires, the murders, the failing structures?"

"Yeah . . . so?"

"There is a great war being waged. The war of dark and light." His eyes flashed. "Good and evil."

The anxiety that I had felt—the roiling nerves and general feeling of idiocy—immediately wore off. "That's nothing new."

"You're right—it isn't. But lately, it's become

much more severe, rising to the surface. It's been breaking the surface. There has always been evil and it has always been eclipsed, even if just barely, by the good."

"Uh. So, do you want me to donate money or something?"

I'm not sure if it was just my general discomfort of being in the shadow of a monk or what, but when Abelard pursed his lips and looked at me, I felt like I should immediately break into a series of Hail Marys. And I would have, had I remembered anything past *Hail Mary, full of grace.*

"Sophie, there is a reason so much malaise has bubbled to the surface."

I raised my eyebrows.

"The darkness has found you, Sophie. The darkness knows about you."

"Meaning?"

"Evil knows who you are. It knows what you are."

"Oh!" I swatted at the air, feeling the cold sweat of relief breaking out all over me. "They—it—evil has known for a long time. I mean, there's always someone trying to kill me or maim me or, you know, shake me by my ankles to get the Vessel out or whatever. Hey, how does that work, by the way? Getting it out? Do I like"—I opened my mouth, tongue wagging, the most elegant way I knew of indicating the act of vomiting—"or something?"

"We need to protect the Vessel of Souls. We need to bring it somewhere more secure."

"Okay, but I don't understand, why now? Why all of the sudden?"

Abelard leveled his gaze. "It's your father, Sophie. He knows and he's coming for you."

As a kid, I had always dreamed of the day someone would tell me that my father was coming for me. I would be in some gray, drab, windowless house for some reason, and my grandmother would be leaning down on one knee, buttoning my steel-gray coat and smiling. I would be nervous, but there would be true joy in her eyes as she buttoned the big black buttons over my chest, telling me, "He's missed you for so long. He was on a secret mission, stuck in some POW camp in a country we didn't even know we were fighting, but he's saved the day and now he's coming for you. He can't wait to see you."

The joy would break through me then. I hadn't been abandoned! I had a mother who'd loved me until her last breath but still looked after me from Heaven—and I had a father who had spent the last years trying to get back to me, clawing against the filthy ground of some horrendous jail cell, the only thing keeping him alive were thoughts of me, his daughter. Of coming back to *me*.

This was not how I had imagined it at all: me, sitting in my office at my cheap metal desk, a monk looking at me with a grave expression. Warning me that the world was crashing into a giant hellish vortex of brimstone, fire, and Kardashian babies and it's all because my father wants me now. Not me, exactly, but what I am. He doesn't want to know me, his only living daughter—he wants to control the Vessel of Souls.

Save the Vessel, not the girl.

"So what am I supposed to do?"

Abelard stood and paced, one hand rubbing over his cleanly shaven chin. "It's a small ceremony to transfer the Vessel of Souls. It would take my whole order, though, and"—his eyes raked over me sadly—"it might not be the most pleasant of experiences for you."

"Not pleasant as in 'it might be a little itchy' or not pleasant as in 'my insides will suddenly be on the outside'?"

"Oh, nothing that dramatic, I assure you. You just might not feel like yourself for a few days. A bit like being under the weather, nothing too terrible." He smiled softly, but my hackles went up.

Nothing about being the Vessel of Souls—hell, nothing about being Sophie Lawson—fell into the "nothing too terrible" category. Likening the removal of the Vessel to fighting a little flu bug didn't seem to add up.

"A little under the weather?"

Abelard's shoulders went up to his ears. "And there is, of course, the release of your Guardian then."

"The release of—you mean Will? Released how?"

"Well, his services will no longer be needed by you."

I thought of Will lying crumpled in that hospital bed. Well, not so much crumpled as splayed out with his Swiss-cheese chest in the air, but still. He had been stabbed, bandaged, and full of painkillers and antibiotics because of me. He had been beaten up and bowled over because of me. If I were no longer the Vessel of Souls, Will's life would no longer be hemmed in by me; his life would no longer be a catalog of soccer games and near-death experiences.

"So the Vessel of Souls is removed from me and re-hidden. Then Will and I are . . . safe?" It seemed too simple, too good to be true.

"Well, not exactly, no."

And of course, there it was.

"Unfortunately, Sophie, you'll always be imprinted with the energy of the Vessel. Those who seek to possess it will still come after you, searching, thinking that you must know where it has been removed to."

"Will I? Know, I mean. Are you guys going to tell me?"

Abelard shook his head. "No. For your safety and for ours."

"So, I go through this, this removal—"

"The ceremony."

"The ceremony, right, yeah, and the Vessel of Souls is removed and I'm back to my regular old Sophie Lawson self and Will is no longer my Guardian and people are still going to come looking for me? No offense, Abelard, but I'm not seeing the upswing on this one."

"Do you not seek to release your Guardian?"

His words shot something through my veins. Was he reading my mind? Abelard's pale eyes were firm on mine, his lips pursed, but there was no animosity there. Nothing that looked like he was quietly poring through the desires of my soul.

"I don't want him to be in danger because of me anymore."

"So then?"

"But if it's not going to do any good . . ."

Abelard pressed the palms of his hands together in front of me. "Perhaps I should clarify. Those who seek the Vessel will always be after you. You are, let's see, the trailhead, perhaps? But once those learn that you no longer possess the Vessel . . ."

"Sorry, Abe, still not seeing the benefit for me in any of this."

He blew out a long sigh, and now I could see that the smile on his face was forced. "Your father wants you. He wants the Vessel. He is stronger than all of us, but so far, we have been smarter than him. As long as you possess the Vessel of Souls, it is within his grasp and the world will continue to crumble until he gets what he wants."

I leaned back in my chair and narrowed my eyes. "But if you took the Vessel and re-hid it, would that stop him?"

"Well, no, not exactly. He will always seek—"

I assumed my bravado and disdain for double-talk and bureaucracy came from shuffling endless papers at the Agency, but I didn't pause to examine it. "Don't get me wrong—it's not like I'm particularly attached to this whole Vessel thing. It's just that"—I cocked my head—"I'm supposed to just trust you to do this ceremony? Trust you to hide it where my fath—or the evil plane or whatever, can't get to it?"

I could see the tension pressing the wrinkles out of Abelard's lips. He eyed me and I locked onto his gaze, crossing my arms in front of my chest. I wasn't a particularly religious person, but it did feel a little heretical staring down a monk. On the other hand, we were underground at the Underworld Detection Agency—my territory—and there were two vampires and a teenage witch huddling on the other side of my office door, pretending not to listen.

Abelard cleared his throat. "Frankly, we're not sure that you have the strength to protect the Vessel of Souls in this particular situation."

A little prick of anger started at the base of my spine. "You don't think I have the strength? Do you know what I've gone through to protect this thing? It's not been a complete walk in the park, let me tell you! And I noticed that you didn't jump up to tell me that you and your little order are totally trustworthy when it comes to moving the Vessel. Do you have some kind of work order I could look at? Can I talk to your superior or something?"

"I appreciate your fierce protection of the Vessel of Souls and your scrutiny of my order and myself. However, we just don't think that when it comes down to your father, you'll be able to think with the same kind of clarity."

I gaped. "Oh, so you think I'm going to go into some little-girl-lost thing, huh?"

"Sophie—"

"No, no. I have protected this thing and kept it safe and out of the hands of your greedy minions and everyone else who's been after it, but now suddenly I'm supposed to give it up because you think I can't face my father? Who are you guys, anyway? Who gave you the authority? You know what? I need to do my own research. How about you leave a card or something and I'll get back to you."

I stood up so quickly that my chair shot out from behind me, its ancient wheels squeaking across the plastic slide mat. "I think it's time you left, Mr. Abelard."

To my surprise, Abelard didn't argue. He stood slowly and waited for me to lead him to the door. We walked in silence to the elevator, everyone at the Agency falling against the walls, giving Abelard and me a wide berth as they stared at us in silent fear. I pushed the up button and Abelard smiled at me, a kind, wide smile, and took my hand in his. He tenderly pressed my hand in between both of his and eyed me. "The fate of the world is hanging on you, child. And you are making a terrible, terrible mistake."

He must have stepped into the elevator and the doors must have closed, driving him upward, but I didn't remember because all I could do was stand there, my hand still outstretched, feeling the cold from where his hand had been.

You are making a terrible, terrible mistake. The words reverberated in my head, shooting terrifying licks of fire down my spine.

FIFTEEN

I wasted at least two hours sitting in my car in the police station parking lot, trembling, and drinking enough pilfered police station coffee to buy Juan Valdez a fleet of Mercedes. I still hadn't heard from Will or Alex, and after Abelard left, I'd gathered what remained of my things and picked my way out of the UDA while Kale and the handful of clients left in the waiting room watched me go.

The fog outside my window was starting to bleed into long fingers of gray drizzle when my phone started blaring "How Do You Talk to an Angel"—a nod to the eighties and Alex's ringtone. I nearly hit my head on the windshield jumping out of my skin.

"Lawson."

"Now you call me? I called you like, ten hours ago. I needed you, Alex!"

"You called me?"

I pulled the phone away from my ear and gaped at it as though Alex could somehow see me. "Of course I did. If you didn't know that, why are you calling me?"

"Where are you right now?"

"I'm in the police station parking lot. In my car."

"Stay there. I'll be there in three minutes."

I had no idea if it was something about being an angel or just that Alex was police-officer anal, but he arrived exactly three minutes later, pulling into a spot close to the door of the station. I hopped out of my car and jogged toward him just as he came around the car to me. His eyes were blazing, his cheeks flushed.

"Lawson, about the other day, back at my office—"

My mind immediately went to Alex backpedaling about our relationship. It made sense that as my UDA family backed away from me, so would Alex.

"Yeah, no, that's fine, I understand. If you want to, you know, be . . ."

"I'm not talking about us. The kid."

I swallowed hard. "The kid?" Oh, God. There was a kid now? Did Alex want me to get *pregnant*? Could that even happen? Would our child be immortal, or like, half immortal? And what did that mean? Would he be immune to illness or just live to one hundred fifty-five? Would he have Alex's ice-blue eyes, his hard, chiseled chin?

"Did you hear me?"

Sweat rolled down my back and was now oozing out of every pore as my skin radiated a fire of embarrassment.

"I'm sorry, what?"

Alex's gaze was steady, his jaw set hard. Everything about him told me he had his cop armor on, and I stiffened, the tension still ratcheting.

"Oliver. The kid."

I nodded. "What about him?"

"He's gone missing."

I took a step back as if his revelation had physically moved me. "What? What do you mean 'gone missing'? Where did he go?"

Alex shook his head. "We don't know. He was being held at the children's ward of SF General. Supposed to have had round-the-clock supervision."

"But?"

"But sometime during the night, someone came in and signed him out. Took everything associated with Oliver—his medical chart, his things, his stuffed animal."

"Well, if someone signed him out, don't you know who it is? Who signed him out?"

Alex fished his cell phone out of his jacket pocket and swiped it on, showing me a photograph of a sign-in log. Oliver's name was written in the PATIENT box with small, sure script. A name was written in the VISITORS box in careful cursive writing: *L. Szabo*.

My lungs popped. I tried desperately to suck in air, but even with my big, fish-face gulps, it felt like I was breathing through a straw. Alex, my car, the parking lot swayed in front of me as a vice tightened around my forehead. I could feel Alex's hands on me again, on my shoulders this time, steadying me.

"Lawson, breathe. Slowly. One breath in, one breath out."

I tried to focus on Alex, on his commands, and after what seemed like hours, I was confident my heart wasn't in my throat, wouldn't flop right out of my mouth and onto the glass-and-condom-littered concrete.

"Lucas took Oliver?"

"There's more."

"More?"

Alex turned the phone to me one more time, swiping the image. He was explaining as my eyes took in the image. Under the box that asked RELATIONSHIP, again in that careful, sure script was the word *father*.

"Father? But Oliver has—had—a father. His father was killed. Was he—was he adopted? Oh, God, Oliver is my brother?"

I had discovered my half sister Ophelia under circumstances that were less than optimal as well. And, as discussed, she'd tried to kill me and our relationship had culminated in a stabbing by trident. Purely self-defense on account of my sister was batshit crazy and clearly took after my father, the devil. I still don't know who Ophelia's mother is, but I would be willing to bet the farm and a half-dozen donuts that her side of the family line included at least one jackal.

"My brother . . ."

"Actually, no, according to his records. There is no indication that Oliver was adopted, and his father—his actual father—is listed on his birth certificate, as is his mother. Medical records match up, too."

I chewed the inside of my cheek, a weird sense of joy and jealousy filtering through me. I was happy that Oliver wasn't the son of Satan, even if unadulterated evil did seem to be his forte. But I was also weirdly upset that my father would devote so much time to a child that wasn't even his when his real child had grown up without a father.

"Are there any leads?"

Alex cracked a half smile. "Look at you with the detective lingo." His smile dropped. "But no, we don't have anything. We weren't even notified that Oliver was missing until about thirty minutes ago."

"But he was checked out last night!"

"Technically, early this morning. The officer on guard has no idea how Lucas or Oliver got passed him."

I cocked my head. "No idea like he was off on a cigarette break or grabbing a donut?"

"Why does it go directly to the donuts with you?"

I raised my eyebrows.

"Okay, no. The surveillance footage shows that he didn't leave his post. And the two times he did, for bathroom breaks, no one came through. No one."

I leaned back against my car. "So . . . I don't understand any of this. What do you need with me?"

"Lucas is your father. Do you know anything— have any idea where he might be?"

I gaped at Alex. "Where have you been the last three years? I don't know Lucas from Adam. Well, I do, but not his haunts. He might be my dad"—it almost pained me to admit it—"but the only thing we have in common that I'm sure of is a couple of strands of DNA. If he has a secret fort or an evil lair, I'm not privy to it."

"Is there anything, anything at all? Think, Lawson."

"I am thinking," I snapped. "I don't know anything about my father except that he's a killer and apparently, he was interested in every other kid except me."

Suddenly, I was crying. I was completely aware of the ridiculousness of the situation, crying because a mass murderer had never taken me to a father-daughter dance, but I couldn't stop myself. I felt pitiful, I felt small. No matter who my father was, one thing was clear: he didn't want me at all.

"Oh, Lawson."

Alex wrangled me into a hug that only made me cry harder. Stupid, body-wracking tears as I slumped against him while he gently stroked my back.

"Wha-wha-what's wrong with me, Alex? Why wouldn't he want me at all?" I snuffled into his neck, forgetting to be embarrassed by the fact that I was soaking the stiff collar of his button-down shirt with snot and tears. "I mean, it's not like I want to go into the family business, but it would have been nice to be asked, you know?"

I blinked up at Alex and he thumbed a tear from my eye. "I know, Lawson. Your father has no idea what he's missing out on."

"But he does. He seems to know everything about me," I wailed.

"No. He doesn't know how amazing and warm and kind you are. He obviously can't even see how beautiful you are. If he knew any of those things, he would never be able to turn away from you. Never." He swallowed. "No matter what it cost him." Alex swallowed and wrapped one of my curls around his index finger with a small smile. I was about to say something witty and poignant—or, since it was me, something would have unequivocally ruined the entire warm and tender moment—when his cell phone buzzed.

And just like that, warm, tender Alex was replaced by all thin-blue-line detective Alex.

"Grace?"

I watched the hint of smile drop completely out of Alex's eyes as he listened to whoever was on the other end of the line. He gave two curt nods, then hung up.

"What was that about?"

"Chief said a call came in. A pretty viable tip. Someone in Fremont said they saw a juvenile fitting Oliver's description with an older man."

"Did that older man fit my father's description?"

Alex shrugged sharply, but I knew his answer was yes. "I'm going with you."

He put out a hand and stopped me. "No, you're not."

I grinned. "I like how after all these years you still think you can stop me from doing things."

"I'm serious, Lawson."

"Alex, I'm a part of this case. And Oliver's kidnapper is my father. I think that warrants a ride along, don't you?"

"Actually, that's exactly why you're not going within twenty miles of the last known location."

"What the hell are you talking about?"

He blew out a sigh. "Look, Lawson, I know we usually do this stay-here/don't-stay-here dance. And usually, I don't really care whether or not you tag along."

A little needle of pain stabbed at my heart, and I crossed my arms in front of my chest, narrowing my eyes so Alex wouldn't see.

"Haven't you ever heard of sugarcoating, ass hat?"

Alex sighed. "Most of the time I'm happy when you tag along because I know you're going to be safe. But we have no idea what we're dealing with on this one."

"But it's my father!"

"Which is exactly why you have to promise me you won't follow me."

I opened my mouth and Alex pushed it back closed. "You're too close to this one. You've got too much emotion to be counted on to act rationally."

"I never act rationally!"

It was out of my mouth before I realized that it wasn't the best argument.

"I'll call you once I get there, and everything I find out, I'll tell you. I promise."

I cocked out a hip. "I'm just supposed to believe you?"

"For God's sake, Lawson, I'm an angel."

"Fallen."

He rolled his eyes. "I've got to go. You're staying here."

It wasn't a question, but I answered anyway. "Yeah, I'm staying here."

Alex stared at me for a long, silent beat before grabbing my purse and fishing out my keys. He slipped them in his chest pocket and spun on his heel, moving toward his black SUV.

"Hey!" I yelled. "I said I was staying here!"

He disappeared around the driver's side of the car, then poked his dark mop over the top of the car, followed by his stupidly mischievous blue eyes. "And I'm just supposed to believe you?"

Alex was out of the driveway, practically on two wheels, thirty seconds before the Muni bus wheezed to a stop. I jogged and boarded the bus, then sunk in my dollar, scanning the assembled riders for even a sliver of empty seat.

There wasn't one.

I edged my way down the center aisle and reached up for one of the leather steadying loops, my arm firmly in place while the rest of my body cursed Muni's apparent disdain for shocks as I thumped against my fellow riders. Three stops and plenty of inappropriate bumps later I was pretty sure the man behind me was my new husband, and either in celebration or desperation, I realized I wanted a drink. And though I knew better than to solve problems with alcohol, today was one of those days when I figured it couldn't hurt. Lucky for me, San Francisco is filthy with bars, specialized for everyone from hipsters to hookers, and the first establishment I walked into fell somewhere in the middle.

It was one of those places that had always been a bar and would always be a bar because the smell of stale beer and old cigarettes had become part of the architecture. The waitresses looked like they were born there and when I opened the door, the patrons squinted at the rectangle of "light" that shone in. The bar was polished wood, long and glossy, and a dozen Naugahyde bar stools were lined up, only two of them taken. One man sat at the crook of the bar, staring into his beer, and the other was halfway down. He glanced over his shoulder when I walked in, and I could feel his eye slide from the top of my head to the bottom of my shoes. Normally, a full-body gaze like that would make my teeth clench and flush my face a pitiful red, but today I didn't care at all. I was the daughter of Satan, a race of being that God wanted washed from the Earth, and my own idiot father who had gotten me in this stupid situation was hiding from me.

I slid onto one of the bar stools.

The guy was looking at me again and when I met his gaze he gave me a slight, respectful nod, then went back to tinkling the ice in his glass.

"What can I get you?"

The bartender looked like she had stumbled into the place one day and never left. She could have been twenty or two hundred and twenty; it was impossible to tell in the dim light and through her pancake makeup and surprised, painted-on eyebrows.

"Um . . ." My eyes wandered to the enormous selection of booze behind her. I supposed I should have ordered something girly and middle-of-the-day respectable, but what the hell? I had evil in my family tree so boozing up at 2 PM was the least of my issues.

"Jack and ginger, please."

The bartender mixed my drink and set it in front of me, standing there, hands on bar, staring me down. Her expression wasn't unkind, but it wasn't puppy-bunny-fuzzy either, so I reached for my purse.

"Oh, I'm sorry. How much—"

She waved me away. "It's on me. Sam."

I was taken aback. "Thank you so much, Sam."

"It's the least I can do for a woman who comes in here before noon looking for a stiff one."

My eyebrows went up and she jutted her chin toward the drink in my hand. My cheeks burned.

"Oh, right."

Sam didn't move. "What's your name?"

I took a small sip, my eyes watering at the ratio of mostly Jack, a few drops of ginger ale. "Sophie," I said, voice hoarse.

"So, Sophie, what brings you into The Clover?"

It was only then that I noticed the giant four-leaf clover painted on the mirror behind the bar. "Just not having the greatest day is all."

Sam harrumphed and the two men at the bar joined in. "Welcome to the club. Cicero over there got fired by the nephew he hired, from a job he had for thirty-seven years. Larry"—she pointed a long red fingernail to the guy who checked me out when I'd walked in—"he was kicked out of his place."

"Can't find a job, gonna live in this shithole forever."

I wasn't sure if he meant a general shithole or The Clover, but I wasn't in any rush to clarify.

"So," Sam said, "what's your story?"

I tried to consider the best way to phrase "a race

of fallen-angel half breeds is stalking me and my father was always too busy shish-kebabing sinners to come to my dance recitals," but any way I came up with sounded weird. Instead I just shrugged, took a hefty sip, and said, "Family issues. My dad's kind of an asshole."

Larry, Sam, and Cicero all grunted their understanding and sipped in my honor. And though I knew it was strangers in a seedy bar, I had already warmed to them, liking the feel of the four of us, relative strangers sharing only an emotion—only our humanity.

I hadn't even finished my drink when Sam poured me another one and Larry sidled two seats over. My guard was up, until he started talking and I started grinning. Cicero stayed in his corner and Sam tended to him occasionally, topping off his drink and dropping updated receipts in a cup.

"My lady took me for everything," he was saying into his cup. "I really shoulda known better."

"No, Larry." I moved one seat closer so that I could clap a hand on his stooped shoulder. "Matters of the heart are difficult."

I didn't realize I had finished my drink until Sam replaced it. I took a few sips and turned back to Larry, turning a little too fast so my thoughts started to swirl in my head.

"Take my life, for instance. I—I know my dad is the devil. Like, the devil, devil. A really bad guy. But I still want his approval. I still want him to be my dad." I frowned. "He was never, ever there for me." I took another swig of my drink and this time, Larry clapped his hand on my shoulder.

"It's okay, sweetie. I can tell just by looking at you that you're a great gal. He missed out."

I pumped my head, feeling vaguely better as Larry and I sat there with our arms on each other's shoulders.

"That means a lot coming from you, Larry. Sam." I turned to face her. "I would like to buy my friend Larry here a drink. And I would like to buy myself a drink for myself."

Sam's smile was warm but a little tight. She looked from Larry to me and set a glass of water in front of me. "I think maybe you've had enough for a little bit, okay, sugar?"

"But you were so nice to me."

Her smile widened. "I'm still being nice to you. Have a few sips, okay?"

I did as I was told, taking two giant gulps after I caught a hint of my own breath and realized it was a fire hazard. My head was starting to buzz—a thousand angry bees working the noise into a deafening roar. I pressed my fingers against my temples and closed my eyes, feeling the entire bar shift a bit too far to the right.

"Are we having another earthquake?"

I felt Larry's hand tighten on my upper arm. "No, hon, I think you've just had a touch too much. Have you eaten anything today?"

I looked at Larry, trying hard to focus my eyes on the Larry that looked most corporeal.

"My dad is the devil," I whispered.

I could see the smile cut across Larry's face as he pushed the water glass to my lips. I drank gratefully, then watched as Larry eyed Sam over my shoulder.

"You got some bread or anything back there?"

"No, Larry," I said, pushing the glass away. "People are hunting me. I am the Vessel of Souls. *Vas animarum.*" I cupped my hands over my mouth. "People think I don't exist, but I do." I glanced over both shoulders, looking for Grigori. "And other people want to kill me. They are many. They are legion." I extended my arms to show the enormousness of the Grigori and swayed on my feet.

Larry clutched both my arms and eyed me. "You got someone I can call for you?"

I saw Cicero moving from the corner of my eye and a cold stripe shot up my spine. I narrowed my eyes. "I think that's one of them," I said to Larry. "You should call Will."

I edged myself against the bar, scanning for something to use as a weapon as Cicero moved closer. My heart started to pound as my stomach roiled against the alcohol.

"You probably should get her outside," Cicero said, holding my eye. "She don' look so good."

Larry took his hands off my arms and Cicero reached for me. I could see something in his eye and a glint of something gold on his belt. I pushed myself backward, feeling my spine arc against the bar.

"Hey!"

Cicero and Larry snapped to attention when Sam came around the bar. I took a little longer.

"Hands off her, guys. Thanks, but I can take care of her." Sam reached out for me, wrapping her thin arms around my waist. "Come on, hon. We'll splash a little water on your face, get you something from the kitchen."

I went with Sam feeling both relieved and slightly nauseous as she steered me toward the back of the bar, toward the lighted RESTROOMS sign.

"I'm sorry," I mumbled. "Drinks don't usually hit me this hard." I pressed my palm against my forehead, feeling a fresh outbreak of sweat. "I don't know what happened to me. Maybe I needed to eat something or something."

"That's okay, hon. Happens to the best of us."

When Sam pulled open the door, I was surprised at the rush of cool air that washed over me. I turned around to ask, but she shoved me, hard. When I was able to focus, we were in a narrow alleyway and Sam's eyes were hard, fixed, her lips pressed in a thin, pale line. She held them that way for a beat before her mouth curved up into a smile that dripped with contempt.

"He's going to love this."

I steadied myself as Sam floated in front of me. The fog was suddenly lifted when I saw the dagger glinting in the choked light of the alleyway.

"Sam?"

Her eyes seared into mine and they were a sizzling blue-red. Though her hand was closed around the hilt, I knew the dagger, I knew the symbol that burned into her palm.

"You're Grigori?"

Sam's smile widened. "Surprise."

She thrust the dagger at me and I jumped, my action feeling slow and lumbering against Sam's sudden litheness. She was faster with the blade than she had been with the drinks, which meant that I sobered up rather quickly, every constricted blood vessel screaming that I was in serious danger and likely to become chop suey in the near future.

"He sent them all after you and I was just supposed to keep watch."

I watched Sam's knife arc in the air a hairbreadth from my nose and reached out, grabbing her by the forearm. Her grin grew even wider, more grotesque, as if she was enjoying the struggle.

"It's no fun to watch."

I didn't see her fist as it came flying at me fast, making contact with my jaw. I heard the sickening sound of bone hitting bone, of my teeth clacking together as my saliva soured and my head lolled back. I lost my grip on Sam's dagger hand, and she lunged again, pinning me against the Dumpster just before I dove right, hearing the excruciating howl of metal grating against metal as her blade struck the can.

She grabbed at me before I was clear, her clawed hand catching my ponytail, pulling until my scalp screamed and I was sure there was blood. I still pulled against her, looking everywhere for something that could be used as a weapon. I turned and kicked out, landing my foot square in Sam's rib cage, hearing her "ooaf!" as her fingers released my hair. She folded at the waist and I stumbled, free now, crashing to the concrete, feeling my palms burn and splinter as I slid. I could make out the glint of a green glass bottle just to my left, and I grabbed it, rolled onto my feet, and blindly swung. I felt the blade slice into my forearm a split second before the bottle made contact with Sam's wrist, bending it backward and sending the dagger flying.

We both heard the metal hit the concrete and both dove for the blade, each trying to snatch it before it slid out of reach under the Dumpster.

Sam and I were bellies down, shoulder to shoulder.

"You bitch!" she growled, while springing on me with superhuman speed.

"Get—the hell—off—me!"

Her thighs were clamped around my rib cage and if we hadn't been locked in a fight to the death, I would have complimented her on her nutcracker-like strength. But that was before she lurched forward and her hands closed on my throat, her thumbs digging into my windpipe.

A blanket of red wafted in front of my eyes and my lungs were aching for breath. Sam kept squeezing, and as I clawed at her, she kept thunking my head along the concrete. I could feel the skin at the base of my head splitting, could feel the warm goo as blood bubbled up and then my head made contact with cement.

My ripping at her palms was futile so I went for her eyes, my stomach lurching as my right ring finger slipped into the socket, mashing into her eyeball. I had the spongy orb against the pad of my index finger, pushing until she howled. She slapped her hands to the injured face and straightened up, giving me the millisecond opportunity I needed to reach for another glass bottle and thwack it cleanly at her temple. The thrashing thoughts in my head, the spastic beating of my heart, the desperate gasps for breath all stopped the second Sam crumpled, her form looking much smaller as she slid off me, a trickle of cherry-red blood oozing from her temple.

I sucked my legs in and crawled on hands and knees toward the door we had come out of, but it was solidly locked. My purse was inside with my cell phone and, probably the sad lineup of empty glasses left as I had drunk my way into Sam's blade.

I limped to the mouth of the alley and onto the street, my eye burning where a rivulet of blood poured from a gash on my eyebrow. My tongue poked around in my mouth, testing for loose teeth, and every single one of them felt as though they had been knocked at the root. My jaw throbbed. My arm stung and itched where the dagger had sunk in, leaving a four-inch slice that was dribbling a trail of red blood spatter as I walked.

I knew my nose was bleeding. When I raised my slightly good arm, my shoulder screamed in protest, but I raked my fingers—gingerly—over my head, pulling a handful of loose locks, sticky and matted with blood.

That's the last time I go drinking alone.

I rounded the corner and stopped at the open door to The Clover, my ears ringing as I scanned the seemingly empty bar, looking for my purse. It was on the stool where I had left it, about eight feet from the door, the open rifts of How Do You Talk To An Angel sailing out of it as Alex rang my phone.

I dashed in while every muscle and cell and fiber screamed, snatched up my purse, and dashed back out, making a beeline for the relative safety of my car while I extracted my cell phone.

"'Lo?" I hadn't realized my lip was puffy and split until I'd forced it to mold around sounds.

"Lawson, it's me."

"Did you find Oliver?"

"I had to send Romero ahead. Where are you? You know what—stay wherever you are. I'm coming to get you. I think you're in danger. I think that there are more than just the one Grigori warrior."

I let Alex prattle on as my tongue rubbed over my teeth, the metallic taste of blood sliding down my throat. I sighed.

"More than one warrior? You don't say."

SIXTEEN

I waited in the shadow of a convenience store three doors down from The Clover until I could see Alex's black SUV peeling through the traffic. I knew I wasn't looking my best, but the expression on his face made the term "train wreck" spring to mind.

"My God, Sophie, what happened to you?"

I opened the car door and melted into the butter-soft leather passenger seat. Every part of my body that didn't feel bruised stung or burned.

"The Grigori," I said. "Another warrior." I worked my jaw around, hearing it pop. "I got some first-hand knowledge that there was more than that one. And, fun fact! The Grigori are letting women into their ranks. Not just a race of men anymore."

The edge of his lips quirked up into a half smile. "At least you've still got your spunk."

He guided the car back into the flow of traffic and I rolled my eyes—though I'm not sure if the action was voluntary or if my eyeballs had really shaken loose.

"She did a number on you."

"Yeah, well, you should see what she looks like now."

I could feel tears edging my eyes, and I gritted my teeth—wincing at the pain it caused—but refused to cry.

"I hate this. I can't live like this. I want to be normal."

Alex didn't look at me, but I could see his jaw relax. "Lawson, with or without an undead race hunting you down, you're never going to be normal."

"Hey!"

Crimson actually colored his cheeks. "I actually meant that as a good thing! A compliment, like 'you're . . . pretty cool.' Or something."

I straightened in my seat, feeling a smile inch up my cracked lips.

"There's an emergency kit under the seat."

I leaned over, retrieved it, then glanced at my reflection in the mirror. "I don't think you have enough gauze here to cover my whole head." I paused. "Wait—Romero!

"What did he say about Oliver? Did he find him—do you . . ." I paused, sucking in a shaky breath that was half hope, half dread. "Do you have Lucas in custody?"

Alex wagged his head, his expression apologetic. "No Oliver, no Lucas."

I frowned.

We coasted to a stop and he turned to me. "You should have called me," he said softly.

I threaded my arms in front of my chest, trying to cock an eyebrow, but it was excruciating. "It's been a busy week."

Alex took the emergency kit from my lap and used one finger to gently guide my cheek into view. He used a bit of gauze to blot the dried blood and gunk from my face, then eked out the last bit of Neosporin and wrangled a few pieces of cotton and gauze from the bowels of the emergency kit, working slowly and deliberately, wincing each time I did.

"Remember the first time I did this for you?" he asked, a slight look of mischief in his ice-blue eyes.

"Hm, the first time? Would that be bandaging my palms outside the Hendersons' house after I ground them in the glass? Oh, no—after Ophelia tried to high-five my face in the diner."

Alex swished an alcohol-dampened cotton ball over a cut at my eye.

"Lawson, Ophelia didn't try to high-five your face. If I remember correctly, she did. And it was less a high five, more of a smacking ten."

I narrowed my eyes. "Has anyone ever told you that your bedside manner sucks?"

He grinned again, the smile going all the way up to his eyes. "It was before the Hendersons and before Ophelia even."

I'd planned on frowning, but was rapidly losing feeling in my swollen face, so my expression could have been the expected frown or a *Real Housewives* post-surgical clown grin.

"Oh," I said, memory inching in. "It was the chief."

"Your little run-in with the chief of police when he was bad. What did he try and convince you happened to you? Aliens? The ninety-nine percent?"

"Gangs, I think. He told me I was attacked by a gang."

"And you believed him."

I shrank back from the sting of Mercurochrome. "Give me some credit. That was my first time out." I gently pressed the pads of my fingers to the cotton ball Alex held at my chin. "I wasn't seasoned like I am now."

I thought about that first time Alex had mopped my wounds, the first time I had woken up, blinking my way out of a concussion. My lower lip popped out on its own.

"What's wrong, cupcake?"

I had a half second of swooning, remembering the sugar-sweet nickname that Alex used to call me before—well, everything.

"That was before all of this."

He raised his brows. "All of this?"

I felt the tears sting at the back of my eyes once again. "That was before everyone was trying to kill me. Before I knew about the Vessel of Souls. Before I knew that all of humanity was in a constant struggle between good and evil that I was destined to lose for them."

I sniffled.

Alex gently took my hand from my chin, taking both of my hands in his. "We're going to get through this, Lawson. We always do."

I felt a tear itch its way down my cheek. "We always did. Those were cakewalks compared to this, Alex. A psycho cop, a vigilante demon killer, my glass-half-crazy half sister. We're up against more now. An army. The Grigori. You said yourself that they'll just keep coming. And . . ." I felt a stab of anxiety. "And there's my father."

Alex's grip tightened on my hands, and his jaw was set hard, the muscle twitching along the line.

"You don't have to face him alone."

I pulled my hands from Alex's and let them fall limply in my lap.

"What if I do? What if that's the whole point?"

He opened his mouth to answer me, but I held up a hand, stop-sign style.

"When I had that dream," I started, "the dream about my father? He was coming for me. Everything was swirling and horrible when he had my mother. He was spinning her and she was dying. But everything went back to normal when he came for me. Then we walked into the water. We walked under it like we were going away. Like we were going to Hell." I sucked on my teeth, my stomach roiling and causing my head to throb that much more. "Maybe he's trying to eliminate everyone so that he can get what he wants—me. Alone."

Alex shook his head. "You never have to be alone. It doesn't matter what your dad wants. You've got Will and Nina and Vlad—"

Suddenly, I was overcome with dread. "And you?"

He paused, and the moment stretched on for hours. "Of course you have me. Lawson." He shook his head, avoiding my gaze. "I love you, Lawson."

My heart clanged like a fire bell. I wasn't sure if it was the declaration of love or the swelling of my nostrils, but I was having trouble breathing.

Alex loved me!

But Will . . .

Instantly, I felt Will's body against mine, his heart beating a steady, comforting rhythm as his arms encircled me. My heart ached and everything inside me seemed to split, moving in opposite directions.

Will and Alex. Will versus Alex. For the first time in my life, I had two men who wanted me. And just my luck, it was Armageddon.

We sat in palpable silence for a beat before I shifted. "So why was it that you came to get me? I mean"—I gestured to my bandages—"this not withstanding."

"Oh, right. Sorry." He reached into the backseat and shimmied something out of the pocket of his leather jacket. He handed the folded sheaf of papers to me.

"What's this?"

"It's about your father. And Armageddon."

Our eyes locked for a terrifically unsexy minute, and I flashed back onto the texts from the library, back to the line drawing of Lucas Szabo in the packet.

"Where did you get this from?" I asked, slowly beginning to sift through the loose pages.

"Around," was all Alex answered.

I raised my eyebrows and he waved me off, pulling a stapled packet from the stack. "This is about your father as—"

"The trickster god," I supplied, nodding. "I knew about that."

In some cultures, Satan was just a fallen angel, no better, worse, or more evil than any of the other fallen. He wasn't the embodiment of evil; he was just a misunderstood trickster.

Well, maybe not exactly misunderstood as his "tricks" would often cause widespread famine, disease, or death while he played a fiddle and collected the souls of the hopeless and greedy. But they didn't think he was all that bad.

"So, I don't understand. How does this change anything?"

Alex flipped a few pages and jabbed at a paragraph that was highlighted.

I read over the few lines, still confused. "So, his main trick is convincing people that he doesn't exist. But he does."

I glanced at Alex, seeing if I was on the right track. He nodded.

"I don't understand how this is going to help anything. Besides, we already knew this."

"Maybe his greatest trick can be yours."

"Lucas knows I exist. He—" I shuddered, my skin crawling with the thought. "He made me." Immediately, I brightened. "But he doesn't know if the Vessel of Souls actually exists."

A pleased grin slid across Alex's face. "So far, it's all just hearsay and legend."

I was moved by Alex's declaration and Will's promise to protect me, but I was jaded and beyond believing anything that wasn't solidly in front of me, smacking me in the face. Tricking my father, and the Grigori, into believing the Vessel of Souls didn't exist—or at the very least, that I wasn't it—was a long shot at best.

I appreciated Alex's hope, but I knew that no one could protect me from the Grigori forever. I knew that no one could protect me from my father or from the world's end, period.

I registered online for Krav Maga classes. Hey, if it was good enough for Madonna and the Israel Defense Forces, I figured it was good enough for learning how to land the occasional roundhouse kick to a rogue vampire's immortal junk or to the immortal warrior in general. The classes were taught at the Fillmore Community Center in a room between an Ikebana class and a digital photography class, both populated by people twice my age. I felt pretty good when I registered. It was a sunny Saturday morning, and I had used my cunning skills to slip out of my apartment undetected. I wanted my new powers to be a surprise to Sampson and the gang, and I didn't want anyone (Nina) to point out that my sudden need to kick and bash at things might have something to do with pent-up sexual energy and general romantic anxiety. I still had "figure out Alex and Will" on my to-do list, and I promised myself I would do that right after class—when I was rife with the self confidence that came from learning to defend myself.

There was a ponytailed woman in cute spandex capris and a matching tank top lightly stretching at the front of the room. She was roughly my height and we had slightly similar builds—hers being of the muscular variety, mine being of the Pillsbury variety. She started to bounce lightly on the balls of her feet, her spunky little ponytail bobbing.

If she can do this, I reasoned, *so can I.*

I tightened my own ponytail and pasted on my most agreeable smile, heading toward Bouncy Spandex.

"Hi," I said, starting to bounce with her and flapping my arms in an attempt to warm them up. "My name's Sophie. I'm kind of nervous. It's my first day."

"Hi, Sophie!" Bouncy Spandex beamed. "You're going to absolutely love Krav Maga! My name's Melody."

Melody. It went with her cute, heart-shaped smile and her bouncy ponytail. If I hadn't known better, I would have sworn that bouncy little Melody, all spandex and sunshine, was a pixie. "I'm glad you're here."

Everything Melody said seemed to be punctuated with an exclamation point; everything I said seemed to be capped with a great huffing gasp of air. The class hadn't even started and already my cheeks were flushing lobster red and sweat was pricking at my hairline. A tiny bead rolled down the center of my sports bra.

"Are we the only two students?"

"No," Melody said, mercifully stopping the bounce to stretch her hamstrings. "Everyone will be here in a few minutes."

As if on cue, the wood door flopped open and two old Japanese women pushed in enormous vases full of single stem flowers artfully arranged. "They must be in the wrong place, huh?"

"Hi, Yuu! Hi, Aikiko!" Melody waved, pushed her legs apart, and did a forward fold that had her hair brushing against the wood floor, and my hamstrings shrinking up in protest.

The two old women deposited their arrangements and slid off their sweaters, then came to join us on the floor.

"They're in this class?" I asked under my breath.

Melody's head bounced. "Uh-huh. Both of them have been here from the beginning. Aikiko's really learning her holds." Melody's eyes cut to the ancient Aikiko. "Isn't that right, girlfriend?"

I kind of hated when people called each other girlfriend, but it was cute when Melody said it (I figured the woman could say earwax and make it sound adorable). Aikiko grinned and slapped Melody a high five.

Okay, I thought. *This class can't possibly be that scary if Aikiko and Yuu are regulars.*

I joined in on the stretching, tuning out Melody's excited explanation of her vegan pineapple soup and slipping into my own head. I stamped out thoughts of the imminent world's end—I wondered how long that was going to take, anyway—and imagined myself after I had a few of these Krav Maga classes under my belt. I'd be lithe and strong, my chocolate-marshmallow Pinwheel pouch replaced by rock-hard abs and maybe a wicked-looking tattoo of a raven or a beady-eyed teddy bear on my rib cage. Whatever big bad that was lurking in the shadows then (provided the world remained spinning and populated) would be nothing but fodder for my sexy, animalistic rage. I would protect the people with my incredible moves, and shock the baddies with my superhuman-seeming strength.

Yeah. I would be *Sophie Lawson: Savior and Ass Kicker.*

I was considering whether I should hyphenate *Ass Kicker* when Melody tapped me on the shoulder.

"Aikiko and Yuu are going to demonstrate some techniques and a short round of sparring. I'll talk you through what they're doing and be your partner since it's your first day."

"Okay, that sounds good."

Something like excitement shot through me, and I grinned, mimicking the ladies' slightly bent knees, bouncy stance, holding my hands in front of my chest the way Aikiko and Yuu did.

Aikiko lunged and Yuu smoothly blocked her advance with a move that looked like she was dancing.

"Hold your hands up like this," Melody sang. "This is going to be your first block, the basic block. See how Yuu does it? Smooth. It's very, very smooth."

I told my arms to do the exact same thing as Yuu was doing, but I couldn't make the command reach the muscles and my arms went sputtering like windmills. Then Melody popped me in the forehead.

"Hey!" I said, rubbing at the warm spot her fingers had left.

"Smooth," Melody said, drawing out the word. "Watch Aikiko and Yuu. Show her again, ladies."

I think I did a pretty decent impression and was even able to block Melody's thin, advancing arms.

I was feeling pretty good when I blocked three in a row.

"Good, good, Sophie!" Melody said, clapping her elfin hands. "Okay, let's switch it up a little bit."

Yuu stepped in front of Melody, and Aikiko stepped in front of me.

"Okay," I said with a half-laugh. "It's just my first day, so go easy on me."

Aikiko smiled serenely and took her fighting stance, and I took mine, my mind ticking through the advances and blocks that I had just learned. I was running through the most basic one, trying to get my feet to unwind when Aikiko advanced on me like a shot. I wasn't able to process anything that happened before I realized I was lying on the floor, cheek pressed up against the sweaty blue mat. Aikiko was on top of me and everything was hurting.

"Great job, Aikiko!" Melody hopped on her tiny sneakered feet and clapped, and I decided right then and there that I hated her.

SEVENTEEN

After class, I hopped on the bus and headed toward the Fillmore District, thinking the overly friendly thoughts that good weather brings. Once there, I picked up a huge bouquet of smiling sunflowers and an armload of celebrity tabloids to appease Nina, and tossed in a few comics featuring chicks with half-exposed huge boobs for Vlad.

I was feeling generous and hopeful even though I had been made to eat mat by a geriatric Japanese lady who went home with my dignity and an Ikebana sculpture in her reusable grocery bag.

I took a seat at a tiny, white-clothed table set outside of a little cafe. The waitress came and filled my water glass, mentioned something about specials, and deposited a basket of warm bread.

"Treating yourself today?" she asked.

"How could I not? This weather is incredible." I dropped my head back, relishing the sun on my cheeks.

"And they say this heat stroke is going to go on until the end of the week."

"Heaven." I grinned.

"Anyway, my name is Luna, and I'll be back to take your order in just a few minutes."

I was sipping my water and making my way through the bread basket when a shadow fell across my table. I looked up.

"Alex."

His face broke into one of his knee-weakening grins, and the sunlight made him even more frustratingly appealing. He sat down across from me.

"Hey, what are you doing out here, Lawson?"

"Having lunch. You?" Before Alex could open his mouth I held up my hand. "Wait. If you're about to tell me you're on a case, investigating this place for supernatural rats, or I'm in mortal danger, I don't want to know."

"You wouldn't want to know if you're in mortal danger?"

"Not today."

"Okay." Alex dug into my near-empty bread basket and tore into a sourdough roll. "But I'm not here for any of that. Good bread."

I snatched my bread basket back. "My bread."

"Grabby." He leaned back in his chair and clasped his hands behind his head. The action made his biceps flex, and I shoved a piece of bread in my mouth to catch the drool.

"Well, hi there. Can I get you a place set up?" Luna was beaming at Alex.

"I'm just going to have an iced tea." Alex eyed Luna for a beat too long and I was stabbed with a pang of jealousy. *You and Alex aren't dating,* I reminded myself. *You're a woman in hot demand! You slept with another man!*

I should have stopped while I was ahead.

I felt the heat wash over me. Embarrassment. Shame. Was he reading my mind?

It was possible. Alex could read minds. As far as I know he'd stopped reading mine when I'd claimed it was truly unfair that I couldn't read his or smite him back with some supernatural power of my own. He'd referred to my (bad) cooking and the whole thing had devolved from there.

"Lawson? Earth to Sophie Lawson?" Alex's rich voice snapped me back to the here and now. I— and my nipples—sprang to guilty attention when Alex focused on me, the cobalt of his eyes catching the sparkle from the sun.

"BLT, please!" I didn't realize I'd shouted it until Luna stepped back, Alex dug a finger in his ear, and every other diner in the establishment turned to glare at me. "Sorry," I whispered. "And an iced tea."

"So you never did tell me why you're here."

He shrugged, and slipped on a pair of dark sunglasses. I expected to immediately miss those gorgeous eyes of his, but instead I leaned forward on my elbows, suddenly loving Alex's "bad boy" look.

"It's a nice day. Thought I'd go for a stroll."

"Oh. Me, too."

There was an awkward pause, and I sipped my water to avoiding breaking the awkwardness with something downright inappropriate. Luna came back with our drinks, and Alex and I made inconsequential small talk until he finished his tea.

"Oh," Luna said, rushing back to our table. "Can I get you more tea?"

"No thanks, I'm going to get going."

She seemed downright sad, and when she returned with my BLT, she all but threw it at me. "Pleasant lady," I said.

Alex grinned and pushed his chair back. "Well, nice to talk to you, Lawson." He paused, still smiling. "I missed this."

My eyebrows went up. "You missed what?"

"This." Alex drew an invisible line from me to him and back again. "Hanging out. Random banter."

I shrank down in my chair, glee oozing out of every pore. "Well, if you want to hang out more, you can call me." I applauded myself for my grown-up lady bravado. "You don't have to be on the trail of a murderer to come over for a pizza."

Alex bobbed his head. "Good to know."

He started down the sidewalk, and I nibbled on my sandwich, my stomach rolling over itself and taking my hunger with it.

"Can I get a box, please?"

Luna looped her way to every other table and filled up a half dozen water glasses before returning to my Alex-less table with my box. I could have sworn she looked mournfully at his empty chair.

I boxed my sandwich, left some cash, and headed onto the sidewalk. I didn't intend to follow Alex; it was just that there were some great stores in the direction he was headed.

"Hey, miss? Miss?"

I swung around when I heard Luna's voice. She

was still in her apron, but now out on the sidewalk, waving the black leatherette case my bill had come in. I took a step toward her, but she trotted toward me—at the exact same time a car decided to whip around a stalled Muni bus. The squeal of the tires vibrated through the street, and when the two wheels of the Nissan Sentra rolled up onto the sidewalk, Luna grabbed me and I pulled her down. We both rolled into the alleyway, and while I was sitting on my butt huffing and gawking after the car that had no idea it had very nearly hood-ornamented us, Luna was already standing and walking deeper into the alley.

"My God, that was close—hey." I craned my neck. "What are you doing?"

Luna seemed to be following something. She was taking dainty steps, her head slightly cocked as she walked deeper into the alley, into the part that was shadowed and hard to see from the street.

Having spent my fair share of time in alleyways being shot at and such, my stomach sank. This was not good. Luna was about to be swallowed by something unholy or raped by a wino with a hook for a hand. I pushed myself up and ran after her.

"Luna, what are you looking for? You should come out of there. We should go back to the—"

But my breath was cut off my a choking gasp, and before I could figure out what was going on, I felt my shoulder blades slap against the brick of the alley wall, my head smacking hard against a protruding brick.

"What are you—"

Luna's eyes were wild with an electricity I hadn't

noticed before. She was gripping my throat and pressing me against the wall. I tried to wriggle, to struggle, to kick away, but she was ready for my every move and was able to dodge and weave without loosening her hold on my neck.

"I've been waiting all day for you, Sophie Lawson."

"What?"

The absolute joy of her actions was apparent in Luna's face, rolled off her in waves. I tried my best to breathe.

"I wasn't sure it was you at first. But then I saw your little angel and I knew."

"Alex." It was barely a breath and my eyelids were feeling heavy, my head feeling light. "What do you want from me? Money?"

I gagged when Luna squeezed harder. "I don't want your money," she spat. "I know who you are. I know *what* you are." She narrowed her eyes, lasering them on mine. Her focus was chilling.

"Son of a bitch! You, too?"

I could feel each one of Luna's fingers digging into my throat. "What's that supposed to mean?"

The term "trickster" spun in what remained of my consciousness.

"Why are you doing this? I don't know what or who you think I am, but I'm not . . . that. Please let me go!"

"Don't play dumb, Sophie."

I sucked in a shallow breath, feeling myself begin to tremble even as I was pressed against the wall. Luna was about my height. I had a good ten pounds on her. She didn't have a weapon.

Luna's other hand rose and I was blinded by the

glint of the enormous blade she was wielding. It was attached to a heavy black handle, the whole thing wrapped with what looked like golden twine. My eyes widened and my legs went rogue; I slipped down the wall before Luna realized it. The hand that was around my throat was now tangled in my hair, and the knife was shoved snugly in the crumbling mortar between two bricks. I chanced a glance up just in time to see the absolute rage on Luna's face. She was working to free her knife. I gave her a swift kick to the shin, hard as I could muster, then clawed at the ground, trying to get my bearings, to get back on my feet.

"Damn it!" Luna yelled, leaning over to cradle her knee.

I started to run, started to will my legs to move forward, but I felt like I was dream running—legs going, but body going nowhere.

"You're fucking dead, Sophie Lawson! You'll never get away from us!"

I was sprinting—finally feeling like I was making headway—and looking over my shoulder at Luna's anger stained face when I ran smack into Alex's hard chest.

"Oaf!"

It was like running into a brick wall, and the back of my head throbbed while my lungs burned. Alex snaked his arms around my waist and held me hard and firm.

"Are you okay?" he asked, staring down at me.

"The waitress." I pushed against Alex until he was forced to take a step back, me Velcroed to him. "She wants to kill me."

Alex looked over my head. I didn't see what he saw, but he broke our embrace immediately and sprinted into the alley. I spun on my heel and reached out for him, Lifetime-movie style, without actually moving. "She's going to get you, too!"

My words bounced off the concrete walls of the narrow alley and sprung back at me. Alex was examining the darkened spot where Luna had been looking before I'd so innocently followed her. "It's a trap!"

Alex didn't seem to hear me so I sighed, steeled my courage and jogged into the alley. My heart thundered with each step I took as I neared the spot where Luna pinned me.

Alex turned quickly and held out a hand. "Stay back," he said.

I opened my mouth—either to protest or to hardily agree, I couldn't be sure—at the same moment a flash of light cracked. It was like a camera flash times a thousand and the sheer magnitude seemed to push against my chest, seemed to pick me up and shove me back.

I don't know when I scrunched my eyes shut, but when I opened them, I was flat on my back on the sidewalk just in front of the alley. A couple slowed, looked down at me silently, and then continued on their way.

By the time Alex trotted out to me, I was breathing heavily, terror infecting my every pore. "What the hell was that?" My body started to shake and my teeth started to chatter. I clamped my knees against a bladder that threatened to betray me and my new Victoria's Secret underwear.

Alex was looking at me hard. "Are you okay?"

"No!" I shouted. "Did you not see that? Someone tried to kill me. Again! And before you say something smart-assed like you'd think I would be used to it by now, don't bother, because I will kick you so hard in the balls."

Alex closed his mouth, working hard not to grin. "Really?"

Anger seemed to eat away at my primal fear. It was better than crying. "What was that? Another goddamn Grigori? They're everywhere, Alex! They're waitresses and bartenders—they're like cockroaches but with weapons and a major chip on their shoulder."

Alex sat down next to me on the cement and blew out a sigh. I looked at him, terrified. "Oh, don't do that. Don't sigh. Don't sit down. Sitting down and sighing means you're not going to say that that was a raving band of LARPers or a rogue group of Dungeons and Dragoners. Sitting down and sighing means this is more than the Grigori. Who is it now? Who else have I pissed off just by virtue of being?"

"I'm sorry, Lawson."

The tears started then. Big, earnest, hopeless. They rolled down my cheeks and plopped onto the cement. "Who?" I asked.

"There's every indication that this attack was also Grigori-based."

"Grigori-based?" I sniffled. "I can't do this anymore, Alex. I can't. I can't live this way. Either I'm running for my life or I'm fighting for it."

Alex wagged his head, but his eyes were sympathetic. "I'm sorry, Lawson. They want you dead."

My lower lip started to tremble. It wasn't the first time I'd learned that someone wanted me dead. Heck, to be completely honest about it, my being dead would be a boon to Alex—he could restore his grace. But really, I was getting pretty tired of it.

"You know what?" I spat. "You know what would be really nice? Some sort of mortal enemies list. A little something that came along with those damn angels' decision to shove this stupid Vessel in my body. Just so I would know how many people—or who, like my dentist, my gynecologist—are trying to kill me. Was that really a routine pap smear? Or is Dr. Harlow trying to kill me? That would be really nice." Rage was coursing through my veins again, cold and hard. I felt my nostrils flare and I fisted my hands, my fingernails digging half-moons in my palms. I didn't care about the pain. Try to kill me once? Shame on you. Try and kill me four times? Well then, I'm really going to get pissed.

"There's a lot of people who think that the Vessel itself is evil."

His eyes flashed when mine widened.

"Not that you're evil. Not at all. Some people—beings—think the Vessel of Souls is just something that perpetuates the whole good and evil thing."

I paused, chewing the inside of my lip. "So what do you think?"

"I don't think anything about the Vessel, Lawson." Alex fixed me with a stare, his eyes the clearest, most crystal blue I had ever seen. His fingers found mine and very gently laced through. "All I think about is you."

A zing went through me. Something that wasn't just physical, but spiritual as well. I felt whole. I felt whole like I never had before, like I, Sophie Lawson, was all there. Not like I was Sophie Lawson, the holder of something else.

"If you take the Vessel, you can return to grace, Alex. You wouldn't have to walk the mortal plane anymore. And I . . . I wouldn't have to run from it. Will would be free. This, this kind of stuff wouldn't happen anymore."

The muscle along Alex's jawline jumped and it twisted my heart. "There is nothing worth losing you. Nothing. I—I've pushed you away for as long as I could because I wanted to protect you."

"From who? The other fallen?"

He avoided my gaze, his handing going limp in mine. "From me."

"What do you mean from you?"

"I fell from grace because I was imperfect. I lusted after the power of the Vessel of Souls."

I straightened. "You were tricked though, you were duped. You didn't know what you were doing."

Alex let out a growling little chuckle. "I knew." Something flitted across his face, something dark settling in his features.

I scooched back on the concrete, and for the first time I could remember, I felt fear when I looked into Alex's eyes.

"At least that's what I told myself. That I was pushing you away because that bad was still inside of me and because of it, I could hurt you. I could take advantage of you and take the Vessel." He shook his head slowly. "But I started to realize that I could never, ever hurt you. I wanted to protect you. I wanted to keep you safe."

A sob choked in my throat. "And that's changed now?"

"I don't exist, Lawson. I'm dead. I'm doomed to wander, to be"—he gestured toward his body as though it were something less than astounding— "this for all of eternity."

"I don't understand."

"I can't give you a life. I don't have anything to give you."

I felt my teeth digging into my lower lip as my whole body thrummed, electric with the adrenaline of the fight, with the carnal want of having Alex this close.

"I can give you something, Alex. I can give you life."

We drove home in silence, and when I walked into my apartment, I went directly for my laptop, popping the thing open and shaking out Abelard the monk's card. I'd thought it was strange that a man who wore burlap underwear would have a glossy business card with a phone number and address, but now I was thankful.

There was something that I could do to step in and stop all this. There was something that I could do to straighten the bad in the world, free Will Sherman, and bring Alex to grace. The fact that I could very likely die while doing it didn't seem like the greatest trade-off in the world, but I would rather die of my own accord than at the hands of a Grigori warrior bartender or waitress.

I plucked up Abelard's card and studied the black raised numbers on the white cardstock until they swam in front of my eyes. I had my hand on the phone, dial tone droning, when Nina poked her head in.

"I'm going to order Italian from that guy that I like. I feel like delivery. Don't want to go out."

I looked at Nina and a lump grew in my throat as my best friend rambled on in her hot-pink velour tracksuit, trying to decide if she wanted the light-colored guy or the darker one for her dinner.

The place she was talking about made incredible homemade pasta with fresh bread, and for deliveries to our place, offered a side of blood from a breathing donor. They also did gluten free.

Nina finally stopped talking long enough to pause and stare at me, fists on her hips. "Something's up with you."

"I've been attacked multiple times in multiple days and I think I'm developing a perpetual goose egg in the middle of my forehead."

"No." She tapped a perfectly manicured fingernail against her pouty lips. "That's not it. You're all weight-of-the-world-y."

I looked away, knowing that Nina could read me, as well as smell me, from eighty paces.

I challenged her stare, but she didn't flinch, so I slid Abelard's card against the desk to her. She snapped it up and immediately dropped it, screaming, "Ow!" and sticking her index finger into her mouth.

I felt my eyes widen. "Did that burn you? Because it belongs to a monk?"

Nina screwed up her face and showed me her finger, a faint little slice down the middle. "Paper cut."

As quickly as it happened, it healed up over itself. She leaned down, picked up the card, and glanced at it. "What were you planning on doing with this?" Nina looked up, her coal-black eyes fierce. "And if you say anything other than starting a prayer circle I'm going to kick your ever-loving ass."

"Well, that's kind of harsh."

"I know what he wanted you to do, Sophie." She flicked the card so it fluttered back down to my desk.

"You do?"

"I heard every word. He wants you to do some ritual. Some ritual that may *kill you*. I can't believe you're actually considering it. You are, aren't you? God, I can't believe you, Sophie! You're so selfish."

I gaped, taken aback. "How am I being selfish? If I—if the Vessel of Souls can be hoodooed out of me, then we'll all be safe. Will wouldn't be tasked with watching over my danger-magnet butt and Alex . . ."

"Alex can get his wings. Ring a fucking bell, Sophie. Neither of those men's lives is worth yours. And you don't even know if this Abelard guy is legit! Did you even check him out?"

"I—I think he has a Facebook page."

I could see that Nina was fuming. She threaded her arms in front of her chest and glowered at me.

"Can't you see this from my point of view at all, Neens?"

"No, no I really can't."

I wagged my head. "Someone will always be after me. Someone will always be chasing me."

"Boo freaking hoo," she snapped, her eyes fierce. "Join the club. Every time there's a *Buffy the Vampire Slayer* marathon or anything starring Wesley Snipes, Vlad and I have to take cover from the hordes of tiny blondes scissor kicking and wielding wooden stakes or, you know, whatever Wesley Snipes did in *Blade*."

"Yeah, but—"

"Yeah but nothing. In addition to that, I've also got to get around all the inanimate shit that wants to kill me, too. Like the sun. And fire. And fucking garlic. Think your life is bad, Sophie? I can be killed by a spice. A spice!"

"Garlic won't kill you, Neens, you just don't like it."

Nina ignored me and ranted on. "And all people want to do is chase Vlad around so they can rip off his shirt and see his sparkles."

"That sounds really dirty."

"It is, if you mean I-just-threw-up-a-little-in-my-mouth dirty."

I sighed. "I'm not as strong as you, Nina."

She batted at the air. "And you're not as pretty as me either. But that doesn't mean that you have to sacrifice yourself to a monk, who, for all we know, could have sewn that awful burlap ensemble in his basement. Hell, he could even be Grigori. Aren't they tricksters, too?"

I shook my head. "No, no, that one is only my pops. The trickster god is my dad."

"So, we're two chicks who have mortal enemies coming out of every corner—"

"Including the spice rack."

"If you give up the Vessel without really knowing what you're doing, you're handing your life over and everybody—the Grigori, your dad—wins. Everyone but you."

I cocked my head, listening, only half-convinced.

Nina slid her tongue over the angled point of one fang. "You promise to do me a favor and not call Burlap Boy until we've had a chance to really figure things out and to make sure he's not evil?"

I paused, looking up into Nina's eyes. There was the typical Nina hardness, that little sheen of attitude and sass, but there was also a warmth that reminded me that we were so much more than friends. We were family.

"Okay," I said, taking the hand she offered. "I promise."

EIGHTEEN

If my life were a big Hollywood movie, this would be the part where we broke into a training montage of me in frumpy sweats trying to sneak a donut, glaring at a jump rope, then ultimately finding joy in exercise and hot pants. But this was my real life, so I lay on the couch and read pro-Satan/pro-killing-Satan books all day, popping ibuprofen and staying as far away from hot pants as the law would allow.

I glanced at my phone when it vibrated its way across the coffee table toward me, and finally swiped it up.

"I'm downstairs. Come out."

Nina's eyes were shining when I met her on the street outside of our building. She was standing in front of her car, her pink-and-black key chain dangling, the little rhinestones on the moustache pendant catching the speckled bits of sun that peeked through the blanket of fog, blurring the harsh outlines of the cityscape. Nina was grinning from ear to ear, too, hands on hips, legs akimbo. I immediately slowed my walk.

"What's up?" I asked tentatively.

She clapped her hands together. "I think I finally know why I was brought back!"

"Brought back? To . . . San Francisco?"

Having recently spent a stint in Manhattan working on her fashion line and evading the police (it's not that long of a story, really, but she can tell it better), plus the whole afterlife thing, I was never really certain what Nina meant when she referred to being "brought back."

"Not to San Francisco," she gushed. "To life!" She spread her arms and burst out with the words as if everyone else thought being brought back to life was normal. Although maybe they did, since the man pushing his *carrito*, hawking chili-sprinkled mangoes, barely stopped ringing his little bell long enough for a passing glance.

I got into the car as Nina slid into the driver's seat, still grinning, still beaming rays of stupid sunshine everywhere.

"What are you talking about?"

She gunned the engine. "You know how I've always been looking for my calling? My reason for being?"

"Re-being," I clarified.

"Whatever. But you know? I mean, I tried being a novelist, which wasn't exactly what I wanted."

"Not exactly what you wanted? I seem to remember the words 'abysmal failure' being tossed around."

She shot me a death glare. "And there was the

musical and the documentary—which would have been epic, by the way, if I had had a more willing cast."

"Documentaries don't have casts, Neens."

"Yeah, you're telling me." She narrowed her eyes at me, the sole "star" of her cast. I hadn't been chosen so much for my optimal work or acting ability as for the fact that I was also pretty much the only member of the Underworld Detection Agency who could be seen on film.

"Anyway," she went on, guiding her little black Lexus through traffic, "I know what I'm here for now. It's to make people happy."

She grinned so enormously that the bloodless veins in her neck bulged.

"To make people happy?" I asked skeptically. "No offense, but your track record is not . . . exactly"—and here I treaded lightly, because my best friend has fangs—"friendly."

"That's because I haven't started yet."

"Oh. Sure. Right."

She swung the wheel and cut off three lanes of traffic, honks and tire screeches sounding in our wake. I gripped the dash. "When exactly are you planning on starting?"

I very slowly, very carefully, made my way over to the Krav Maga studio for my second lesson with the bouncy Melody and the terrifyingly strong Aikiko and Yuu. This time I managed to mostly stay on my feet and not get attacked by either the Grigori or

Aikiko, so I was feeling pretty good when I stepped out into the crisp San Francisco night.

I was painfully aware that an undead theological army was hunting me and that there were grumblings of my father making his grand debut among the debris of the city, so I kept my head up, my keys spiked through my fisted hands, and I wore an old Jesus Jones T-shirt. I didn't exactly go to church, and I had a vague fear that a crucifix would burn through my flesh due to my bloodline, so I thought the shirt might be a fair compromise—or at the very least, a tick mark in the "trying not to be evil" box.

The city was teeming with energy and life like it did every evening around this time. The buses were loaded with business people in suits and sneakers, throngs of them heading out at every stop, mixing into the crowd of diners, shoppers, tourists, and wanderers. I scrutinized every face that passed me, wondering which one was going to advance, to attack; which one was listening to my father whispering horrible, murderous things in his ear right now.

Somewhere, sirens rang out. Car horns honked. People chattered. Church bells rang. The city moved in harmony, nothing so obvious or showy as strangers striking up conversations or people bursting into song, but a peaceful, moving coexistence.

I found myself boiling with anger.

My father, for whatever reason, had chosen now to pull the strings. He had abandoned me and worked his evil away from me, but now it was here, in my city, and blood of mine or not, I wanted him to leave.

I had to find him. I had to stop him. And I knew that for the good of everyone—San Franciscans, Nina, Vlad, Alex, and Will—I had to do it on my own.

I sucked in a deep breath and felt the heat roil through my body. I made a beeline for the little shop in the back of an alley in Chinatown.

I hadn't been to Feng and Xian's shop since the massacre that had killed Xian. The place was boarded up with huge sheets of graffiti-covered plywood, but even behind the wood and spray paint smells, the place carried the bitter stench of death. It invaded my nostrils as I closed in, and as I shimmied down the narrow alleyway I paused, listening. My hackles went up, suspicion pricking at the back of my neck. When I didn't hear anything, I sucked in my stomach and pushed myself all the way through the narrow tunnel to the alleyway behind, and landed with a breath-stealing thud on my back.

I blinked twice and saw stars, bright pinpoints of glorious white light and then I saw Feng, eyes pulled into narrowed slits, eyebrows angry slashes.

"Sophie Lawson?" she said.

There was more than a hint of distaste in her voice, but she leaned over and offered me a hand. I let her help me up and brushed off the rotting vegetables and general garbage that litters every San Francisco alleyway.

"Hi, Feng. Thanks for not . . ." A starburst of pain

shot out at the back of my head and I let my words trail off.

"What do you want? Finally want me to kill that rabid dog?"

The "rabid dog" to which she was referring was Sampson. Feng and Xian were werewolf hunters and, up until Xian's fairly recent death at the hands of a nutcase, had been the sole reason that our werewolf files at the Underworld Detection Agency were painfully slim.

"No. I need to talk to you about something else." I jutted my chin toward Feng's workshop, a cement block room with all the charm and warmth of a jail cell. "Privately."

She studied me for a beat, then offered a sharp, quick nod and pushed me into the workshop.

"I—I think I need weapons."

Feng glared up at me, clearly taking me in, clearly certain that a weapon and me would only result in one thing: me shish-kebabed.

"I don't do weapons, I do bullets."

They were all lined up in glowing Lucite cases behind her. I was rather impressed at this swanky new addition, even if was a collection of body-shattering ammunition. But they were shiny and silver and glinted under the lights, looking both elegant and dangerous—and I liked shiny things.

"Why did you come here?"

"I think I need something . . . special."

Truth be told, I wasn't exactly sure why I had come to Feng. She made silver bullets that tore through werewolf hide and were made to eradicate a species. I didn't know if I would need a weapon against my father, or if there even was one available.

Feng's eyebrows went up. "Explain special."

I swallowed, not sure why I was nervous that this nut job would think I was a nut job. "I need something—a weapon, or protection, or some kind of defense against the devil."

Feng's tight lips quirked up into a smile. "What kind of devil?"

I blinked. "*The* devil. Satan, Lucifer." I stopped going, suddenly worried that using too many names would Beetlejuice forth my jackass of a dad. I wanted to meet him, to defeat him, but I wanted the opportunity to have some sort of defense or chain-mail underwear or something when it happened.

She snorted, her teeth showing through her wide grin, and shook her head. "There is no defense against that evil. There is nothing you can do when you face it. If *T'an-Mo* wants you, he will have you."

I took a step backward. "Oh. Oh. Well." I waved like we had just shared a remotely normal conversation. "Thanks anyway."

I turned and had my hand on the doorknob when Feng spoke again. "It's not a weapon like you think."

I looked over my shoulder, eyeing Feng as she advanced, the hard meanness gone from her expression. She almost looked . . . thoughtful.

"It's not a weapon like you think that will stop him. He cannot be stopped with mere force."

"I don't understand—"

"He is force. He is violence and hate and danger

and pain. He cannot be stopped with blades or bullets."

"Oh. Well, thanks for that." It wasn't that I'd had my heart set on getting a weapon from a woman who, not very long ago, had been my mortal enemy. But I really hadn't expected her to drop the "basically, you're totally screwed" knowledge on me either.

I turned back to the door.

"But he can be stopped. He can be pushed back to where he belongs."

This time, I didn't bother turning around. "And how would one go about doing that, if there isn't a weapon that can be used against him?"

I heard Feng let out a long, slow breath. "Like kind," she said slowly. "The trickster tricks."

My shoulders sagged. "Thanks, Feng. Have a nice Armageddon."

I heard the door snap shut behind me, and as if on miserable cue, the rain started in cold ribbons. I pulled my hood up over my head and trudged to my car, suddenly feeling the weight of the situation sinking into my muscles.

My father was going to get what he wanted. He could pull the strings and bring his darkness to the world and there wasn't a damn thing I could do about it, Vessel of Souls or not. I was *Sophie Lawson: Total Waste of Skin and Tear Ducts.*

As the rain continued to sail down, it hit my cheeks, burning there, mixing with the tears that were already there.

I drove home with the radio off, listening only to the thudding sound of rain on the hood of the car, to the sound of tires splashing through puddles and my windshield wipers scraping drops away. I wanted to formulate a plan, but my mind kept rolling, kept flashing images of little Oliver Culverson, of the maniacal grin of the man in my dream. I had longed for a father my whole life. I was desperate for his approval, his love, and now I was ready to kill him to defend my friends, my city, from this man who I had spent my entire life dreaming about, building up, and wishing for.

By the time I got to my apartment building, the rain had grown into heavy sheets that reflected back the streetlights and pelted my car in a whooshing cacophony. The rush of the water mimicked the rush of the blood going through my ears, and I tried to focus on the road in front of me even as it swirled and blurred. I didn't care what it took; I was going to make this right.

I was going to find him.

I had no other choice.

Unfortunately, I wasn't exactly sure how to find the devil right off the bat. Sure, I had a hollow, terrifying memory of the homeless guy who'd turned himself into a human torch calling forth my father, but being completely engulfed in flames wasn't something that interested me.

There was always a couple of guys at the Powell turn who claimed that Satan lived in the strip clubs or Congress or in J.K. Rowling books, but I was pretty sure they were just guessing or had their own agendas.

So really, where does one go looking for the one from whom everyone else is trying to hide?

I really had no idea.

Once I'd pulled the car into the underground lot—and said a prayer to the god of apartment buildings to thank him for sending me a dry spot to park my car—I was more focused and more determined. My jaws hurt from the constant clench and I was chomping to get in front of my laptop to start my research another way. Feng had said it was going to be hard to stop my father—she hadn't said it was going to be impossible.

I plodded up the stairs, exhaustion lingering in every muscle, but when I got to our floor, I straightened. I felt the familiar tingle on the back of my neck that meant something bad—something really bad—was happening. But it wasn't so much a feeling as it was a scent. A horrible, noxious scent. It seemed to permeate my every cell, filling my nose with its bitter stench, making my eyes water.

I paused, trying to place it. I had smelled the sickly sweet stench of death that comes, seconds before, to claim the living. I knew the wretched scent of flesh decaying, the dull, copper-penny scent of blood. Even the sharp, enveloping smell of fear. But this wasn't it. It was bitter, but smelled like rot—mold, maybe. There were traces of fear and fire and—chocolate?

I raced across the floor just as Will threw his door open, a panicked look on his face. His hair was disheveled, his eyes slightly red, and he was shirtless. It wasn't until he sprung through the doorway that I realized he was also pantless, clad in nothing but an excruciatingly well-fitting pair of boxer briefs and a fire extinguisher. He dashed past me, rested his palm flat against my door, and then yelled, "Is anyone in there?"

We both heard the clatter of metal as the sickening stench of fire that must have enveloped something horrific puffed from under the door. I thought of Nina and Vlad, of what the burning flesh of a vampire might smell like, and my stomach went to liquid. I didn't think, I just moved. I body-checked Will and sunk my key into the lock. I was pushing open the front door when Will grabbed me.

"Stay back!" he barked.

Tears were blurring my vision. "She's my best friend!"

He raised the extinguisher and pulled the pin at the same moment the front door opened. Nina, in a frilly apron that was splattered with something that must have once been alive, grinned from the doorway.

"Oh, you're home! And you brought Will!" She scanned him, her smile beginning to fall. "Who didn't exactly dress for the occasion."

"Nina! Get out! Something is in there! There's fire! Fire!" I was panicked, screaming maniacally. I threw my arms around Nina's still-cold skin, throwing all my body weight backward, trying to move her from the throes of death.

I couldn't budge her.

"So, nothing's burning then?" Will asked.

"Burning? No, of course not. But I'm so glad you're here. Sit, sit!" She bustled us into the apartment, shoving us toward the dining table that had been set with pink napkins and a fistful of wilting flowers shoved in an empty Prego jar.

Once Nina turned her back on us, heading toward the kitchen, Will leaned in to me and opened his mouth. I abruptly held up a hand and shot him a warning glance. "Don't talk. You never know what's going on when she's like this."

"I heard that," Nina sung from the kitchen.

We stayed silent and Nina returned, oven mitts up to her pin-thin elbows, something horrendous in a nine-by-thirteen-inch metal pan between her hands, the noxious odor wafting up from it. She dropped the pan on the table between Will and me. It landed with a dead-weight thunk.

"I made brownies!"

"Out of what?"

I elbowed Will hard in the ribs and tried to keep my eyes averted from the smoking pile of whatever in front of us.

"Mmm, Neens, thanks! It—that—they look fabulous."

Will gaped at me. "What is wrong with you?"

"What is wrong with *you*?" I hissed under my breath. I took a pink napkin, laid it on my palm, and held out my hand. "I'd love one, Neens."

Nina preened like a peacock hopped up on antidepressants and dug a spatula into the brownies. Her smile faltered just the tiniest bit, but she lifted out a brownie and slapped it into my palm. It kept its shape for a half-second before melding into the napkin, hunks of something that could have been chocolate chips or asphalt sliding over the edge of my hand and falling onto the table. I pinned my lips together and smiled, forcing myself to utter an "mmm."

Nina wasn't convinced. She dropped the spatula on the table, bits of brownie shooting over Will and me. She slumped into a chair, holding her wobbling chin in her hands.

"This is awful!"

"Oh, no, Neens, don't be so hard on yourself!" I looked at the slopping mess in my hand. "They're just a little undercooked. A lot of people do that on purpose because they like their brownies gooey."

She looked hopeful and I painfully realized I had cheered myself into a corner. I leaned forward and took a little nibble.

I couldn't stop my gag reflex. "Oh, God, Nina!"

Her lower lip popped out. "It wasn't my fault! We didn't have any stupid cream of tartar. I had to make my own."

I stopped guzzling everything liquid in the house and looked at her.

"You can't make cream of tartar," Will said. "Can you?"

"How did you make cream of tartar?"

Nina groaned and threw open the refrigerator door. "Okay, so I didn't make it from scratch. It just seems so ridiculous. You know, cooking wasn't this difficult when I still chewed."

She slapped a bottle of tartar sauce—mainly just little chunks of pickle in the few sad wisps of mayonnaise—in front of me.

"Do you know how long it took me just to get the cream?"

After the brownie debacle was redeemed by an extra-cheese pizza and a side of crazy bread, the conversation switched from what star was liposuctioning what body part and turned, as it does, to Armageddon.

"You made it through the day unscathed, so that's a plus, right?" Nina said cheerfully.

I immediately grabbed the box that was holding all of my information on the case and plunked it in the center of the table. Two hours later, everything we had, all the information I'd gathered, was spread out on the dining room table, and Will, Nina, Vlad, and I all took turns staring at it blankly.

"None of this really fits together," Will said.

"Yeah, it's like Lucas has evil ADHD. First he lights a vampire on fire, then he's got crazy people starting fires, and the dog and the kid, and then he sets off the Grigori. . . ." Vlad frowned, leaning back in his chair.

Nina cradled her head in her hands. "It's like he's just throwing random stuff at you, Soph, then just, hiding out. Frankly, I'm a little disappointed. I kind of thought the devil would be way more organized. You know, strategic attack, A-plus-B-equals-C kind of thing. Even I can plan a more sinister and orderly attack plan."

I nodded. "Every text says he's smart. Brilliant, even. But he's . . ." I let the word trail off as something hit me. "But he's not unorganized. He's not stupid. He's playing tricks."

Will's brows shot up. "Come again?"

I was about to answer when there was a quick, insistent knocking on the door. I pulled it open and Alex shoved past me. "I've got to talk to you about some—"

He paused in the foyer, his leather jacket in mid slide over his arms as he took in the assembled crew. "Am I interrupting something?"

"Actually, you just interrupted Sophie's big breakthrough, bloke."

My cheeks reddened as Alex stiffened. Will kept his gaze fixed and none too warm.

"I wouldn't call it a breakthrough, exactly. Just a thought. But why—what do you need to talk to me about?"

Alex narrowed his gaze at Will, then back at me.

Vlad groaned. "The weight of the world hangs in the balance here, guys. How about you do your pissing contest if we survive Armageddon, okay?"

"It's the guy from the video. And the girl. The people from the fires."

"I don't remember there being a girl, but okay."

"They have absolutely no recollection of what happened. None. They don't know Latin, don't know anything about the fires."

"Pretty sure the guy that burned himself knew about the fires," Will put in.

Alex shot him a withering stare. "He had no idea why he was burned."

"Great," Nina said, "so yet another total non sequitur."

"It's a trick," I said simply.

"A trick?"

"He needs us to believe that he is recruiting an army. The Grigori, sure, but humanity? And Oliver? He's playing a game."

"Trickster god," Alex said with a slow nod.

"All of this is a ruse. It's just fun for him or something."

"So he doesn't want to take over the world?" Nina wanted to know.

"No. All of these things have one thing in common," Vlad said, looking pleased with himself. "Sophie."

"So he's throwing all this shit at her to . . ." Will let his words trail off.

"To exhaust her. To weaken her. To realize that if she joins forces with him, she can stop it. She can stop everything and, essentially, save the world."

Nina sprang from her chair. "Sophie, you're like the golden ticket!"

NINETEEN

I pinched the bridge of my nose. "That's just . . . excellent."

"No offense, but being around this many breathers for this length of time is really getting to me." Vlad snapped his laptop shut, fished a couple of blood bags out of the fridge, and disappeared out the front door. Nina looked mournfully at the remains of her ruined brownies and plopped herself on the couch and clicked on the Food Network. That left just Alex, Will, and me, and the way Alex and Will were staring each other down, I wasn't sure that they even knew I was there. Both were doing that manly puffed-out chest thing, nearly circling each other like dogs.

"I think I'll just hang around here a bit and make sure you're all right, Lawson," Alex said.

"That's all right, mate. I'm just across the hall. Easier for me to just hang around here, make sure everything is okay."

Alex's smile was thin and forced. "Not a problem. I'm a cop. It's my job. Serve and protect and all."

"Funny thing is, it's my job, too. Guardian, and all."

Alex flashed the smallest bit of his leather holster. "I think I'm better prepared."

Will shrugged. "You know as well as I do that that thing isn't going to do a thing to stop what we're dealing with."

I waved my hand and inched my way into the male catfight. "Guys? I'm okay. I'm fine here."

"Sophie, let us handle this."

"What?"

"Will and I can deal with this. You're going to be just fine, Lawson."

I gaped, fury boiling over. "I *am* just fine. I'm safe here in my apartment, probably a lot safer here with Nina than I would be if both of you stayed here beating your chests and glowering at each other."

That snapped both the guys to attention, and they stared down at me as if surprised that I was there. I put one hand on each of their backs and shoved them toward the door. "The world can crash down outside. I've got fanged protection over here."

Nina waved from the couch, and the guys stepped into the hallway, looking back at me plaintively.

"Are you sure?" Will asked.

"It's no trouble."

"Probably for your own good, love."

"Out!" I slammed the door with a groan, then flopped down on the couch next to Nina.

"Can you believe those two?"

"Yes." She paused. "You know, you're really going to need to make a choice soon. You know, if the world doesn't end and all."

I raised my eyebrows. "What are you talking about?"

"Look, Soph, you can't keep doing this back-and-forth thing. First Alex, then Will, then Alex, Will, Alex—"

I held up a hand. "I get it, Neens."

"Seriously. This whole thing is starting to get a little old. And if it's old for me—someone who has an exciting life and plenty of other things to do—can you imagine what it must be like for them?"

I shot her a glare before clamping a hand over my forehead. "We're seriously talking about this now?"

Nina gave me a hard look, and I flopped forward. "It's hard, Nina. I don't know what to do."

"Just choose one!"

"I'm worried about—"

"Looking a little slutty?" Nina patted my hair. "Stop worrying. You passed Slutville and careened into Skank City a long time ago."

"I'm worried about hurting one of them."

Nina wrinkled her nose. "Who?"

"I don't know! Isn't it possible to be in love with two people at once? Because I am. I love Alex, Neens, I really do. I could see myself with him. He just gets me, you know?"

Her eyebrows went up. "I don't think anyone actually gets you, Soph."

"But Will . . . I feel so safe with him, so protected. And he makes me laugh. But Alex has always been so loyal. . . ."

"So Will is doing his job and Alex is a golden retriever. And need I remind you that your future with Alex is finite? He's a fallen angel. He's immortal. And he's going to stay pretty while you droop and age and are no longer able to control your bodily functions."

"Thanks for the reminder, friend."

"But"—Nina put out her hands like scales—"on the Will front, he'll probably get old and decrepit, too. He's mortal, right? Through and through? Or does he get special powers because of his Guardianship? You should find that out. Because if you're choosing between two immortals, well, frankly sweetie, you should hop on OkCupid right now. The whole die, never-going-to-die thing can be a real deal-breaker."

I blew out a sigh. "With all that being said, what would you do? I mean, I really do—I love them both, Neens." I bit my bottom lip, feeling the lump forming in my throat. I knew it was only a matter of time, and in theory, two amazingly hot, just-this-side-of-dirty men fighting over me was like winning the slut lottery. But in actuality, it hurt my heart and made me wholly dependent on Tums and climbing out bathroom windows when things got too deep.

Nina pursed her lips together, considering. "Well, I suppose if it was me . . . I'd move to Northern Nigeria."

I cocked an eyebrow. "What? So you can hide out in a mud hut for the rest of your life? Way to go with the solution, Neens."

She spat out an annoyed puff of air. "No, because Northern Nigeria still practices polyandry. I'd marry them both."

I rolled my eyes and the doorbell rang.

"Told you you'll have to make a choice. There they are now." She swept by me while I trembled, as terrified about showing down the two men I loved as I was about the end of our doomed world.

But Nina flew back into the living room, an enormous, Miss America-style bouquet in her arms, her cheeks a heady pink. It would have been a lovely scene if I weren't totally aware that the rush of blood in her cheeks belonged to someone else.

I gestured toward the flowers with my chin. "Who sent those?"

The bouquet was huge and Nina's upper body was practically swallowed in the assortment of fist-sized lavender roses, baby's breath, and various frilly green things. A silk bow was tied around the trunk of stems, the white and lavender ribbon trailing halfway to Nina's knees.

"I'm not sure. They're gorgeous, though, aren't they?" She pressed an impeccably manicured index finger against her full lips. "I bet they're from Austin."

I scrunched up my face. "Austin? The were-vamp? I thought you guys had a falling-out."

Nina's flesh seemed to ripple as her lips curled up into a snarl. "He gave me fleas." She glanced down at the bouquet. "This is the least he can do for something like that."

Before I had the time to consider that I was sharing seven hundred square feet of living space with a flea-ridden vampire, Nina whipped out a card, eyes gleaming.

Then her face promptly fell.

I sat up, feeling a nervous flutter in my stomach. "Neens, what is it? Who are they from?"

Nina looked up at me, truly dumbfounded. "They're for you."

"For me?" My mind immediately raced in a thousand different directions. They were from Will! They were from Alex! I had won the Miss America Pageant by a slew of write-in votes (that happened, right?).

Nina shoved the tiny card back in its envelope and unceremoniously dumped the flowers into my lap. I cocked an eyebrow. "What happened to you working on being more gracious?"

Her eyes raked over me and the bouquet before she flopped into the chair-and-a-half. "I brought them over to you, didn't I?"

I grinned, savoring one of the few moments in my life when I could trump Nina. I made a show of finding the card and whipping it out myself. My name was typed on the front and I waved it at Nina.

"So this, my actual *name*, typed on the front, didn't clue you in on the fact that these might not be for you?"

"No offense, Soph, but when it comes to flowers coming to the house, what is your first thought?"

I blew out a resigned sigh. "Who sent Nina flowers now?'"

Nina batted her eyelashes and pulled an *InStyle* magazine into her lap. "It's not that I'm shallow or self-centered; it's that I was following historical precedent."

"No," I said, yanking the tiny card from the ecru

envelope. "No one would ever consider you shallow or self-centered."

She glowered at me and snapped a page of her magazine, but there was a hint of a smile on her lips.

Then I stopped cold.

I could feel my eyes widen, could feel the heat prick out all over my skin. Somewhere, I heard Nina calling my name, but it was as if I had vaulted backward, a hundred miles away. The image of Nina's wide, concerned eyes and the apartment were a tiny pinprick of light in front of me. There was cotton in my ears and a thousand-pound weight pressing against my chest.

It wasn't until Nina's icy-cold hands were on me that I sucked in a deep, choking breath.

"Breathe, Soph, breathe!"

Nina was kneeling in front of me and my lungs were aching from lack of air.

"What—who are they from?"

I didn't know it—didn't feel it—because my limbs were stiff and numb, but somehow I had dropped the flowers. They were scattered in a weird arc, the lavender-purple petals glowing against our grain-colored carpet while the stick-straight stems scattered like desperately pointing fingers, each one pockmarked by stiff thorns. Nina picked around them until she found the card. I looked on incredulously as a drop of velvet blood fell from the sky, staining the perfect ecru.

Nina looked up at me. "You're bleeding."

"What?"

"You. Are. Bleeding."

I stared blankly at my hands, unseeing, until Nina wrapped her hands around my index finger, cocooning the slit in my skin, catching the next drop of blood before it fell.

"You must have caught a thorn."

"Right." I pulled my hand away. "I should get a Band-Aid."

I watched Nina stare at the little smear of vibrantly colored blood that dribbled and formed a tiny puddle in the palm of her hand. She was mesmerized and I could see her every muscle tighten, could see her making every effort to avoid the primitive need that raced through her head. A terror simmered behind her deep onyx eyes. I tore my eyes from her and stared at the card lying amongst the fallen roses.

Everything inside of me screamed to pick up the card, to reread it, to smell it, to taste it, to see if I could glean anything of my father from it, and yet any motion toward it was terrifyingly paralyzing.

Nina and I were statue still in our living room, wrestling our greatest fears-slash-desires for moments that felt like hours.

Finally, I broke the silence. "Read the card," I whispered.

The spell was broken. "What?"

I yanked a Kleenex and wiped the blood from Nina's palm, then cleared my throat. "The flowers."

Once the stain was gone from her palm, Nina's whole body seemed to relax. She plucked the card.

"*My dearest Sophie,*" Nina read, "*I've waited so long and now it's time.*" She looked up at me, her eyes wide and soft, and I struggled to suck in a decent breath. "*Always, Dad.*"

Now Nina dropped the card as though the very thing were made of skin-searing acid. "Dad?"

I nodded solemnly. "My dad."

I thought how, just this afternoon, I had been thinking about my father, ready to track him down. And here he was. Telling me "it's time."

I could see Nina hitch her chin, the flitter of fear that crossed her face. "It's really happening."

Now my heartbeat was speeding up and I was breathing in tiny, short bursts, thinking of everything that had happened in the last couple of days. Finally, my mind settled on one image. "Alex—Alex—the case. The homeless guy."

Nina's eyebrows went up. "The guy who was burned up? What does he have to do with anything?"

I hadn't bothered to tell Nina everything about the business card because, as I'd told Alex, it was no big deal. I worked at the Underworld Detection Agency and I had business cards with my name on it for just these kinds of circumstances. Well, circumstances that involved vampires looking for the Agency more than vampires being burned alive, but still. But suddenly I was beginning to think that the business card might have been a bigger deal that I cared to admit.

"The guy—the homeless vampire who got—"

Nina's eyes flashed with fear, and I stopped, cleared my throat instead.

"He had my business card."

She nodded. "Yeah, I know. You said that. Your whole 'not freaking out' thing, remember?"

"I think it's time I started freaking out."

Nina's pale face went even paler. "Do you think the vampire—what was his name?"

"Armentrout," I intoned. "Lance Armentrout."

"Do you think Lance Armentrout was looking for you to warn you?"

My heart did a wild spasm of double thumps. "Or he was working for my father."

We sat in tense silence for what seemed like hours. Finally: "Neens?"

"Yeah, Soph?"

"As a vampire, do you have any . . . like . . . connections?"

"Connections? Me?" She splayed a pale hand against her chest. "Of course I have connections. Tons of them. What do you need? A new wardrobe? A panini? A decent dye job?"

I glanced at a lock of my fire-engine-red hair and frowned. "All of those things might be nice, but that's not what I was talking about." I rubbed my palms against my thighs and cleared my throat. "What I meant was, do you have any connections to—you know . . ." I cut my eyes to the carpet.

"To a carpet cleaner?"

I shook my head and gestured a little more vividly.

"Linoleum? A vacuum cleaner? Soph, I really don't have any idea what you're trying to—"

"To Hell, Neens, HELL! Do you have any connections to Hell or anyone, I don't know, Hell-adjacent?"

Nina narrowed her eyes. "Because I'm a soulless vampire?"

"I don't mean to be offensive, but—"

"We have lived together for seven years, Sophie. Don't you think you would have caught on by now if I had some kind of frequent Hell calling card? Don't you think I would have told you if I ran into your father at the yearly Bastions of Hell family picnic?"

I had to smile despite the fact that I had hurt my best friend and was now being read the riot act for it. "There's a family picnic?"

If blood could rush through Nina's veins, it would have. Instead, she shot me one of her even more terrifying dark-eyed glares.

"I'm sorry, I'm sorry!" I held up my hands placatingly. "It was just a question."

Nina softened then, rolling off her knees and onto her butt beside me. She grabbed my hand and gave it an icy squeeze. "I just hope you know that if there was something I could do—anything to help you find your father sooner—that I would do it. You know that, right?"

Nina had been in my life for only a few years, but she was the closest thing that I had to family. She was like a sister to me, and soulless or not, the depth in her eyes made me certain that her feelings, our sisterhood, went beyond her afterlife.

I squeezed her hand back. "I know, Neens."

The flowers had been gathered up and stuffed in a coffee can with a few splashes of water. Nina and I had gone back and forth on whether I should toss them or enjoy them, and we decided on a sort of halfway, which was why the sweet-smelling blooms sat just outside the bathroom window.

I had studiously avoided them while I brushed my teeth and washed my face and tried to put them out of my mind when I crawled into bed. Minutes later I was in the bathroom again, window cracked as I stared at the bouquet as though there were some secret to them, some message that would let me know what Lucas meant—what he wanted.

I exhausted myself and went back to bed eventually, ChaCha snoozing by my side while I watched the red numbers on my digital clock shift hour after hour. Everything that I had compartmentalized so well came crashing down in an earthquake of unease: Armentrout. *Find Her.* The murders in the Marina. *It's time.* The fire. Oliver.

Nothing made sense.

I may have slept, but it didn't feel like it. Everything ached as I trudged into the dining room the following morning, only for my sleepy, droopy face to be met with Will's grinning, charming face. He was seated at our table, feet up, crossed at the ankles, half of his body hidden behind a newspaper. He poked his head over the top, glanced at me, and gave me a slight grimace.

"You don't look so well, love."

I pressed my fingers to my temples. "I don't feel so well. I got—"

"The flowers, I know."

"How did you know?"

He shrugged folding up the paper and laying it on the table. "I'm your Guardian. It's my job to know. And Nina told me."

"You're welcome," Nina called from her room.

"You okay?" Will asked.

"Should I be?" I sighed. "I honestly have no idea. I mean, my father is back? Does he want to see me or is this all part of his elaborate scheme?"

"With all due respect, love, dear ol' dad is the devil. There's a pretty solid chance he's up to something."

I don't know if I'd expected—or hoped—the flowers to be an innocent attempt to connect from an arcane father to his daughter. But they seemed even more tainted and hideous now.

"What could he want with me?"

Will's eyebrows went up.

Face palm. "Right. Vessel of Souls. But what about this 'he's looking for you' and 'it's time' stuff? Does the Vessel have some kind of time limit? Am I supposed to like, spit it up on my thirtieth birthday or something? Does he want to be there to catch it? I don't get it."

"If we could understand pure evil, love, then it wouldn't be so scary."

Will's statement was simple, but it fluttered something like butterflies in my stomach.

I bit into my lower lip. "Have you ever wished you could do something else, Will?"

He turned and looked at me, his expression confused. "I'm a fireman, love. That's pretty much every little boy's fantasy." He smiled salaciously. "And every big girl's." He waggled his eyebrows and, when I didn't react, rolled his eyes. "I get to spray shit with a hose. It's good fun, pays the bills."

"Not do something else instead of firefighting. Do something else instead of being my Guardian."

Will kicked his feet off the table and clapped his palm over his chin, considering. "Not be your Guardian? I guess I'd never considered it."

"How could you not? You're saddled with me and your job is to protect me by fighting to the death. *To the death*, Will. You can't tell me you're totally cool with that."

He shrugged, as nonchalant as if I had just described the duties of a hot dog vendor. "I suppose it would be nice to do something a little less punchy." His fingertips gently brushed over the wound on his chest. "And a bit less shooty."

"And to not be stuck with me."

He slung an arm roughly over my shoulders and pulled me to him so that I was half balancing on his lap. "Ah, but come on. Hanging out with you is the only perk I get on this route."

It was sweet, but I couldn't help but hate the fact that every ache Will had gotten since he walked into my life was because he was protecting me. And this last time, he had nearly lost his life because of it.

Thoughts and ideas were percolating in my head.

I was curled up on the couch starting my second sleeve of chocolate marshmallow Pinwheels when Nina came through the front doors like a tiny, well-dressed hurricane. She was loaded down with shopping bags that were leaking glitter and streamers, and I was immediately suspicious as Nina was both anti-party, and anti-cheap decorative cut-outs and confetti.

"What's all this?"

"Oh! Remember how I found my calling? You know, because I'm so giving and so good at helping people?"

I remembered most of those words being thrown around. Not in that particular order, but I nodded anyway.

"Well, I was talking to Vlad and he just seemed so sad and everything. I mean, everything that has been going on has been pretty heavy and"— she made a cut-throat motion and stuck out her tongue—"blech. So I thought, what would Vlad want?"

"A girl Vlad with boobies?"

Nina rolled her eyes. "The world may be ending, Soph, and you know what—"

"Wait, wait, time out. We're going with 'the world may be ending' now?"

She blinked at me and went right on talking. "So I thought, what does Vlad not have that every other kid his age—you know, his littler age—have?"

"Blood, a heart, life, breath, the ability to pick up socks or go to the beach, a reflection . . ."

"No." She upturned the Party City bag. "A birthday party!"

I scratched my head. "A birthday party?'

"Uh-huh."

There was a quick rap on the door and then Will came strolling in. "So, any news on the big bad?"

I shook my head. "Not having the greatest luck contacting my father."

"So we're having a party?" he asked skeptically.

"Nina apparently bought the whole store out."

She slapped at the air. "He's my nephew! And this is his first birthday party in almost a hundred years. It has to be special."

"A birthday party." He shrugged. "Well, seems like as good a time as any to break out the noise-makers. Come to think of it, as all signs are pointing to imminent doom, maybe I should go out and buy a lottery ticket or something."

"Why? It's going to be useless if you win. I'm pretty sure the great overlord Papa Satan won't allow you to run around with extra bills in your pocket."

Both Will and Nina turned to stare at me.

"What?" I said, pulling a packet of Pop Rocks candy from the melee of party supplies on the table. "I'm on edge. Give me a break."

Will poked through the plastic-wrapped contents on the table and flipped up a stack of plates. "Cowboys? You went with a cowboy theme?"

Nina put her hands on her hips and narrowed her eyes. "What did you expect? *Twilight*?"

I pressed a hand over my mouth but couldn't hide my laughter. "That would have been awesome."

Nina swung her glare to me and I snatched up some cocktail napkins emblazoned with a giant cowboy boot. "But this is even more awesome . . . er."

"I know it's a little bit juvenile given his age and all, but I just wanted something really classic. And red looks great on me. See what else I got?" She produced another bag and pulled out a fitted red plaid blouse, some brand-new worn-looking denim shorts, and a pair of red leather cowboy boots. She topped the whole ensemble off with a hat, shiny silver sheriff star glistening in the overhead light.

Will grinned, swigged his beer, and leaned back into his cheer. "That's brilliant."

I yanked a red plastic cowboy hat from the Party City bag and smacked Will with it. "Get your mind out of the feed trough, you ass."

Nina pointed at me and nodded appraisingly. "That's getting into the spirit. And to get you further into the spirit, you"—she handed me a notecard with an address written on it—"are getting the cake. And invite Alex, too. And you." She cut her eyes to Will. "You'll be picking up the kegs."

Will waggled his eyebrows. "Keg service? That I can do." He tossed his empty bottle into our recycling. "Just don't expect 'em to be full when they get here."

"They'll be O-neg, Vlad's favorite."

Will paled and tucked the notecard Nina handed him into his back pocket. "Noted."

She handed him a twenty. "Why don't you grab a six-pack for the breathers?"

"Brilliant." He skulked across the room and right out the door.

I sat down. "I'm really excited about this. I don't think we've ever had a party here."

"Not a good one. I figure we'll get balloons and hang the streamers from there." She pointed to our IKEA bookshelf. "And we can hang the piñata from that sword you left stuck in the door. It'll be so festive!"

Cowboy hats, a keg full of blood, and a piñata

hung from a long sword. Oh yeah, apartment 3B really knew how to party.

I headed downstairs while dialing Alex.

"Lawson?"

"Grace?"

He signed into the phone. "Can I help you?"

"Yeah. Nina is on a new kick. She has decided now that her reason for being brought back—"

"Brought back where? To San Francisco?"

I snorted like that was the dumbest thing I ever heard. "No, for being brought back to life. It's to make people happy."

Alex was silent on his end of the phone for a beat. "Did you tell her that she was brought back to life because some vamp saw fit to open a vein for her?"

"No, weird, I didn't think of mentioning that because I like being alive this time around. Anyway, the first stop in Nina's happy-go-round is a birthday party for Vlad."

"A birthday party? For Vlad?"

"I know how ridiculous it sounds, but it's tonight, you're invited, and we're supposed to pick up a cake."

Alex blew out a breath. "I seriously don't know why I let you talk me into these things, Lawson."

"So, you're on your way?"

Alex pulled to the curb not more than twenty minutes later, and I was reminded that that was one of the things I truly loved about this city: at seven square miles, it was always bound to take twice as long to get anywhere.

I jumped in the passenger-side door and started

reading from the note Nina had written for me. "Apparently, it's at a bakery in Noe called La Sucrene and it's a horse cake. I really, really hope that the cake is shaped like a horse and not made of one. Especially since we're likely to be the only ones eating it."

Alex pulled off into traffic and I poked at his shoulder. "You're supposed to turn there. Noe Valley, Alex. It's that way."

"We have to make a stop first."

There was a tight set to Alex's jaw so I folded the paper in half and stayed quiet while we zipped through the city, lights flashing on his unit, siren quiet.

"Is it an emergency? Crime scene? Shouldn't we"—I raised my hand, making the universal motion for a siren going around—"whew-whew-whew?"

He finally cracked a grin and cut his gaze to me. "Is that supposed to be your impression of a police siren?"

"Yes. And it's obviously pretty good because you got it right off the bat."

"Well, I wouldn't have if you weren't making those finger sirens, too."

I slugged him in the shoulder. "Are you at least going to tell me where we're going? Oh! Is it a stakeout? Are we going to watch a drug deal go down?"

He didn't answer me.

"Pick up your dry cleaning, what?"

Alex maneuvered the car through a choked street on the outskirts of Japantown. I craned my neck to see where he was going and tried my best to predict his next move as I was always keen to work my own investigative skills. From the looks of it, we were either going to a McDonald's or the Orchid Emporium. I deduced it was probably the McDonald's as there was likely more crime happening there. It wasn't very well lit and it backed up to a semi-shady area.

And then Alex turned into a church.

"We're going to church?"

He pulled into the first parking space and stopped the car, then leaned back in and said, "You can stay in here if you want."

I paused for a half second and kicked open my own door. "Okay, but is this investigative or . . . ?"

"Biblical?" That smile played at the edges of his lips again. "It's about the case."

I'd never gone to church as a child, what with my mother not claiming a significant religious affiliation and my father being the devil, but I had always been fascinated by the buildings, the old, stone structures that held more whispered prayers and theological knowledge than anything a half-evil orphan could ever conjure. The buildings were hallowed, and I had long since gotten over my fear of churches imploding on me should I set foot inside, like Shirley Maxwell had said was going to happen back when we were in the third grade.

I followed close behind Alex when he walked in and strode directly up the front aisle toward an older man who sat praying in the first pew. The man turned when we approached, and he and Alex shook hands and embraced. I felt completely awkward and out of place so I attempted to blend in by waving like an idiot to a priest in a Catholic church.

At least I didn't give him a high five.

"Thank you for coming," the white-haired man said, nodding to both Alex and me. "This is what I want to show you."

The man retrieved a thick envelope from the pew beside him and slid out a sheaf of papers. I inched closer to see that they were crayon drawings—bright slashes of waxy crayon done by kids. I felt a little warmth when I thought about what the children must have been drawing—their interpretations of peace or love or God—and then I squeaked like an idiot when Alex paused on a drawing.

I tried to point to it, but my hand was locked at my side, my outstretched index finger pointing at the concrete ground. Alex shot me a look and slid the pages back into the envelope.

"Thank you, Father. I will take these in for analysis. I think they will be very helpful."

The priest nodded as we turned on our heels, me biting the inside of my cheek the whole way out. When we opened the double doors, I snatched the envelope out of Alex's hand and started to sputter.

"Who did these? What are these? Oh my God!"

The crude drawings started with pink, smiley women with bell-jar-shaped hair and triangle dresses. There were men by their sides in boxy suits and wide smiles, stick feet jutting out from their trousers. Progressively, the pictures got darker until the woman and the man were covered in thick red and yellow slashes and two new characters were drawn into the picture: a little boy and an older man. They were smiling broadly, their smiles getting bigger with each progressively more heinous picture until the triangle-dress woman and the boxy suited man were completely engulfed by angry-looking red slashes.

"These were Oliver's, weren't they?"

Alex nodded solemnly.

"And that's Oliver." I pointed. "And that . . ."

The man holding Oliver's hand had pale red hair and red eyes. He was wearing a hat, a little, stocky fedora, and even though his expression was child-artist crude, there was something unsettling about it.

"Oliver says that's his friend, Lucas."

Alex and I got back into the car, and the air in there seemed solid, incredibly dense. I could feel it pressing against my chest, and as much as I wanted to cry, to scream, to say *something*, it snatched at my breath and sucked the moisture from my eyes. We started to drive.

"No." I heard myself saying the word and then I was shaking my head. "I can't believe that he's going after a little child like this."

Alex pulled the car over on the shoulder of a road that abutted a park, and I hopped out immediately, relishing the cool air.

Alex came around the car. His eyes slipped over mine but wouldn't focus on them. "Lawson . . ."

I pushed myself back, still shaking my head. "I can't believe he did it. I can't believe that little boy did it. He drew Lucas. It was Lucas who probably killed the kid's parents, not Oliver. Not Oliver. He's just a kid, Alex. Why—why would my father come after a little kid?"

I knew that Alex wanted to tell me something, but I also knew there was nothing left to say. Evil was evil, and whenever Lucas Szabo was around, even the innocent weren't safe.

Alex raked a hand through his hair, the loose curls springing back under his palm and I remembered the first time I saw him standing in the Underworld Detection Agency, his badge winking on his belt, those curls lolling over his unlined forehead, licking the tops of his ears. If I had known then that I would be standing on the precipice of Armageddon—or possibly causing it—would I have turned away? I knew the answer would be no. Even at this moment when the world was whirling toward a giant sinkhole of doom, I wanted to get lost in those eyes; my fingers ached to feel his silky hair wrapped around them.

"This can't be happening." My voice came out meek in the darkening cab and in a half-second, in a heartbeat, Alex's arms were around me and I was crushed against his chest, my body instinctively curling into his. His arms were around my waist and then his hands found their way up my spine, fingers gliding over my neck and tangling themselves in my hair. For once, my body didn't spring to inappropriate sexual attention. It was more than that. I didn't want Alex near me; I needed it. I couldn't bear the tiniest bit of space between us, and I felt myself press against him, felt his body respond with equal pressure.

"I'm sorry, Lawson."

I nodded against his chest, tears running over my lips. I still wasn't sure what to believe. I had spent the last five years of my life on high alert, jumping to crime-fighter attention when even the slightest thing seemed off. But now, in the face of earthquakes and hellfire and aged rock stars falling from the sky, I didn't want to believe. I *couldn't*. If I did, it would mean that my father really didn't love me and he was everything everyone else said he was. Evil. He didn't see me as his daughter with a life and feelings and friends. He saw me as an item, a stumbling block to his essential power, and my life was only valuable as long as he could manipulate me into doing everything he wanted.

The sad thing was, as a daughter who never could give up the need to please an absent father, I would have done anything for his approval if only he had asked.

Alex kissed the part in my hair, the gentle brush of his lips sending shivers throughout my body.

"Lawson, this is happening. This is real. You can't deny that the gates of Hell have been blown wide open."

I unclenched the fists that were holding him to me and blinked up, pushing away. "With all due respect, Alex, I think you underestimate me."

Alex paused for a beat, and his lips edged up to that familiar half smile. "Lawson . . ."

I sniffed and used the heel of my hand to wipe at my wet cheeks. "I know. But can't we pretend for a few more minutes?" I took a step closer, my arms snaking over his neck, my hands playing with his hair. "Just a few?"

I felt the heat surge through his body even before the sly smile reached his eyes. He slid his hands around my waist and yanked me toward him, his hips firm against mine. The feeling was amazing, intense, and every nerve ending in my body shot off like Fourth of July firecrackers.

"What exactly did you have in mind?" he asked.

I walked my fingers down his well-muscled back until I came to the waistband of his pants. I paused on his belt, then inched toward his navel. I felt his breath break over my cheeks as his sighed, a slight groan escaping his lips.

My smile grew.

I took two fingers and dug into his front pocket, snatching out his keys. He cracked open an eye, his eyebrows rising.

"Someone's got to get the cake."

I spun on my heel, warm but smug, and went for the door. But Alex's arm slid around my waist before I could. He pulled me against him, his every inch on fire and lighting mine as his lips found my ear, nibbling gently.

"If we're going to Hell anyway, the cake can wait."

I'd thought the weirdest thing I would ever see was a vampire blowing purple Hubba Bubba bubbles through her fangs, but I've amended that. The weirdest thing I've ever seen is a one-hundred-and-thirteen-year-old vampire wearing a shiny red cowboy hat and gleefully tearing the pony-printed wrapping paper off a *BloodLust* game. And then doing a keg stand of O-neg. If the world wasn't going to Hell in a hand basket already, it was now.

Even Will and Alex were making nice, and that unnerved me more than an upside-down, blood-stained Vlad did. I was staring at them both as they leaned up against the wall directly across from me, deep in conversation, and I was torn. I loved Will. He was easy and uncomplicated, and being with him was fun. But Alex pushed my buttons and got on my last nerve and struck something inside of me that made everything right with the world.

Both of them deserved more.

While Nina had an arm thrown over Kale's shoulder as the two cheered on Vlad's chug, I disappeared into my bedroom, found Abelard's card, and took my phone into my closet.

My hands were shaking and my chest was tight, but I dialed, slowly, carefully. I pushed my phone to my ear and listened to it ring, the tears rolling over my cheeks, rolling down my chin.

"Ms. Lawson, I was hoping you'd call."

"The ritual, Abelard. Tell me about the ritual."

Satan, hellfire, and murderous children had been mercifully quiet for two whole days and while the time-out should have calmed my jangled nerves and soothed me, all it did was ratchet up my blood pressure and made me jump and scissor kick anything that snuck up or frightened me.

Which was why the Xerox machine had a size-seven-and-a-half dent in the side of it.

I had spent my free time Googling Lucas Szabo as if I hadn't been doing it all month. I found a few listings, including the address of a house that Lucas once lived in with my half sister Ophelia, but that had since been blown sky high. Possibly while I was there, huddling under Alex and a shower of flaming debris.

Considering I was a city girl, there was an awful lot of flaming debris in my life.

I tried old-fashioned searches, too, using actual books and library data, and even scanned a few biblical passages that gave general areas (i.e., "Hell") but no actual specifics.

My head was swimming in a mass of unanswered questions and aborted quests, and it throbbed while my fingers cramped as I started yet another search. Finally, I pulled out my phone and dialed.

"I need to see you," I said, my voice low. "It's important."

TWENTY

I wrapped my hands around my steaming-hot paper cup, letting the hot liquid sear my palms. When Nina dropped her size-of-Long Island shoulder bag onto the table, I jumped, my tea burning my hand.

"Okay, I'm here. What do you need?" Nina frowned. "Blush, obviously, but I'm assuming your need extends beyond the cosmetic."

I rubbed at the throbbing ache that was starting on my forehead. "I feel like I'm going crazy, Neens. This whole apocalypse—"

"I thought it was Armageddon."

"Pretty sure they're interchangeable, and if not, pretty sure the confusion will clear up once we're all burned to a nice, charcoal crunch."

Nina shuddered, nostrils flaring. "Way to paint a picture. So, what do you have in mind? A caper? I love a good caper."

I took a delicate sip of my coffee, wincing when it burnt my tongue. "Armentrout, Oliver, the Grigori, the fires—if all of those are happening because"—I tried to breathe, tried to squeeze an inch of air into my already screaming lungs— "because of my father, then I have to stop him."

Nina's eyes flashed and I could see the real fear in them. Seeing terror reflected in the eyes of the blood-sucking undead didn't make me feel any better about my decision, but I knew what I had to do.

"Sophie, he'll kill you. He'll kill you and then he'll possess the Vessel of Souls, and creep-o kids and weeping statues will be the absolute least of our worries."

I bit my thumbnail, the coffee feeling as though it were burning a hole in my stomach.

"He's not doing all this to play around, Neens. I mean, why now, right? He's been—I don't what you call it, dormant?—for all this time and then suddenly he comes calling? Suddenly 'it's time'?"

Nina drummed her fingernails across the wood grain of the table. "Vlad and I were thinking the same thing. It's not like it's your thirteenth birthday or you got your period or one of those momentous moments in your life. It's just you, on a Tuesday in November. What's special about that?"

I shrugged. "I don't know. I just wish I had some answers, you know? Or at least some way to know where he is or where's he headed. Is he watching us now? Inside, outside, through binoculars?"

We both looked around the sparsely populated coffeehouse. A teenage girl in a white tee was intently studying her cell phone. A man was sipping an iced latte while looking over his laptop and loudly smacking his lips around a hunk of strawberry coffee cake. A blind man was maneuvering his walking stick amongst the chairs.

"None of these people could be him."

"Maybe someone could be working for him?"

We did a scan again, this time factoring in the skinny barista with the fire-engine-red hair tied at the nape of her neck, a leafy peace sign tattoo poking out from her tight-fitting tee, and the matching soccer moms with their strollers outfitted with off-road tires. In the middle of the city. On a stroller.

"I don't know," I sputtered, the tension sinking into my every muscle and making my left eye twitch.

"Okay, so maybe he's not here and maybe none of these idiots are his minions. But there is a way we can find him."

I raised my eyebrows, expectant.

"The flowers."

"The flowers?"

"They were sent from Lola's on Harrison." Nina whipped her cell phone from her purse. "All we have to do is ask who sent them and from where."

"They're not just going to give out that information, Neens."

But Nina was already on her way, her sparkly black and pink phone pressed her ear, her index finger raised in the universal sign for "hold please."

"Okay. I still don't see how that is going to help us."

Nina brushed me off, and I could hear the nasally voice of the information lady on her end of the phone. I heard Nina ask after Lola's Flowers, then watched her grab the paper bag that, until very recently housed a maple scone, and jot something down.

"Satan's number?"

Nina rolled her eyes, our special sisterly moment obviously over. "Lola's Flowers. Call. Ask who sent the flowers."

"I thought we were pretty sure it was . . ." I felt the saliva in my mouth turn sour, my stomach rolling over as I swallowed. Instinctively I wanted to say "dad," or "my father," but my lips wouldn't form the word. "Him."

Nina held the paper bag out to me. "Well, now we can be sure, and not only that, we can get the address where the flowers came from. Then it's just a matter of a Sassy Stakeout!"

I stopped. "A Sassy Stakeout?"

"I know, but it was the best I could come up with on such short notice."

"I don't really think our stakeouts need names."

"No." Nina put her hands on her hips, nodded defiantly. "They definitely do." She waggled the paper again.

I started toward it and then pulled back. "They're probably not going to tell me anything."

"Maybe, maybe not."

My stomach was still wobbling, but I took the paper anyway, staring at the ballpoint-printed blue script. It was only the number of a flower shop, but it seemed like the start of something—something I wasn't sure I was all that ready to deal with.

I folded the bag in half. "I'll call when they're not so busy."

"How do you know they're busy?"

"Oh, it's common knowledge . . . among breathers. Everyone knows that people always order flowers at"—my eyes cut surreptitiously toward the clock—"four twenty-seven p.m."

Nina crossed her arms in front of her chest. "You know I've been alive a lot longer than you have, sweet cheeks." She held her phone out for me.

I took the phone, then flopped back into my chair, sliding the phone across the table back to her. "It's not that I don't want to, Neens. It's just that I'm not sure that I can." I stuck out my lower lip. "And I'm not sure that I want to. I mean . . ." I worried my bottom lip, trying to garner sympathy from Nina, who sat glaring down at me with those dark, fearless eyes. "What if, after not talking to him for most of your life, you were faced with the possibility of finding out where your dad was?"

I stopped, immediately, the stupid truck bashing into my forehead. Nina tried to keep her face neutral, but I could see the almost imperceptible look of sadness that flittered through her eyes. She hadn't been able to speak to either of her parents since she was twenty-nine years old. And she had been twenty-nine over a hundred years ago.

"Oh, Neens, I didn't mean—"

She held up a hand, her entire countenance back to her effortless cool. "Not a big deal. I get it. And not only could this be the start of a very quick trail to your father, and whether or not he's planning on sucking us all to a fiery grave, but you also have that other thing to deal with."

"That other thing?"

"Yeah, you know? The whole 'unable to commit wholly to a man yet always in need of male approval' thing." She shot me a smug smile, and I crumpled and tossed a napkin at her, missing her by a mile.

"Okay, okay." I pushed myself up into a more sitting, less slumping position. "I can do this."

"Besides, even if Lola gives you your dad's number or address, it's not like you have to use it."

"You're totally right. I mean, after more than thirty years he can't just get to walk into my life whenever the hell he wants."

"Right!"

"And you know what? Maybe I don't think it's time. Maybe—maybe I decide when it's time. I mean, why now, anyway? Why now, out of blue, huh? Did he even consider that I have a life? And maybe I have things to do?"

Nina paused. "What kind of things?"

"I was going to give ChaCha a bath on Wednesday and I've got a Bed, Bath and Beyond coupon I should probably use."

"Maybe just leave that part out."

"*If* I decide to call him." I tossed the paper, watching it flitter down to the table. "I call the shots now."

I got to absorb my second round of badassedness for approximately thirty-four seconds before Nina thrust the phone and the bag at me all over again.

"Do it now, badass."

I grabbed the phone but took my time carefully typing the numbers on the keypad. Nothing ruins a devil-may-be crackdown like a wrong number.

"This century, Soph."

I typed in the last number, then held the phone to my ear, every single ring searing into my brain.

"Lola's Flowers?"

The voice on the other end was sweet. The singsong quality of it should have put me at ease, but it didn't. I started and stopped several times and cleared my throat until Nina snatched the phone from me, put on her sweet-as-pie voice, and asked for the sender's address.

"I'm sorry, I can't do that," the woman on the other end of the phone said. I saw Nina's lip twitch, showing off the smallest hint of angled fang.

"Oh, but I think you can," she answered, her sweet voice now tinged with something slightly sinister. "You see, the man who sent these flowers is a sexual predator. And while I can certainly run on down and slap you with a search warrant, that would take a few moments and in those few moments a woman could be dead and you know who would have blood on their hands, dear? That's right, Lola's Flowers. So I suggest . . ."

The woman began to backpedal, though whether it was because she believed Nina's episode of *Law and Order: Special Vampire Edition* or just because she wanted to free up her phone line I couldn't be sure. Nina leaned over and scribbled down the address the woman read off and then thanked her gratefully and commended Lola's commitment to the community and willingness to keep law and order. Once she hung up the phone, Nina pushed her dark hair over her shoulder with an elegant flourish and dangled the page between forefinger and thumb.

"Care to go for a ride?"

I was too nervous about tracking down Lucas Szabo to fear for my life as Nina pinballed her little Lexus coupe down the 280 freeway. The address wound us through town onto a weird exit, then dumped us into a nondescript section of town that looked like it masqueraded as the set for *Happy Days*.

"Make a left over there."

Nina pointed. "Six-six-three-three. Should be right there."

I followed Nina's gaze. "Oh."

My father's original house had been in a chichi section of Marin and was firebombed about a year ago. Even with the new address pinched in my fingers I didn't have a high expectation of finding the spot where the devil kicked up his cloven feet, but I didn't expect this.

"Haven Crest Mortuary." Nina blinked. "So . . . your father is an undertaker? Isn't that kind of unfair?"

I shook my head, bat wings in my stomach going bonkers. "This can't be right."

Nina kicked open the car door, then turned and looked back at me. "Only one way to know for sure, right?"

I sucked in an uneven breath and attempted to shake some blood into my frozen fingertips. "I guess so," I said to the dashboard.

Nina was rearranging the arc of her Peter Pan–collared vintage blouse when she stopped and looked at me, lips pursed, hands splayed on her small hips.

"Are you coming?"

I licked at my bone-dry lips. "Of course I am. What makes you think I'm not?"

"Because you've been rooted to the cement for a solid three minutes." She held out a hand. "Come on."

"I don't know if I can."

No one else save a vampire with super-vamp hearing could have heard me. Nina was at my side in a millisecond, her cold, stony hands rubbing comforting little circles on my back. "You can do this, Soph. I'm right here for you. We wouldn't even have to tell anyone who you are."

I worked to swallow. "What if he already knows?" My hands flew to the corkscrew curls of my bright red hair. "What if I look just like him?"

Nina cocked her head, her lips pushing up into a motherly smile. "I don't think you look a thing like Satan. I would think he's more"—she made little wispy motions with her hands—"smokey."

She wound an arm through mine and began to budge me forward—inch by miniscule inch. "It'll be fine," she coaxed. "Just breathe. I can hear your heart hammering from here."

I supposed I'd walked along with Nina, though once on the base steps of the mortuary, I couldn't remember crossing the street. I was suddenly raging hot and I prayed to God that it was a nod to early menopause rather than the crackly glow from the Hell-bound. Nina whipped up the stairs and had her hand on the doorknob. I followed her up and put my hand on her arm.

"Ready?"

I wagged my head. "No. But I'm going in there. Alone."

Nina's arm dropped to her side. "Are you sure?"

I nodded, trying to muster up a touch of confidence with my certainty. "Uh-huh."

Nina was my best friend and I'd already put her through too much. She'd risked her afterlife for me once already, and I wasn't about to let her do it again—Satan or no.

"Just wait out here. I'll try not to get turned into a flaming pile of ash."

Nina forced a smile. "That's comforting." She pulled me into a tight hug anyway. "I love you. No matter what happens, I love you, Sophie."

I nodded, feeling the emotion well up behind my eyes. I pulled open the door and stepped into the mortuary.

TWENTY-ONE

I suppose I wasn't expecting an actual mortuary when I walked through the door. The room was heavily wood paneled and cool, with just the faintest scent of dampness intermingled with the sickly sweet stench of wilting flowers. It was deathly silent and the air felt heavy, punctuated by a thousand souls or a thousand tears or perhaps just a thousand sentiments never said as families looked over the lifeless bodies of their loved ones.

I expected more.

I expected fire and brimstone, and possibly something with neck chains and giant boulders. I didn't expect the older woman who sat at a huge mahogany L-shaped desk moving her mouse, her wrinkled lips held tight as she studied her screen, the computer giving off the familiar "blip!" of a game of *Solitaire*. I cleared my throat and the woman looked up at me with a welcoming smile, her eyes milky with practiced compassion.

"Hello, dear. May I help you?"

I cleared my throat again, my voice choked off

by the dead flowers, by the overwhelming, silent announcement of death all around.

"Yes," I finally forced out. And then, "I think." I wrung my hands and crossed the room to the woman—whose name was Gertrude Viet, I learned from her nameplate—and pasted on a small smile.

"I'm looking for someone."

Gertrude looked up at me, lips still pursed, head bent slightly forward, listening.

Lucas Szabo. My father. My dad. Lucas. Mr. Szabo. The man who married my mother. The man who abandoned his child. The words and monikers tumbled head over heels in my brain and each one sounded wrong—too formal, too personal, too strange.

"Szabo." It came out like a shot and died on the air. "Lucas Szabo."

Gertrude's smile didn't falter. "And you are?"

"My name is Sophie," I said. "I'm Sophie Lawson."

Gertrude's smile was still staunch, and I realized then that it wasn't welcoming or empathetic or businesslike. She held it hard, teeth clenched behind those pursed lips. I swallowed.

"And what business do you have with Mr. Szabo?"

My bones melted away with the hot wax that tore through me. "He's here?"

An eyebrow raise. Eyes challenging mine. "What business do you have with Mr. Szabo?"

"I need to talk to him about . . ." The word *daughter* stuck behind my teeth, and I couldn't hold Gertrude's eye any longer. "A coffin." I coughed out the word as my eyes set on the open catalog to Gertrude's left. "I'd like to buy a coffin."

"For yourself or for a family member, perhaps? Your mother, maybe?"

Icy fingers of fear clawed their way down my spine. "My mother?" She was behind my eyes in a flash—my mother laughing, my mother with her head thrown back as the sunlight caught the blond streaks in her hair. The day my mother died, her naked big toe drawing tiny circles a half-inch above the hardwood floor.

"Do you know?" I whispered.

But Gertrude was hefting the catalog in front of her, flopping the glossy pages backward. She held up a single finger and cocked her head. "You just wait right here one moment, won't you? I've got something I think you might like better. Stay put, okay?"

I watched Gertrude back away, that smile held taut on her lips. And then she was gone. The air in the room seemed to get heavier, if that were possible—seemed to press harder against my lungs. I sucked in a tiny gulp of air and started when I heard the shuffle of feet. I whirled toward the sound and almost feel over, stunned.

"Oliver?"

He was half-hidden behind a heavy velvet curtain in the showroom. A little child with wide eyes and an impish smile clutching a length of olive-green cloth while he stood between two coffins, staring at me.

"Oliver! The police have been—" I headed for him, but he pressed a finger up against his lips. I paused, crouching down to his level.

"You want me to be quiet? Are you scared, honey?

You don't have to be—I'm going to get you out of here. You'll be safe with me, I promise."

Oliver shook his head, and I could see the crook of a smile behind his index finger. "I'm hiding," he whispered. "So shush." He shrank back into the curtain.

"Who are you hiding from?" I whispered back. "You don't have to hide. You don't have to be afraid."

I reached for the curtain, trying to push it aside, but Oliver's grip on it was surprisingly strong.

"Oliver, it's okay."

His nostrils flared and the smile was gone. His eyes were dark storms and his lips were tight. "Stop it," he said, voice a low growl. "I'm hiding. It's a game. I'm winning." His eyes locked mine and my stomach went to liquid. There was nothing pure in those eyes, nothing but darkness and hate, nothing human. "And you're going to lose."

My blood ran cold, and when Gertrude sang out, "Here it is," I stumbled backward, terrified of Oliver, more frightened than the night he'd killed his parents. He was evil now; it was apparent—evil through and through.

"We have all sorts of models. Do you have a price range in mind?"

Gertrude said other things too—something about cedar and polished brass that I could barely hear above the rushing of blood as it coursed through my skull. I felt each toe touch the carpet through my shoe; I felt each step, each breath of ice-tinged air, and then I was running, my lungs screaming against the sear as I held my breath and pushed through the double doors. The sunlight on my shoulders, on my face, burned me and I hurled myself into the street, my eyes focused on Nina's black car, which looked a thousand miles—a hundred blocks, a lifetime—away. I vaguely heard her calling me, heard the screech of tires and the blaring of horns. Someone yelled, someone screamed, and I was clawing at the door handle, my palm burning from the sunbaked steel, my fingernails clawing at the slick black paint. Finally, the door popped open and I huddled inside, legs curled to my chest so my heart thundered against my thigh, arms curled around my legs, head buried.

"Sophie, Sophie, what happened? Are you okay?"

"Go. Just go." I was shaking, and then I was screaming. "Go-go-go-go-go!" There was more screeching, more honking, more yelling, and when I dared to look again the mortuary was inching away behind us, the curtains twitching as Oliver stepped into the window, arm raised, hand waving jovially.

Nina and I had been sitting in bumper-to-bumper traffic for over an hour. We were dead silent the whole time, she tapping her fingers against the steering wheel, me staring out, seeing but not seeing the city outside the passenger window. Every time I blinked, the image of the mortuary flashed in my mind. The cloying smell of the lilies choked me and I started to hyperventilate. Nina reached out and took my hand, her cool one bringing down my temperature at least two degrees.

"It's going to be okay, Sophie," she said softly.

"Oliver was in there."

"Oliver? The kid?"

"He was evil. He was horrible. I just don't understand any of this. Why—? If he has Oliver, what does he want with me? And he sends me flowers, but he's not there. What the hell does he want with me? Is he just playing?"

Nina shook her head. "I was initially thinking he was trying to flush you out with the fires and the destruction. You know—you'd see them all, know that you were somehow responsible, and come out and solve them or bumble them or whatever, and then bam, he'd swoop in and get you." She bit her thumb. "At least that's what Will and I think."

A niggling jealously caught the back of my neck. "You talked to Will about this?"

"We were just shooting the shit. Will kind of thinks that Lucas wants you on his own terms. Like, the flowers were an introduction."

"And then bam." I settled back in the seat, my saliva going sour.

The sun was setting and the sky was an electric pink. It looked unnatural, and I laughed at the observation since there seemed to be nothing anymore that was natural. I was born of the devil. I was born of evil.

"Screw this." Nina yanked the wheel hard and drove half on the shoulder, the other half of her car a quarter-inch from the screaming drivers on the other side. "Sorry, sorry," she said with a dazzling smile. She guided us off the off-ramp in record time while a symphony of honks and obscenities rang out in our wake.

"Feel like going shopping?" she asked. "My treat."

I shook my head, the veins in my neck like steel rods from all the tension I'd been carrying. I was mildly certain that I would have to unhinge my jaw from the outside if I ever wanted to open my mouth again.

"No thanks, Neens. Would you mind just swinging by the house and shoving me out?"

"Not at all."

She maneuvered the city streets like a pro and when I say, "like a pro," I mean a pro in any field other than driving or maneuvering. We chased down an old lady in a crosswalk, nearly took out two parking meters, and for some reason when we arrived in front of the house, there was a wilted head of lettuce stuck to one of the headlights. I peeled it off and waved. Nina rolled down the window and craned her neck out before pulling away from the curb from which she had "parked" perpendicularly.

"Promise me you won't sulk tonight, 'kay?"

"I don't sulk," I sulked.

Nina pursed her lips. "You have real family, you know? Vlad and I wouldn't know what to do without you. And King of Darkness or not, your bio dad is really a dick."

I smiled and gave Nina a peck on the cheek, scraping a few more bits of lettuce from her driver's side door.

I was upstairs and stretched out on the couch with ChaCha on my lap and a sleeve of mini powdered donuts under my arm when someone knocked on the door.

"Jusa-minoot," I said, mouth full of mini donuts. I snatched the spare house key from our unlimited stash since Nina was famous for losing hers on a weekly basis, usually during her Indy 500–style driving endeavors.

I yanked open the door. "Did you lose—"

The donut that I had eaten sat like an enormous black mass in my gut. The tension that I was holding exploded and pinpricks shot out, tagging every inch of my bare skin. My hackles went up. Sweat beaded on my upper lip. If the entire world hadn't dropped into animated suspension, I'm sure my heart would have been thudding out of my chest.

Lucas Szabo was standing there, staring at me.

I don't know what I'd expected, exactly. On the one hand, this was the being charged with the contamination of all mankind, the epitome, the example, the *symbol* of evil. I guess I'd thought he would look more badass or have hellfire flying up behind him like some kind of Broadway show or AC/DC concert. There were no minions, the waft of brimstone didn't float up from his cheap-looking suit, and his hair—though thinner and far wispier than mine—was the same pale red I usually sported. He had kind, interested-looking eyes and a comb-over. No horns.

On the other hand, I was staring at my father. Once I had dreamed that he would be a lithe, sinewy six-foot-three with a body like a cyclist or a James Bond iteration. He would wear the suits fashionable in the *Father Knows Best* fifties and smoke a pipe while tousling my hair and calling me a little scamp. My mother would fix him a martini. Norman Rockwell would immortalize us in the *Saturday Evening Post.* I'd never dreamed of this man who was stocky and a little short. He stood with his shoulders back and his chin hitched; he was a rather commanding presence if a very short one. He was barely an eyebrow taller than me.

We stared at each other for a good long minute. In my mind's eye, we circled each other like curious dogs ready to strike. He sized me up, I sized him up. All the anger and hate and betrayal that had simmered in my gut for my entire life bubbled to the surface, and I was hurling questions, insults, accusations while this man—my *dad*—cringed and begged and tried to answer, tried to apologize. In actuality, he raised his anemic eyebrows and gestured with the hat he carried in his left hand.

"Oh," I started. He wanted me to let him in.

There were so many emotions associated with this man walking into my home. Once he crossed that physical threshold, he was crossing a mental one, too, and so was I. This was my life, my every hope in tangible, physical form in front of me. The decision that I made in this split second, in this moment in time would stand for all eternity—

"Sorry to be a bother when we're just meeting like this. But may I use your restroom?"

I felt my mouth drop open. I felt my heart plummet and then swell, warming to the kind voice of this man—of *my father.*

"Y—yes, of course," I stuttered, stepping aside. "It's right there." I pointed like a ninny, still standing with the door wide open as Lucas crossed the living room and disappeared into the bathroom. Eventually, I shut the door. Eventually, I made it to the kitchen and put on a pot of coffee.

My father was in my house. *My father* was in my house!

Joy flittered around my chest like I was a little girl and my daddy had just bought me a pony. I pulled on my hair and tried to straighten my bangs, did a quick stain scan of my T-shirt and skirt and pinched my cheeks so they would be rosy.

The devil is in my house.

That second voice was darker than the first, and it shot a nauseating wave through my stomach.

Trickster god, Alex's voice pinged around my head. *He cannot be honest, Lawson. He cannot be good.*

He doesn't care about who you are, love. Will's voice joined Alex's. *All he cares about is what you are.*

I was blinking hard and trying to swallow down the raw feeling in my throat when Lucas opened the bathroom door, offering me a broad, if unnerving, smile.

He'll kill you just as soon as kiss you. He's the devil, Lawson. He's evil incarnate. There is no redemption for him. He was cast out and he liked it that way. He'll pull you onto his side, he'll pull you into his world and then there will be no redemption for you either. Regardless of the Vessel of the Souls, that can't happen. I won't let it happen. You're too good, Lawson.

"Can I get you a cup of coffee?"

Lucas seated himself at the dining table and knitted his fingers, looking up at me. "I'm sorry if this is awkward. But"—his eyes slipped over me, taking me in from head to toe, his expression curious—"I just can't believe how much you look like her."

My breath hitched. "My mother?"

Lucas nodded and I steadied myself against the counter. I knew very little about my mother even though I had grown up with *her* mother.

"Your eyes, your smile." He clucked his tongue and shook his head. "Looks like all you got from dear old dad is our red hair." He patted his head.

Oh, I wanted to shout, *and eternal damnation!*

The coffeepot dinged and I poured two cups, sat down across from Lucas, and slid one to him.

"Do you want to ask me anything?"

I wanted to ask him why. I wanted to ask him if he was sorry for leaving, or sorry for having me. I wanted to know if he really had killed my mother. I wanted to know what had happened that day, if he ever thought about me, if he really was who they said he was. The questions kept percolating but lodging in my throat, and all I could do was stare. Outside, a war was being waged on me by a warrior race of fallen angels. Outside, a trickster god was fooling people—children, even—into doing things, evil things. But in here, across from me was just a man with my same red hair and the same unfortunately Vienna-sausage-like fingers bringing a coffee mug to his lips.

"Are you him?"

Lucas sipped, his eyebrows going up over the rim of the cup. When he put it down, his lips were ruddy from the heat and twisted into a hint of a smile.

"My little Sophie, always so inquisitive."

Fire shot through me. I wasn't his little anything. He didn't know if I was inquisitive or not. I felt my fist tighten around my coffee cup.

"Why did you come here?"

Lucas frowned, looking immediately sorry. "I thought it was time. The guilt—leaving you alone for all this time—it was eating away at me. I should have come sooner, but I was a coward."

"Sooner?" I spat. "You shouldn't have left at all."

"Things were different then."

I looked away, gritting my teeth against the hot tears that rimmed my eyes. I wouldn't let him see me cry.

"Some things never change. Like a daughter needing her father."

Lucas shook his head. "I was in no position to be a father to you, Sophie. Your mother knew that, I knew that."

"My mom was in no position to be a single mother, either, but you didn't give her any other option now, did you?"

The anger that had been simmering over the last thirty-three years was at a full boil now, and I could feel that hate welled up inside of me. I could see my mother's sad, exhausted eyes and my grand-mother as she tried to do something to help. To pat my mother's back, or say soothing things, but my mother was always there with those sad, hollow eyes and Lucas was—where?

"I was hoping we could start fresh. We are family, you know."

"No, we're not. I have my own family."

Lucas's lips crept up and I could see the evil in

his smile, the darkness in his eyes. "And what family would that be my dear, dear child?"

"The family I chose. The one who chose me."

Lucas pressed his palms together and cocked his head. "The Underworld Detection Agency, hm? That your little family? A collection of misfits, the undead, my castoffs?" He took a step closer, and I was rooted to the ground, somehow cowering in his shadow. He drew his index finger along my jawline, his touch making my skin crawl.

"Get away from me."

Another step closer and I was inexplicably drawn to him. Fire shot through my body and I felt alive, I felt the breath of life—and death—tear through me. I felt my father's power.

He grinned. "You like that, don't you? This is family, Sophie. This is what you are born of. Me."

Lucas's face shadowed and then swirled into a grotesque kaleidoscope of horrendous images. The tongue that slid out of his mouth was serpentine and forked. He wasn't moving his lips, but he was still talking, advancing on me, and I was bending backward, my spine protesting.

"You were the seed of evil born into humanity. You took root and grew. You infected this world."

I tried to close my eyes, but they were pulled wide open and I could see my friends—Nina, face contorted in agony as her soft, human features edged out and hardened, her teeth growing and sharpening. Vlad glared up at me, his mouth glossy with fresh blood, the broken flesh hanging from his teeth as the woman beneath him writhed and bucked until she paled, her life force gone. Alex was next, moving fast, the darkness wafting from his shoulders and legs as he walked, decimating everyone in his way—stomping out the light, tearing at the throats of the saved.

"Please stop."

A much younger Will was next, hanging back as a woman before him struggled and reached for him. There was a man on top of her, his hands tightening on her throat. Her lips didn't move, but I could hear her begging for Will to intercede. He stood there, rooted, watching the light leave her eyes. Her killer looked up and locked eyes with Will, his grin maniacal, pure evil—the grin that was looking down on me now.

"You did it to them. You made all of this happen," I spat.

"You can't be damned without the King of the Damned, Sophie girl. They all gave in to the darkness. They all gave into the power. The strength. Just like you will. You think your wisp of goodness will protect you?" He gnashed his teeth. "I stomped your mother's genes out. You snuffed out her goodness."

"She was good. They're all good," I managed to whisper. "They're good. Free will. They can choose. We all can choose."

That made Lucas smile. "How about you choose this then, for your little family—all their souls for yours."

My head snapped up. "And Oliver?"

He grinned. "My little protégée. There is no goodness in him. No humanity. There never was."

"He's a child."

Lucas's smile was smug and horrible. "He's a new breed. One of many. One of legions. Evil is winning out. So I ask again, daughter—all their souls for yours?"

I pinched my eyes closed, the images burning behind my closed lids. "They'll all be freed? Every one of them?"

"And you will have everything you've ever wanted. Power. Prestige." He raked his fingers through my hair. "And I'll have everything else."

My mind exploded with the sounds of millions of voices, lost souls, waiting to depart.

"The Vessel."

Lucas snapped his fingers and my spine snapped, the pain shooting from both ends. I was sure the bone was sticking out, could feel the blood as it oozed and poured over my skin as the back of my head met my ankles.

"Give it to me."

I gritted my teeth, the pain unbearable in my ruined body. "No."

"Didn't anyone ever tell you that you should always, always obey your father?"

Blood gurgled in my mouth and trickled out of my nose.

"Please, no."

Lucas was enjoying himself as every image I had ever seen—every depiction of the devil—came to life and leered over me, changing one from the other like a heinous slide show that would never end. He used that serpentine tongue to lick his lips, his saliva spitting onto my face. "Give in to the darkness. Give in to who you are. To what you are."

I tried to avoid looking at Lucas, tried to break his gaze, but he kept grinning and I was mesmerized.

"You always had the darkness inside of you, waiting to get out."

I felt his palm close against my forehead and my whole body went into a spasm, my lungs on the verge of collapse. I was back in my grandmother's home, in that attic room. I could see the grain of the wood floor, could see my mother's bare feet as she stepped on the ladder and wrapped the noose around her neck.

"Oh, God, no," I was whimpering, crying. "God, no."

And inside the image I pushed myself to my feet, and watched the ground move as I stepped closer to my mother, closer to the stool, closer to her bare feet. I saw a hand reach out—my hand, plump and young—and I gripped the edge of the stool she stood on and pushed.

TWENTY-TWO

"Sophie!"

Nina was on the floor beside me, pulling my broken body to her, crushing me to her chest. I couldn't see her, couldn't focus my eyes or move my head. I was there, I was awake, but I was floating, free of my body, watching over.

"Will!" Nina screamed. "Vlad! Alex!"

The image tattered and shook like a Super 8 reel, and then Will and Alex and Vlad were surrounding me. I tried to push them away. I tried to tell them that Lucas would be back, that they had to save themselves, but they weren't listening. They were moving me and yelling, and I could barely hear them, floating high above them.

And then you were at the door.

Lucas.

Hat in hand, looking meek and apologetic.

Trickster.

I woke up on my living room floor gagging and clawing at the carpet, desperate for breath. My body and was tight and tense, but I was okay and

Lucas wasn't there. I crawled on hands and knees to the phone and pulled it toward me.

"Nina. Get Alex, Will, and Vlad. Get everyone and meet me at the Underworld Detection Agency. Get there as fast as you can." I hung up, made one last call, then headed out the door.

I took the stairs two at a time, constantly looking over my shoulder for my broken spine or the horde of Grigori that I knew would be attacking me at every turn. I slammed myself into my car and stepped on the gas, not worrying about traffic lights or red lights, driving like Nina on her worst day. My heart was slamming against my rib cage and I knew what he was doing, I knew that he was picking them—my friends, my family—Lucas was plucking them each to torture until he got to me, until he got what he wanted from me.

And for the good of my friends, for the good of all humanity, I was going to give it to him.

I pulled into the police station parking lot and yanked the balled-up sweatshirt that I had stuffed under my seat. I pulled out the first sword, the dagger of the Grigori, and admired the razor sharp blade. It hadn't taken much for me to slip it out of Alex's trunk and right back into my purse the night he "took" it from me. After all, I had grown pretty slick under Alex's tutelage—a fact that he failed to recognize.

When I saw Abelard cross the parking lot, I slid the dagger in my pants and went directly down to the UDA. Nina was there, as were Vlad, Will, Alex, Kale, Lorraine, and Sampson. There was a hint of a noxious odor, and Steve stepped from the doorway, little lichen-covered troll arms crossed in front of his barrel chest.

"Steve will not let him take you," he said defiantly.

I felt the prick of tears at my eyes. "You guys—"

"We're in this together," Sampson said defiantly. "We're part of you just as much as you're part of us."

"Well . . ." Feng stepped out from the other side of the group. I gaped.

"Feng?" I looked from her to Sampson, another wave of fear crashing over me.

Sampson held up a hand. "We have an unofficial twenty-four-hour truce."

I raised my eyebrows and Feng nodded. "I can kill him any day. But you and Satan?" She shook her head, clucking her tongue. "You're going to need help."

I blinked back tears. "This isn't your fight. I love you all, but I brought this on. Lucas will never stop coming after us—the Grigori, they'll never stop coming after us."

"Then we'll keep fighting. Every day if we have to," Alex put in.

"Twice a day," Will rejoined.

"I'm just here for the show," Vlad said, blank faced.

Nina jabbed him in the gut and he rolled his eyes. "I'll stand up for you, too," he finally groaned.

The elevator dinged and we all turned in a single mass toward it. The heavy doors slid open, and Lucas was standing inside, hands clasped in front of him, hat pinched between two fingers. Once again he looked like a man, a weak, pitiful man. And then he smiled.

"Oh," he said, nodding appraisingly. "This is nice. This little grouping of demons and rejects. Cute. But useless."

He flicked his hand, and Vlad and Sampson doubled over, holding their middles and moaning in agony. My breath hitched when I saw the blood clouding their eyes, dripping red-black from their sockets.

"Stop!" I said.

Lucas did, and as quickly as it began, Vlad and Sampson straightened, looking no worse for the wear.

"You can't stop me, Sophie girl. I am so much more powerful than you've ever imagined. You never knew, but I was always there. That voice in the back of your head. That fleeting thought of killing, of destroying? It was me. It was you."

"I'm not going to stop you," I said, taking a step forward. "Why should I? You're my father. You're back. You offered me everything I've ever wanted." I glanced over my shoulder, gazing at the demons behind me with disdain. "You're my family. You're my father."

Lucas breamed like a nurse had just handed me to him. "The Vessel?" he said, his tongue slipping in and out over his lips. "Bring me the Vessel."

I stopped. "The Vessel? You didn't ask for that. You asked for me."

"I want both. We'll have both and we'll control everything."

I paused for a beat, then nodded. "Yeah. Okay, yeah."

"Lawson!" Alex said. "Don't do this!"

I turned to him. "Why not? So that we could continue on with this little game of ours? You pull me in, you push me out? Shampoo, rinse, repeat? Uh-uh." I shook my head. "Tired of that. I want to be protected. I want to be revered."

The power pulsed through me and it made me smile, made my every fiber vibrate and hum. "You can come with me, Alex. It's all you've ever wanted, isn't it?"

His lips pressed into a hard, thin line, and I wavered an equal distance between The Underworld Detection Agency and Lucas Szabo as the legions began to surround him. Dark forms, dark warriors who appeared out of nowhere.

"They will do anything you ask, daughter."

"God, Sophie, don't you remember us? Think about us!" It was Nina now. Her voice was high and tortured, and it pulled at something deep inside me. I didn't want to hurt her, but the pull of the dark side—of a family and a home—was too much.

"My daddy wants to be with me, Neens," I said, blinking. "You understand, don't you?"

Will was behind her, not looking at me. I went to him. "You're awfully quiet, Will. Don't you care whether you live or die?"

He sucked in a deep breath and seemed to rise up before me. "I'm a Guardian of the Vessel, love. My job is with that, not with you."

He gripped me by the arms and yanked, but Alex raced forward, trying to break in between us.

They were jostling me. I knew Lucas was watching

carefully, and then he was right beside me. I could feel the heat when he laid his palm on my arm.

"We're going now."

I snapped toward him. "But the Vessel."

"Come on, Sophie girl. We can leave them all. We can." He flicked his fingertips and the ground started rumbling. The walls started to buckle; bits of ceiling and debris started to fall. Lucas grinned. "Ashes to ashes," he said.

"But the Vessel!" I shouted.

"I just need you," Lucas said, taking a step closer.

His face continued to reflect every hateful image of Satan, of the trickster god, that I had ever seen. I reached out and yanked the Grigori dagger from my pants. Lucas's eyes went to it and his smile broadened.

"Are you going to fight back now? Going to stab me with that?"

He ran his finger along the blade, making a clean slice on his index finger. He watched the blood bubble, then pushed the injured finger to his mouth. His forked tongue made a grotesque sucking sound, and he lapped up the blood.

"Go ahead. You can't hurt me."

I nodded, the weight of everything that Lucas had said crashing over me. I took one last look over my shoulder at my friends, all assembled, all at the ready—and I drove the Grigori dagger straight into my gut.

I felt my skin pucker and split as it took in the sharp end of the knife. I felt it cut smoothly, right through me. I felt Abelard's hands as he reached out and removed the dagger before I fell to my knees.

There were flashing lights everywhere, and sound. Popping and cracking and screaming and sirens and a bright white light. It was blinding and beautiful. It hummed with comfort and warmth. I wanted to go toward it, but something was holding me back. Something was keeping me tied down, close to the noise, the trauma, the screeches and the sirens. I wanted to go toward the light.

Trickster.

When I woke up I was in the hospital, pinned down in a stark white bed, tubes and wires taped to my hands and arms, and something uncomfortable shoved up my nose.

"Where am I?" I asked and blinked as the room slowly came into view.

I heard the snap of a magazine and saw Nina sit upright, her coal-black hair glossy against the sun that filtered in through the blinds.

"She's awake," I heard her say. "Guys, she's awake."

I struggled to sit up, but just as quickly Nina pinned me back down to the bed, throwing her arms around me.

"You're alive! Oh, thank God, you're alive! Vlad! Vlad! Come here, you don't have to eat her now!"

"Vlad was going to eat me?"

Nina held her thumb and forefinger a half inch a part. "Just a little bit. This much. So you could stay with us forever."

The sentiment was incredibly sweet even if the follow-through was unbelievably creepy. I tried to move and winced, pressing my hand against the enormous bandage at my waist. "Ow."

"Don't you remember what happened, warrior girl?" Alex said as he came through the door.

"You stabbed yourself," Vlad said, more life in his eyes than I'd ever seen. "You were like, 'wah!'" He made the motion of me stabbing myself. "And Lucas was all, 'nahhh' and then that weird monk guy was all, '*sayonara*!' and then Will was all, 'me too!'"

"Wait, what? What did Will do?"

Nina's eyes clouded. "Sophie, you know that you're no longer the Vessel of Souls anymore, right? You kind of handled that with all the shish-slice stuff. And Will—well, Will goes where the Vessel goes."

A sob choked in my throat. "So he's gone?"

Alex looked at me, his eyes soft. "You didn't know it would happen that way?"

I shrunk back into my pillow. I had known that it would happen that way. Abelard had told me that was how it would happen. Will had told me that was how it would happen. But I hadn't expected he'd really go.

"Where—where did he go? Did he leave a number or—or . . ." I leaned over on the bedside table and shifted stuff around, looking for my cell phone. "I can just call him." I hit the speed-dial button and immediately, the triple dial tone came up telling me that I had reached a number that had been disconnected.

My heart broke.

Alex came to my side and took my hand in his, giving it a gentle squeeze. Nina touched my shoulder softly, and Vlad stood at the foot of the bed, looking at me with alternating gazes of respect and good old teenage-boy annoyance.

"I just didn't think he'd really disappear."

Alex looked away and coughed, then fished a folded-up piece of binder paper from his pants pocket. He gently laid it in my palm, then walked to the foot of the bed and sat in a chair, avoiding my gaze.

I unfolded the note.

My Dearest Sophie, who has been both the greatest charge and the greatest pain in my ass of this life—

I was made to guard, to watch, to revere above all other things the treasure of the angels. All along I thought that thing was the Vessel of Souls (which, by the way, looks like a funky old hookah vase). But on this mission I learned what a treasure truly is: you. You have been trusted with more than anyone should ever be forced to bear and yet you do it all with glory and grace. Well, less grace than glory. Well, not all that much glory, either, but you get where I'm going with this.

From the moment I took charge of you, I wanted—needed—to be near you whether or not the Vessel was in danger because to me, you were it. You were the life force of all the good in the world, of every soul waiting to find its plane. You must never forget that because that is where your power lies.

Years ago your grandmother left you a letter that explained the story of your life—the story of your power. You were born from an angel to an angel, and the evil that Satanalia speaks of was never able to take hold in you. Because of you, it was never able to take root in the world. You, Sophie,

*brought out the good that was once in him, the
fallen angel who once sat at the right hand of God.
You are the light. You give grace.*

*You know that Angel Boy and I never saw eye to
eye. It was my job to defend you from him, from the
fallen, and I did until I learned that when he fell,
he stayed for you. You gave him his wings a long
time ago, love, but he kept them clipped, kept them
low for you.*

I folded the page and looked at Alex, my eyes wet
with tears. "You—you could have gone back?"

He stood and came around the bed, taking the
hand opposite the one Nina was holding. "No," he
said shaking his head. "I really couldn't have." His
eyes were a bright, intense cornflower blue. "I tried
not to love you, Sophie Lawson. I tried. But there
was no Heaven—no grace without you there."

"Oooh!" Nina sighed at my left shoulder. Alex
squeezed my right hand. Vlad groaned.

"Look, we successfully averted Armageddon.
Sophie shoved her father back down to Hell with
her inner evil."

I blinked, slightly sheepish. "Like kind. Feng
told me."

Alex's eyebrows went up, but I batted explanation away.

Nina threaded her arms in front of her chest and
pinned Vlad with a glare. "So what are you suggesting, Vlad?"

He looked around, shrugged, unaffected. "I don't
know. We saved the world. There should be cake."